COME AWAY WITH ME

RACHEL LACEY

COPYRIGHT

Content Warning: This book contains reference to a suicide. It occurs off page and is mentioned only as backstory and without detail.

Piper Sheridan stood on a darkened Brooklyn sidewalk, staring at the bar on the opposite side of the street. A lavender dragonfly-shaped logo gleamed above the door, announcing the bar's name. Through the window, Piper could see a handful of people on stools, laughing and sharing conversation, out for a drink with friends after work. Maybe a date. Piper used to be one of those people.

Now she was standing outside, heart pounding, palms damp as she summoned the courage to cross the street and go inside. It had been six months since she'd gone out in public like this, but she was going to change that statistic tonight. She and her therapist had talked through all the details ahead of time. They'd covered every possible scenario and how Piper would handle it. She was doing this.

One step at a time. That's what Dr. Jorgensen said. Piper glanced both ways to ensure the street was clear, and then she took that first step. And the second. She crossed the street, gaining speed with each stride. With a quick tug at the black wig covering her distinctive auburn locks, she grasped the bar's heavy wooden door and pulled it open.

Immediately, she was enveloped in the murmur of conversation undercut by strains of jazz music. A pink-haired bartender waved in her direction with a friendly smile. Piper spotted an empty stool against the back wall, and she made her way to it before she could lose her nerve and bolt back out the door. She took off her jacket and hung it on the hook under the bar before sliding onto the stool. Then she reached for a lavender drink card on the lacquered bar top in front of her, not because she didn't know what she wanted to drink, but because she wanted something to do with her hands, something to focus on. If she fidgeted, she'd only draw unwanted attention to herself.

Piper wasn't exactly a household name—not yet anyway—but after four seasons as Samantha Whitaker on the legal drama *In Her Defense*, she was fairly recognizable here in New York, and for tonight, anonymity was key. If she made it through the evening without a panic attack, she'd be one step closer to going out in public as herself again.

She wanted to reclaim that freedom, but even more urgently, she needed to get her panic attacks under control before her audition next month. This movie could launch her career, and it was ultimately what had driven her out of her apartment on this Thursday night.

"Welcome to Dragonfly," a cheerful female voice said. "I'm Josie."

Piper looked up to see the pink-haired bartender standing in front of her. "Hi."

"Know what you're having?" Josie asked.

"A negroni, please." She'd chosen her drink before she left her apartment. Tonight, she was following her own script, no unnecessary decisions to elevate her anxiety.

"You got it." The bartender turned around to mix the drink.

Piper darted a quick glance around the bar, relieved to find that no one was paying her any attention. Her chest was tight, and claustrophobia pressed over her, the feeling that everyone was just *too close*, even though she had the wall to her left and an empty stool to her right. She had to recondition herself not to react this way in public places, and tonight was a first step toward achieving her goal. She blew out a slow, measured breath.

The door to the bar opened, and a petite brunette entered. Piper tugged a strand of black hair into her face as recognition dawned. That was Eve Marlow, the host of *Do Over*, a popular makeover show on the *Life & Leisure* channel. She and Piper didn't exactly know each other, but they'd met in passing at industry events, and Piper didn't want to be recognized tonight. Her entire strategy for the evening hinged on remaining anonymous.

"I see who you're looking at, but don't get any ideas," Josie said playfully as she placed a glass tumbler on the bar in front of Piper. "She's married."

"She is?" Piper was genuinely surprised at this news. She hadn't heard anything about Eve getting married, but sure enough, as her eyes tracked to Eve's left hand, she saw a gold band glinting there.

"I'm her wife," the bartender said with a wink, and Piper wasn't sure whether or not she was joking. "It was a small, private event."

"No shit?" Piper said as she spotted a matching ring on Josie's finger. "You're married to Eve Marlow?"

"I am," Josie confirmed as she moved down the bar. Perhaps to make her point, she leaned across the counter and kissed Eve.

Well, that was interesting, and Piper was glad to have Eve's attention elsewhere tonight. She lifted her drink and sipped, feeling the burn of liquor all the way to her stomach. She blew out another breath, and some of the rigidity left her spine. This was okay. She was okay. She'd finish her drink, maybe have another, stay long enough to be able to report tonight as a success to Dr. Jorgensen, and then she'd go home.

"Is this stool open?" a woman's voice asked, and Piper became aware of someone standing beside her, uncomfortably close.

Her muscles stiffened, tension prickling across her scalp. She kept her eyes on her drink, watching the reddish liquid as it glistened beneath the bar's track lighting. "Yep."

"Thanks," the woman said cheerily as she slid onto the stool.

Piper caught a glimpse of jean-clad legs and knee-high black boots. She lifted her drink for another sip. Maybe she'd only stay for one drink after all. A hand strayed across her vision as her new neighbor reached for the drink card.

"These specialty drinks sound so good," the woman said after a moment. "What did you get?"

Piper darted a glance in her direction to see if that question was meant for her. The woman sitting beside her had shoulder-length blonde hair and hazel eyes, which were crinkled at the corners as she smiled at Piper. "Mine's a negroni," she said, answering the woman's question, grateful that she found no hint of recognition in her neighbor's eyes.

"Oh," the woman said, lips pinching. "Too bitter for me."

Piper hummed noncommittally as she returned her gaze to her drink.

The bartender approached. "Welcome to Dragonfly. I'm Josie. Do you know what you'd like to drink?"

"Hm," the blonde said. "I'm torn between the Midnight in Manhattan and the Broadway Bubbles."

"They're both really good," Josie told her. "The Midnight in Manhattan is cooler because of the mint, where the Broadway Bubbles has a bit of a bite."

"Let's go with the Midnight in Manhattan," the blonde said. "Lemon and mint sounds like a winning combination to me."

"Perfect," Josie said. "I'll be right back with that."

The blonde sighed as she settled on her stool. "Come here often?"

Piper glanced to her right, and sure enough, her neighbor was making another attempt at starting a conversation with her. Maybe she'd come in looking for a hookup. This was a gay bar, after all. "No. You?" She surprised herself by tacking on that little question, since she really wasn't trying to get into a conversation.

"First time," the blonde said. "I'm a flight attendant, just in town for the night. One of my coworkers recommended this place, so I decided to pop in for a drink."

Did she even know it was a gay bar? Maybe she was just talkative. That was probably part of her job description. And maybe Piper should indulge her to keep from focusing on the fact that she was in a room full of strangers. Actually, this was one of the scenarios she and Dr. Jorgensen had rehearsed. "Seems like a nice place," Piper said.

"And bonus, I don't have to worry about being hit on by any of the men in the room," the blonde said with a sly wink. Okay, so she did know.

Piper let out a soft laugh. "That *is* a nice bonus."

Josie reappeared in front of them, setting a glass containing an opaque liquid on the bar.

"Thank you," the blonde said, tapping her finger

thoughtfully against the drink menu. "So, what's the deal with this rumor about the Midnight in Manhattan? Did you make that up?"

Intrigued, Piper peeked at the menu, noticing the italicized line beneath the blonde's finger: *Rumor has it, it you drink one at midnight, you'll fall in love before the end of the year.*

Josie laughed. "I could tell you I made it up, but I could also tell you that it worked on me and several of my friends, so I wouldn't discount the rumor." With a wink, she walked off.

"There's no way a drink could make me fall in love," the blonde said, "but I guess it can't hurt, right?"

"You want to fall in love?" Piper asked.

"Well, not tonight, obviously, since I don't live here, but I'm a romantic at heart, so I wouldn't complain if the right woman were to come along and sweep me off my feet."

"Where are you from?" Piper asked, because it seemed the only safe part of that statement to respond to. She thought she'd detected a hint of a southern accent when the woman spoke.

"North Carolina," the blonde said as she sipped her drink. "Mm, this is delicious. Ever been?"

"Once," Piper told her. She'd filmed a bit part in a movie there a few years ago. "The mountains are beautiful, although I only got to see them in passing."

"Oh, that's where I live," the blonde said. "My family's just outside Asheville. I love it there, even though I'm hardly ever home."

"Do you fly somewhere new every day?"

"Almost. I'm a long-range flight attendant, so I typically travel for four or five days at the time, then go home for two to three days, and then I'm off again."

"That sounds exciting but exhausting," Piper commented.

"It is both of those things," the blonde agreed with a laugh.

"How did you get into that line of work?"

The blonde swirled her drink, staring into its opaque depths. "I'd always wanted to see the world, and since I was young and on a budget, this seemed like a good way to make it happen. It's been amazing, but I'm actually moving on at the end of next month."

"You're quitting?" Piper asked.

"Yep. I think it's finally time to stay in North Carolina long enough get my own place and put my interior design degree to good use."

"Ah," Piper said, intrigued by this woman who'd spent however many years flying around the world, traveling so often she had no home of her own. "Where do you live now?"

"With my parents," she said, scrunching her nose. "I know that sounds super lame for a woman my age, but I couldn't justify paying rent when I'm only home two days a week."

"It's not lame," Piper said. "It sounds practical."

"I guess it is." The blonde smiled, drawing Piper's attention to her lips, soft and full and glistening with a combination of lipstick and her drink. "I'm Chloe, by the way."

Piper dropped her gaze to her negroni. *This* was why she'd intended to keep to herself tonight. She could give Chloe a fake name, but somehow that felt disingenuous. They'd only just met, but Chloe seemed so open, so honest, so *real*. It was refreshing. "I'm...trying to be anonymous tonight. Sorry."

∼

CHLOE CARSON SIPPED HER DRINK, cheeks puckering from its tart flavor as she watched the mysterious woman sitting beside her. She was about Chloe's age, probably late twenties or early thirties, with striking blue eyes. A cascade of shiny black hair tumbled over her shoulders, but it was a bit *too* shiny, and it didn't match her eyebrows, leading Chloe to think it was a wig. What kind of woman came to a bar in disguise and unwilling to share her name?

The kind Chloe wanted to get to know, apparently.

"Why didn't you just give me a fake name?" she couldn't help asking.

"Good question," the woman said with a shrug. "That would have been easier, wouldn't it?"

"Yep," Chloe told her. "But this way is more intriguing. So, tell me something less revealing. What brings you to this bar tonight?"

"Trying to prove something to myself," she said as she sipped the reddish liquid in her glass. "And you?"

"Just didn't want to be alone in my hotel room," Chloe told her. "I like to be around people."

"I guess that makes you good at your job."

"It certainly helps," Chloe agreed.

"So you aren't here looking for someone to take back to your hotel room?"

Chloe narrowed her eyes at her neighbor. Was she flirting? She looked vaguely familiar, which gave Chloe the impression she might be a public figure of some kind. And she was probably in the closet. Why else would she be in a gay bar, hiding her identity? "Not necessarily, no," Chloe answered her question. "I'm not usually a one-night-stand kind of girl, but my job makes it hard to maintain relationships, so I've been known to indulge occasionally if I meet the right person."

The raven-haired woman held Chloe's gaze. "I'm not the right person."

"No?"

The woman shook her head, looking away. "I'm just here for a drink."

"That makes two of us, then," Chloe said.

"Tell me one of your favorite places to fly to."

"The Caymans," Chloe answered without thinking. She loved all the tropical islands she'd visited, but the Caymans were on her mind because she'd be flying there next weekend. "I love the sea breeze and the turquoise water and the fact that there aren't any sharks."

"No sharks?" The woman lifted her drink, swirling it so the ice clinked against the glass.

"Almost none, or so I'm told, and there's a sand bar you can visit where the rays literally eat out of your hand. It's so fun. I went out on a boat to feed the rays and snorkel on the reef, and it was amazing."

"That does sound nice," the woman agreed. "It's been too long since I took a vacation."

"You should go sometime," Chloe suggested. "Maybe whatever drove you here tonight should also push you to take that vacation."

"I'm certain my therapist would agree with you."

"Yeah, I have one of those too," Chloe told her with a casual shrug, hoping to maintain the easy banter between them.

"Do you?"

"Mm-hmm. She's my longest-running relationship, aside from my family."

The woman laughed. "I guess I could say the same."

"See? We have something in common." Chloe tapped her glass against the woman's, and they both polished off their drinks.

"Do you get to see much of the places you visit while you're working?" she asked.

"It depends. Often I don't even have time to leave the airport, or—like tonight—I'm here just long enough to grab a drink and sleep before I fly on to my next destination. Sometimes I get to spend a day or two, though. Especially when I visit someplace new, I try to schedule a day off to explore when I can."

"Have you gotten to explore New York?"

"Not this time," Chloe admitted, "although I've done some sightseeing in the past."

"Ah." She fiddled with her empty glass.

"Do you live here?" Chloe asked.

She nodded. "I've lived in Brooklyn for about ten years."

"Like it?"

"Love it." Her gaze darted around the room before returning to Chloe. "Are you having another?" She gestured to Chloe's empty glass.

"Probably shouldn't. Flying with a hangover is a bitch."

The woman nodded. "I'm heading out too. I need some fresh air."

"Want to take a walk?" Chloe asked impulsively. "Maybe you could show me some of Brooklyn I haven't seen before."

She stared at Chloe for a long moment, eyes slightly narrowed, and then she nodded. "All right."

"Great." Chloe knew absolutely nothing about this woman, and maybe that was part of the draw. Certainly there was an undercurrent of attraction running between them, but that wasn't what this was about, not for Chloe, and she didn't think it was for her companion either. It was about sharing an unscripted evening, having an adventure, and that was something Chloe had always cherished.

The woman reached beneath the bar for her purse and her jacket. She slapped a couple of bills on the bar, catching the bartender's attention as she pushed the bills toward her. "Let's go, then."

"Wait. I didn't mean for you to pay for my drink," Chloe protested. "This isn't a date."

"No, but you're helping me achieve a goal tonight, so consider it my token of thanks," the woman said, rising from her stool.

Chloe watched her for a moment in silence. She was tall and slender, graceful like a dancer in her snug-fitting black jeans and a turquoise blouse. As Chloe watched, she shrugged into her black jacket and zipped it. "The lady in black," Chloe commented, watching as she swept her ebony hair out from beneath the jacket. "Thank you for the drink."

"Any time." She smiled, and it lit up her whole face. She was fair skinned with a faint smattering of freckles over her nose and cheeks. Her reddish eyebrows made Chloe ridiculously curious as to what her natural hair looked like. Who was this woman, and what was she hiding from?

"Is there somewhere you'd like to walk, or should we just wander?" Chloe asked as she put on her own jacket, grabbed her purse, and followed the woman out of the bar.

"I have someplace in mind."

"Where?" Chloe asked.

"You'll see," came her response as she struck out down the sidewalk, walking with the swift, sure gait of a local.

"You know, it's not exactly recommended to follow a stranger to an unknown location," Chloe teased as she fell into step beside her. It was true, but the sidewalk around them teemed with people, and whatever Chloe thought of this woman, she couldn't imagine that she was in any sort of danger.

"I guess you'll just have to trust me, then," the woman said slyly. "Or not."

"Very funny," Chloe said. "I do trust you, but I reserve the right to change my opinion if you try to take me down a dark alley or something."

"Fair enough, and not even remotely what I have in mind."

"That's good, because I don't like dark alleys."

"If I could tell you who I was, I could tell you a funny story about a dark alley," the woman said as she glanced over her shoulder at Chloe.

"You're so strange." Chloe shook her head in mock exasperation. Everything about this evening was strange, but she was having fun. This kind of uncharted adventure was the reason she'd become a flight attendant in the first place, and she was going to miss it once she quit her job.

They passed all sorts of people as they walked. Chloe saw couples strolling hand in hand, groups of teenagers laughing and taking selfies on their phones, and plenty of people who appeared to be on their way home from work, heads down and walking with purpose. Chloe had stayed in Brooklyn before, but she'd never been to this part of town. Up ahead, the street opened unexpectedly into a park, complete with grass and trees and... "Oh look, the waterfront!"

"Yes," the woman confirmed. "This is Brooklyn Bridge Park. The views here are stunning, especially after dark."

Chloe was already entranced by the glimmer of water visible through the trees. They walked down a paved path together, and Chloe had another vague thought that she was blindly following a stranger, but the park was well lit and filled with enough people to keep this from feeling weird. Benches lined the path, but the woman kept walking.

Eventually, they came out onto a wider paved walkway that bordered the river. This path was full of people out walking and jogging as Manhattan sparkled from across the glistening expanse of water like an image on a postcard. Unlike a photo, though, this image winked as cars passed through the streets, headlights popping in and out of view. Lights flicked on and off in various buildings, and boats chugged up and down the river, brightly lit bubbles on the dark waves. To her left, the Brooklyn Bridge loomed large and bright, as iconic as the city gleaming behind it.

"This is beautiful," Chloe said quietly.

"It's one of my favorite places." The woman led them across the greenway and onto the rock-strewn shoreline. "This is Pebble Beach."

"Aptly named."

They sat side by side on a bench facing the river, and for a few minutes, they just listened to the splash of the water against the rocks and the hum of conversation around them mixed with the rumble of engines. A gull squawked, and someone nearby laughed. Overhead, a jet blinked across the night sky.

Chloe glanced at the woman beside her, curiosity getting the better of her. "Did you accomplish what you were hoping to tonight?"

She exhaled, looking down at her hands. "Yeah."

"I'm glad."

"I walked into a bar full of strangers and had a drink. Simple enough, right?"

"Sometimes things that sound simple can be the most difficult," Chloe said.

"God, that's so true," she said with a choked sort of laugh.

Chloe gave her a sympathetic smile.

"I..." She exhaled, shifting restlessly on the bench. Then she nodded as if she'd just made up her mind about something. "About six months ago, I was waiting for the subway, and I saw someone commit suicide."

Chloe sucked in a breath at her unexpected confession. "Oh my God."

"I was standing right beside her, and when the train pulled into the station, she just...jumped."

"Shit," Chloe whispered, horrified as she tried to imagine what it would be like to witness such a thing.

"After that, I started having panic attacks in crowded places. They got so bad I basically quit going out in public." She looked away, posture tense beneath her jacket.

Chloe reached over, resting her hand on the woman's wrist, giving it a reassuring squeeze. "That's so understandable, truly. And I can't believe you wouldn't tell me your name, but you just told me something so incredibly personal."

"I guess I told you *because* you don't know my name," she admitted. "Sometimes it's easier for me to talk about difficult things with someone who doesn't know who I am."

"Not to be nosy, but is this the first time you've been out at all? I mean, do you ever leave your apartment...or wherever you live?"

"Believe it or not, I work full time," the woman told her. "About sixty hours a week this time of year. So yeah, I leave my apartment, but that's a familiar environment with familiar people. There's another job I want for the summer, though, and I have to get a handle on these panic attacks before I can...apply for it."

Chloe wondered at the hesitation before *apply*. What did this woman do for work? Was her job part of what made her so secretive? Chloe was a naturally curious person, and it was killing her not to know. Maybe that was why she found herself hanging on her new acquantance's every word. "I think that's very brave of you."

"I don't know if brave's the right word," she said. "My therapist helped me come up with a plan, goals to check off and strategies to help if I panic in public."

"I think brave is exactly the right word," Chloe told her. "I've never had a panic attack, but I know people who have, and they've given me an idea how terrifying it is. Plus I've seen plenty of passengers panic during flights. So yeah, I think it's pretty brave to put yourself out here, knowing it might happen."

"I need my life back," the woman said, her eyes locked on the waterfront before them, hands clasped tightly in her lap.

"And it seems like you're on your way to making that happen," Chloe said. "What's next on the list?"

"There are a bunch of public situations I need to conquer...including a flight."

"You should fly somewhere fun," Chloe said. "I mean, wouldn't you rather have a private beach villa to recover from a panic attack than be in a crowded city? Assuming you can afford that sort of thing."

"You seem to make a lot of assumptions where I'm concerned," the raven-haired beauty said, casting an amused glance at Chloe, but she didn't refute Chloe's assumption that she had money.

"I'm just forward that way, I guess," Chloe told her. "Or maybe you bring it out in me."

"I think it's you, not me," the woman told her, but she

was still smiling, looking much more relaxed than she had in Dragonfly. There was an energy in the air between them, a sizzle of chemistry that had been there since they met.

And Chloe found herself wondering if her mysterious companion had been kissed during her months of self-isolation. Had she been touched, even for a hug? Did she have anyone in her life, or was she alone when she wasn't working? Chloe wasn't sure if she'd leaned closer or if the other woman had, but their shoulders were flush together on the bench now, transferring warmth and connection between them.

Chloe turned her head, dropping her gaze pointedly to the woman's lips. "Is this too forward?"

"No," she whispered, eyes sliding shut as she leaned in for a kiss.

2

Piper rested a hand on Chloe's thigh as their lips met. Electricity surged through her body, something she hadn't felt in too long. Her pulse quickened, flushing her skin with an all-consuming warmth. It felt good, *so* good. Chloe lifted her head, grinning at Piper, and she felt herself smiling back. What had this woman done to her? Of all the scenarios Piper had rehearsed for tonight, she hadn't expected to have fun, and she had Chloe to thank for that.

"Not sure I've ever kissed someone without knowing their name," Chloe said, eyes glittering with the reflection of the city. "And not to be too forward again, but could I give you my number? Maybe we could grab another drink sometime when I'm here in the city."

"I can't make any promises," Piper told her as she unlocked her phone. If Chloe had asked for her number, she would have said no, but by presenting it the other way around, Chloe had given her control of the situation, and control was something Piper needed right now, especially when it came to personal relationships, even one-night stands. She opened a new entry in her address book and handed the phone to Chloe, who tapped in her number and handed it back. "How often do you fly into New York?"

"It depends on my schedule," Chloe told her. "This month, I'll be here every Thursday night, just like this one."

"Good to know." Piper filed that information away, not yet sure what—if anything—she would do with it. Before she could stop herself, she leaned in for another kiss.

This time, Chloe's lips parted, and Piper's tongue slipped into the citrus-infused depths of her mouth. One of Chloe's hands found its way into Piper's lap, squeezing her thigh over her jeans. Her body awakened beneath Chloe's touch, reminding her how long it had been since she'd had sex. Right now, her heart was pounding for all the right reasons, and it was intoxicating.

"I think I like kissing mysterious strangers," Chloe whispered, but there was something hesitant in her expression. Maybe she wasn't ready to take this any further without knowing Piper's name, and that was fine, because Piper wasn't ready for more than a kiss either.

"And I like being kissed by flirtatious flight attendants." She brushed a hand through Chloe's hair, tucking it behind her ear, and then she sat back, returning some space between them. "Do you like pretzels?"

Chloe's brow wrinkled. "Sure."

"The big, soft kind," Piper clarified. "Because if you do, I know a great place, and then I'll walk you back to your hotel."

"Oh." Chloe straightened on the bench.

"Just to be chivalrous," Piper told her. "I'm not coming in."

"You are so confusing." Chloe shook her head, but she was smiling. "And I love soft pretzels, so lead the way."

Piper shivered as she stood. The temperature had dropped since they left the bar, which was typical for March in New York, and she wished she'd worn a thicker jacket. Beside her, Chloe reached into her purse and pulled out a knit hat, which she tugged over her ears. Piper would ordinarily wear a hat too, but her head was warm enough beneath the wig.

She led the way out of the park, hoping the little shop on the corner that sold her favorite pretzels was still here. It had been six months, after all. But the familiar yellow logo greeted them as they left the park. She got her pretzel plain and unsalted, keeping her hair in her face while she ordered even though she didn't recognize the teenager behind the counter. She used to come here often, and the owners knew her by name. Chloe went for cinnamon sugar, which seemed to suit her personality...sweet with a hint of spice.

"You don't really have to walk me to my hotel, you know," Chloe told her as they left the shop, pretzels in hand. "I'm used to wandering unfamiliar cities on my own."

"I bet you are, and I'll say goodbye here if you prefer, but I'd like to walk with you. I could use the exercise...and the company."

"Well, in that case." Chloe nudged a shoulder against Piper's as she bit into her pretzel. "Mm, you're right. This is amazing."

"Told you," Piper said. "Where's your hotel?"

"Oh, um." Chloe fumbled with her phone in her free hand, holding it up so Piper could read the address on the screen.

She nodded, leading the way down the street. They had about a thirty-minute walk ahead of them, but as she glanced over at Chloe, munching happily on her pretzel, Piper realized she'd assumed Chloe was going to walk because of her own issues, when in fact, Chloe had probably planned to hop on the subway. "You don't mind walking, do you?"

Chloe shook her head. "Nope. I took the subway to the bar, but I totally get why you don't want to."

"Sorry." Piper dropped her gaze to her pretzel. "I haven't ridden the subway since that day. It's another thing on my list."

"Understandably so," Chloe said.

This was...strange. Piper wasn't used to talking so openly about what she'd witnessed or the havoc it had wreaked on her mental health. Luckily, despite being interviewed by the police, her presence had never become public knowledge, so she hadn't had to address it in interviews. Most of the people in her life—her friends, family, and costars—knew. They'd all been sympathetic when they heard, but beyond the initial shock of the story, their lives went on unscathed.

For Piper, it hadn't been that easy, an unfortunate fact she'd increasingly begun to keep to herself outside of therapy. She'd been more open and honest with Chloe tonight than she had been with anyone but Dr. Jorgensen in recent months, except for the fact that Chloe didn't know who she was, of course.

Her therapist had been pushing her to open up to someone, though, and somehow it felt less threatening to talk to a stranger. Piper could cross two items off her list tonight.

Ahead of them, a man darted into the street, and Piper's body turned to ice. She froze on the sidewalk, unable to draw air into her lungs, unable to do anything but stare as the man...climbed into a car parked on the opposite curb and drove away.

"Hey, you okay?"

Chloe's voice filtered through the cotton in Piper's ears.

Her lungs were heavy and tight. She closed her eyes, focused on drawing in a slow breath through her nose and exhaling through her mouth, forcing air into her lungs, forcing her body to move past the panic.

"I'm here if there's anything I can do to help," Chloe said, and her voice sounded clearer now that Piper wasn't deafened by the blood pounding in her ears.

She wiggled her toes inside her boots, grounding herself to the feel of her socks against her skin, a trick Dr. Jorgensen had taught her. She'd worn her fuzziest socks tonight for this reason, because they gave great sensory feedback. She focused on her fluffy socks, on the weight of her cell phone in her right hand and the warmth of the pretzel in her left. She licked her lips and tasted lemons, a reminder of Chloe's kiss.

Piper opened her eyes. "Sorry." She sounded breathless, and suddenly, she couldn't bear to look at Chloe. She didn't want to be here, didn't want to have to explain herself to a stranger. She just wanted to go home.

"Don't be sorry," Chloe said quietly. "Is there anything I can do?"

"No." Piper started walking again, rolling her shoulders, which were so rigid, her muscles screamed in protest. "I'm fine."

"Okay." Chloe fell into step beside her, not pushing, not prying, not pitying.

And Piper finally dared to glance in her direction as she slid her phone into the back pocket of her jeans. Chloe was midway through poking a bite of pretzel into her mouth. She grinned at Piper before her lips closed over the pretzel, leaving a smattering of cinnamon sugar on her lips.

Piper had the irrational urge to press her against the side of the nearest building and kiss her until the chaos in her brain had calmed. Chloe's lips quirked as if she'd just read her mind, and then she tripped over a crack in the sidewalk, dropping to her knees on the pavement before Piper could react.

"Dammit, I'm sorry," Piper muttered. "Are you okay?"

"Ouch. Yeah, I'll live." Chloe scrunched her nose as she accepted Piper's outstretched hand and stood. "I guess I should pay more attention to where I'm walking instead of making eyes at the pretty lady beside me."

Piper laughed. "Maybe."

"We're quite a pair, aren't we?" Chloe swiped at her knees, but her jeans didn't seem to be ripped, which hopefully meant her skin wasn't either.

"I guess we are. Still want to walk?"

"Yep. I'm okay, although I kind of feel like I should be walking *you* home, instead of the other way around," Chloe told her.

"But you don't know where I live."

"And you want to keep it that way," Chloe said.

"Sorry." But she felt so much better now, it was almost laughable to think she'd been halfway into a panic attack a few minutes earlier. They walked on in silence, eating their pretzels. Piper wondered at the easy comfort that seemed to resonate between her and Chloe. She hadn't experienced anything like this in so long. "Where will you fly tomorrow?" she asked finally, both to get the conversation going again and because she was curious.

"Tomorrow, I have a boomerang flight from JFK to Chicago and back, then home to Charlotte," Chloe told her.

"Charlotte's not in the mountains, though, is it?" Piper asked, remembering that Chloe told her earlier that her family lived outside Asheville.

"No, it's about an hour and a half drive from Charlotte to

Hendersonville, where I live, but I usually only have to make it once a week."

"That's quite a nomadic life."

"I know," Chloe agreed as she popped the last bite of the pretzel into her mouth. "I've been doing it for eight years, and it's been so much fun, but yeah, I'm ready to slow down."

"You're going to get whiplash, going from constant travel to none," Piper commented as they stopped to wait for the light ahead to change.

"I'm a little worried about that," Chloe admitted. "I hope I don't get bored, but I couldn't live like this forever, you know?"

They crossed the street, stepping to the side as a teenager on a skateboard darted past them.

"No, I don't see how you could," Piper said, "unless you lived closer to the airport and had a schedule that at least allowed you to sleep in your own bed most nights. I mean, some people could maintain your current lifestyle indefinitely, but probably not many."

"Exactly. Oh, here we are. That's my hotel." Chloe gestured to a tall gray building ahead. "Are you sure you're okay to walk home alone?"

"I'm positive," Piper told her, irrationally disappointed that it was time for them to say goodbye.

"I'd tell you to text me and let me know you made it home okay, but..." Chloe gave her a goofy smile.

"I'll be fine. Promise."

"Okay. Well, thanks for a very unusual and fun evening," Chloe said as she turned to face Piper, taking her hands. Her grip was firm and warm. Chloe's hands would be a great grounding tool to use during a panic attack.

"It was unexpectedly nice for me too."

"I'm glad," Chloe told her. "You've got my number, but I do have one request."

"Oh yeah?" Piper asked, holding tight to Chloe's fingers.

"If you want to see me again, I need to know your name."

Piper nodded. "Fair enough."

"Okay, then. Good luck with everything," Chloe told her. "I hope you knock those panic attacks on their ass and get that job you want."

"Thank you. And I hope you find a house and job you love near your family in the mountains."

"Me too. Goodbye, Mystery Woman." With a wave, Chloe walked toward her hotel, disappearing through its brightly lit glass doors.

Piper turned around and started walking. Exhaustion crashed into her as she strode down the sidewalk, the kind of bone deep tiredness that followed a flareup of her anxiety. Tonight had been stressful from start to finish, with a brief respite in the form of Chloe. Piper smiled as she remembered the warmth of Chloe's lips, the calm she'd found in her touch. Chloe had been a very happy addition to her evening.

But now she was so tired, she had to concentrate to keep her boots from scuffing against the sidewalk as she walked. She'd worked a long day on set before she went to the bar, and it had all just caught up with her. She was tempted to call an Uber, but she also knew the exercise would do her good. It would help her sleep. So she walked.

Twenty minutes later, she pushed her key into the front door of her building and let herself inside. She entered the stairwell and trudged up to the third floor, where she inserted another key and let herself inside her apartment. Once the door was bolted behind her, she released a deep sigh.

What a day.

She leaned against the door, touching her lips as she remembered Chloe's kiss. It wasn't just that, though. She found herself replaying her whole evening, drinks and Pebble Beach and pretzels. It had all been unexpected and unexpectedly fun.

When was the last time Piper truly had fun? Not just a good day on set, but the kind of evening where she came home and relived every moment with a smile on her face? Certainly it had been *too* long, which was exactly why she was determined to get past this panic-ridden chapter in her life.

With a sigh, she reached up and tugged the wig from her head. She pulled out the pins holding her hair in place, releasing it down her back. Immediately, the tension on her scalp was relieved, and she gave her head a shake for good measure.

She walked into her bedroom and changed into a tank top and sleep shorts before freshening up in the bathroom. Scrubbing the makeup from her face was another relief. It really had been a long day. As she crawled into bed, she grabbed her laptop from the nightstand to pull up her checklist. Tonight, she had a couple of big ones to check off. She'd successfully gone out for a drink. And she'd opened up about her panic attacks. She'd made a connection and shared a kiss.

The kiss wasn't on her checklist, but it felt like an important milestone nonetheless. She remembered Chloe's suggestion that she should take an impromptu trip, go somewhere warm and tropical to unwind away from the stress of New York. Suddenly, that felt like an excellent idea, but when would she ever find the time? Probably not until after filming for season five of *In Her Defense* wrapped in May, two months away.

Her audition for *Tempted*, the movie role she wanted so badly, she'd finally been inspired to leave her apartment and start working to overcome her panic attacks, was next month, though. Maybe she should try to squeeze in a weekend trip between now and then to keep her forward momentum.

But where? Chloe had mentioned the Caymans. Piper had never been, and suddenly, she wanted to. She doubted she'd hand feed stingrays, but an island with no sharks sounded great, and when she did a quick Google image search, the results were stunning.

After spending half a year oscillating between this apartment and the *Defense* set, Piper couldn't bear it for another moment. Tonight had reawakened something in her, and she couldn't force it back into hibernation, nor did she want to. She pulled up her calendar, surprised to see she was only on the schedule until noon next Friday.

She toggled her browser window to pull up flights, finding a flight out of JFK into Grand Cayman island that departed at three o'clock that afternoon. It was kismet, because she never wrapped so early on a Friday. A few clicks later, she had booked her ticket.

Tropical getaway, here I come.

3

"Goodbye. Thanks for flying with us today!" Chloe repeated the sentiment as passengers shuffled past her and stepped onto the jet bridge. She was exhausted, and her feet ached from a long day, but she spoke to each passenger as they deplaned, even crouching to exchange a high five with a little girl who'd just taken her first flight.

Finally, the cabin was empty except for the flight crew. Chloe walked to the rear of the plane and grabbed a plastic bag. She started at the last row, checking for leftover trash and straightening the contents of each seat back pocket. Nisha, Chloe's friend and fellow flight attendant, was already working her way down the aisle from the opposite direction.

"Got any plans this weekend?" Nisha asked as they met at the middle of the plane. Because this Embraer 170 only had seventy seats, Chloe and Nisha were the only members of the flight crew. They often worked this flight from New York to Charlotte together, and it was always one of Chloe's favorites.

"House hunting, actually," Chloe told her. "You?"

"Working," Nisha said with a sigh. "I picked up a few extra flights."

"Ugh, I'm sorry. How's your mom?" Chloe asked. Nisha's mom had been battling breast cancer for over a year now, and Nisha was working herself to the bone to help support her family while her mom was sick.

"If her numbers go down after this round of chemo, she might have rounded a corner," Nisha told her. "We're hopeful."

"Well, I'll keep sending healing thoughts her way. You guys are due for some good news."

"Thank you," Nisha told her with a tired smile as she tucked a loose strand of black hair into her bun. "I appreciate that. So, house hunting, huh?"

"Yeah, I'm excited. My Realtor scheduled a full day of showings for me tomorrow, and a few of them look really promising."

"I hope you find one you love," Nisha said as she followed Chloe to the galley.

"Me too." They worked side by side as they cleaned and straightened the area for the next crew. After a final check of the cabin, they retrieved their bags and rolled them onto the jet bridge. Chloe heaved a happy sigh as they walked into the terminal. It was good to be home, or almost home, anyway.

After a quick trip to the bathroom, she and Nisha left the airport together, parting in the parking garage. Once she was inside her car, Chloe slipped out of her uniform jacket and released her hair from its tight twist, rubbing at the soreness in her scalp. As she began to drive, her thoughts drifted to the mystery woman she'd met last night.

That *kiss*. Chloe's pulse quickened just thinking about it.

It had only lasted a few moments, and yet, there had been something inherently electric about it. Maybe it was just the aura of mystery surrounding the entire evening. Maybe Chloe got off on kissing women she didn't know.

But she already knew she didn't. She enjoyed flirting with women in bars, but she rarely left with a stranger. Chloe thrived on making connections with people, getting to know them. She'd definitely connected with the woman last night, although her gut said she'd never hear from her again, and maybe that was for the best. Chloe was about to put down roots here in North Carolina, and her mystery woman lived in New York. Still, she'd provided fodder for Chloe's daydreams for the near future, or at least until she found a girlfriend of her own.

As she drove, Charlotte's bustling suburbs gave way to open farmland and soon, the Smoky Mountains darkened the horizon ahead. Chloe's foot nudged the accelerator. No matter how much she enjoyed traveling—and she really did love it—the mountains were her happy place. This was her home.

The sun had sunk below the horizon by the time she pulled into her driveway. Well, her parents' driveway, but Chloe had lived here her whole life too. The front door flew open before she'd even gotten out of the car, and her ten-year-old niece, Caitlynn, came racing down the steps, blonde hair trailing behind her. "Aunt Chloe, I can't wait for you to meet Oreo. He just woke up, so it's a perfect time for you to hold him."

Chloe grinned as she drew her niece in for a hug. Oreo was Cait's new hamster, and she'd been texting Chloe pictures all week as she detailed the process of taming him. "I can't wait to meet him," she told her niece.

"His cage is in my room," Cait said as she led the way inside.

"Let me just take a quick shower, and I'll be right in to see him, okay?"

"Okay," Cait said with a sigh as she jogged upstairs toward her bedroom.

"Chloe, is that you?" her mom called from the kitchen.

"It's me," she confirmed as she kicked off her shoes and walked toward the kitchen in her stocking feet to say hello.

"There's a plate for you in the fridge," her mom said. "How was your week?"

"It was good, the usual insanity," Chloe told her. "And thanks. You're the best. I'm just going to shower and meet Cait's hamster, and then I'll be back down."

Her mom smiled. "She's been waiting to introduce you to that thing for days now."

"I know." Chloe headed upstairs, waving at Cait before she went up the stairs to the attic, which had been converted into her makeshift apartment after she graduated college. It wasn't the most traditional arrangement—three generations under one roof—but they'd needed each other after Cassie's death, Cait most of all.

Chloe rolled her suitcase into her bedroom and closed the door behind her. As tempting as it was to sit on her bed and catch up on the messages on her phone, she knew she'd only feel more tired if she sat. Instead, she stripped out of her uniform and headed into the bathroom to shower. Ten minutes later, she slipped into cotton lounge pants and a T-shirt.

Her gaze caught on the framed photo of her and Cassie on her dresser. It had been taken their freshman year of college, shortly before Cassie got pregnant. They'd been inseparable for the first nineteen years of their lives, two halves of a whole, distinguishable only by the small scar on Chloe's forehead, the result of a childhood fall.

Chloe felt like her life had been turned upside down when her twin sister dropped out of college to have a baby. For the first time, they weren't together. Their lives had diverged, and she had no idea how to get by at college without Cassie by her side. Chloe actually considered dropping out in solidarity, an idea her parents quickly dismissed as ludicrous.

So Chloe had muddled through her sophomore and junior years on her own. She had foolishly thought it was a big deal that Cassie became a mom at nineteen. She'd shed so many tears over the fact that she'd have to find a new roommate, that Cassie was experiencing this major life event without her, that she and Cassie wouldn't graduate together and become flight attendants like they'd planned.

And then came the call that *truly* changed her life. She'd just gotten back to her dorm room after a Zumba class at the campus gym and was desperate for a shower.

"Chloe." There was a kind of raw anguish in her mom's voice Chloe had never heard before, and it turned her stomach to ice. "Honey, I'm so sorry. I don't know how to tell you this, but your sister was killed in a car crash tonight."

For a moment, Chloe had almost laughed, because she and Cassie had that twin connection. They'd always been completely in tune with each other, so there was no way this was really happening, because Chloe would have *known*.

Except, as it turned out, she hadn't. She'd danced and sweated her way through a Zumba class while her sister died, and she hadn't felt a thing. At Cassie's funeral, Chloe realized how naïve she'd been before, lamenting that her sister had become a teenage mom instead of cherishing every moment with her.

She'd fallen into a deep depression, barely leaving her bedroom for weeks, but eventually she'd been saved by a brown-eyed toddler who genetically might as well be her own daughter. Caitlynn had saved them all with her bubbly personality and big heart, Cassie's legacy.

Chloe had briefly lobbied to adopt her, but her parents talked her out of it, reminding her that she was an unemployed college student, barely an adult herself. Instead, they'd adopted Cait, and Chloe finished college and became a flight attendant, the way she and Cassie had planned to do together.

Chloe touched the photo of her and Cassie, wishing desperately that she could tell her sister about her night with the mystery woman. Cassie would have *loved* that story. Instead, Chloe padded downstairs and went into Cait's room. "Is Oreo still up?"

Cait, who was sitting cross-legged on the floor next to a wire-sided cage, waved her over. "Yep. He's nocturnal, so he'll be awake for a while now."

On cue, the hamster scampered across the cage, pausing to look up at Chloe.

"Oh look how cute he is, and the name totally fits." She sat beside her niece, watching as the hamster climbed into his wheel and began to run. He was a deep chocolate brown with a band of white around his stomach, just like the cookie he was named after.

"Do you want to hold him?" Cait asked.

"Duh." Chloe held her hands out.

"He's still shy, so be careful with him, okay?"

"I'll be very gentle, promise."

"Here, I made these treats for him. You can give him one." Cait handed Chloe a hamster-sized cookie.

"You made these? What's in them?"

"Flour, raspberry puree, oats, and water," Cait told her. "Oreo loves them."

"I bet he does," Chloe agreed. "Lucky hamster. So how's school?" she asked as she opened the door on the cage and stuck her hand in with the treat visible on her palm. The hamster ran right over and hopped onto her hand.

"He likes you!" Cait announced. "School's good, except Mrs. Goodman redid our seating plan, and now I have to sit next to this really annoying girl, Rebecca. She always knows the answer to every single question, like *always*."

Chloe laughed at the vehemence in her niece's voice. "I remember girls like that. Is she nice otherwise, though?"

Cait shrugged. "I don't know. She doesn't talk much except to show off by answering all the questions."

"Well, maybe she's shy. You should ask her if she likes hamsters. Maybe she'd like to hear about Oreo."

"Maybe." But Cait didn't look convinced.

"Well, *I* like Oreo," Chloe said, smiling as the hamster sat on her palm and ate the treat Cait had baked for him. "But watching him eat is making me hungry. Want to keep me company while I eat dinner?"

"Sure," Cait said.

They went downstairs, and Cait sat at the kitchen table with her while Chloe ate dinner, before her parents shooed the girl to bed. Chloe sat and chatted with her parents for a little while before climbing the stairs to her room. Before she got into bed, she checked her phone, hoping against hope that the mystery woman would have texted, which was silly, because she knew she wasn't going to hear from her.

There was a text from Nisha, though. *Picked up an extra flight next week – looks like I'll be joining you from Charlotte to Atlanta on Friday.*

Yay that I get to see you, but you need a day off, friend, Chloe replied.

It's true! Hoping to fix that soon.

Good. See you on Friday!

Chloe put her phone on silent and went into the bathroom to wash up. She climbed into bed and snuggled her face against the pillow, drifting to sleep with her mind full of happy thoughts about her upcoming day of house hunting. The next morning, she had breakfast with her family before she headed out.

"Can I come with you, Aunt Chloe?" Cait asked between bites of oatmeal. "Please?"

Chloe looked to her mom. "Unless Gram needs you for something."

Chloe's mom shook her head. "If you don't mind letting her tag along, it's fine with me."

"I'd love some company, and Cait has impeccable taste." Chloe meant it too. She loved spending time with her niece. It was one of the main reasons she'd pushed herself to quit flying and settle down here in Hendersonville this year. Cait was growing up so fast, and Chloe felt like she'd already missed too much time with her.

"Yay!" Cait stood to put her oatmeal bowl in the sink.

Ten minutes later, they were ready to go.

"We'll need to make sure my new house has a nice guest room," Chloe told her as they got into her car together. "Because you're going to be staying over a lot."

"I'll make sure," Cait told her as she buckled herself into the backseat.

Unfortunately, their morning didn't get off to a great start. The first house they visited smelled musty and was surrounded by enough poison ivy to make Chloe itch just thinking about going outside. The second house was adorable, and Chloe was just starting to get excited about it when her Realtor was notified that it had gone under contract. They saw two more houses that Cait accurately summarized as "meh" before taking a break for lunch.

"Met any girls lately?" Cait asked as she disassembled her burger, momentarily sounding so much older than ten that Chloe just blinked at her. It was almost a relief to see that Cait was carefully removing the lettuce, tomato, and onions from her sandwich, leaving behind only the meat and cheese, because it was such a kid thing to do.

Chloe knew her niece was on the verge of tweendom, but she wasn't quite ready to leave behind the little girl with pigtails and a gap-toothed smile who hated vegetables on her burger. "Not really, no," she answered Cait's question. "But I hope I'll have more time for dating once I'm living here full time."

"My friend Lucy likes this boy Brandon who sits in the back of the class, but I think he's gross," Cait told her.

"Well, dating *is* gross when you're ten," Chloe told her with a laugh. "Take your time. Enjoy being a kid, and then enjoy being an adult too. Honestly, there's no rush."

After lunch, they got back in her car and drove to meet her Realtor at the next property.

"I think we're going to like this one," Cait told her from the backseat.

"We haven't even seen it yet," Chloe protested.

"But it's on Cicada Lane, and 'c' is our lucky letter—Chloe, Cassie, and Caitlynn Carson. Plus I really love the sound cicadas make. It makes me think of hiking with Pop and making s'mores on the grill."

"Well, now I really hope we love it," Chloe told her as she turned onto Cicada Lane. Her RAV4 chugged as she aimed it uphill, curving and twisting along the mountain road. "It sure is steep along here."

"I like that too," Cait said, gripping her seat rest with a grin.

They rounded a corner, and the house came into view. It was small, with dark wood paneling and white shutters. Firewood was stacked beneath a shed beside it, and the yard was covered in pine straw, dropped from the looming loblolly pines that surrounded the house.

"I love it," Cait proclaimed.

"I do too," Chloe agreed. Her Realtor's car was already in the driveway, and she pulled in behind it. She and Cait got out of the car and met Sandra on the front steps.

"This one's been on the market for a while," Sandra told her. "There was a dispute over the property line in back, but that's been resolved. Also, it's being sold as-is, so bear that in mind as we walk through, because it does need some work."

"Okay," Chloe agreed, her excitement dampening slightly at this news. She didn't know a thing about home renovations, but as she stepped inside, she had a feeling she was going to have to learn, because this was the one. She was pretty sure about it.

"You know who's good at fixing things?" Cait said behind her.

"Who?" Chloe asked.

"Pop."

"Yeah, you're right about that." Chloe's dad was definitely handy around the house. She'd hoped to be fully independent for a change after she moved out, but maybe it wasn't the end of the world if she had to ask her parents for a little help.

She and Cait wandered through the house, falling more in love with each room they saw. The kitchen was small and seemed to still have all the original appliances from when it was built in the sixties, but she could live with that until she had the cash to upgrade them. There was a wood-burning fireplace in the living room and gorgeous hardwood floors throughout.

In back, there were two bedrooms, a bathroom, and a patio that led into a small backyard, bordered by the forest beyond. There was a whole lot of hideous wallpaper and an issue with the heating system that Chloe didn't entirely understand, but she was determined to make it work. This place felt like home. And Cait was already in the guest room, deciding where all the furniture should go.

Chloe turned to her Realtor. "I'd like to make an offer."

4

O n the following Friday, Piper set her alarm an hour earlier than usual, much as it pained her to lose that sleep, so she'd have time to finish packing before she left for the set. She would go straight from there to the airport, and as she climbed out of bed and went into the bathroom, she was already oscillating between excitement and panic.

Ever since her impromptu evening with Chloe last week, she'd been impatient to get out there again, to keep pushing herself, and she could hardly wait for her weekend on the beach. If only she could hurry up and *be* there, because she wasn't looking forward to the flight. She'd never enjoyed flying, and she liked it even less the more famous she became. Usually, if she covered her hair and waited to be one of the last people to board, she could go unnoticed, but occasionally, someone still recognized her, and that might be more than she could handle today.

She'd dealt with anxiety since she was a teenager and had been in and out of therapy since. It was just how she was wired, and she generally managed it well. That had changed with the onset of her panic attacks six months ago. She was determined to overcome this setback, though, and this trip would hopefully be the next step in that direction.

She dressed in jeans and a tank top before pulling up the packing list on her phone and getting to work. Once her duffel bag contained everything she needed for the weekend, she fixed herself a bowl of cereal and some much-needed coffee. She had about twenty minutes before the car would arrive to drive her to the set.

As she ate, she tapped through notifications on her phone, typing a quick response to her mom to confirm that yes, she'd come home for a visit after she'd wrapped filming for the season. Then she went into her bedroom to finish getting ready. She paused in front of Master's tank.

The red fish stared back at her, wide-eyed.

"Be good while I'm gone, okay?" She opened the container of freeze-dried bloodworms while he tracked her every move, fins flaring in anticipation of breakfast. It was one of her favorite things about betta fish, their ability to see outside the tank. It gave her a sense of connection with him. Master knew she was standing here, about to feed him. It also helped her feel less like a weirdo when she talked to him, because maybe he could hear her too. Who knew?

She sprinkled several worms over the surface of his water. Since he only ate every other day, he'd be fine until she got home on Sunday, another thing she loved about having a fish. Then she grabbed her bag and went downstairs, where the car was already waiting.

Thirty minutes later, she entered the Brooklyn sound-stage where *In Her Defense* filmed. After dropping off her bag in her dressing room, she headed straight to the hair and makeup department to begin her transformation into Samantha Whitaker, defense attorney and all-around badass. Sam—and the rest of her firm—specialized in representing women who had been victimized, hence the name of the show.

Piper settled in her chair next to Eliza Cummings, who played Claire Burroughs, another lawyer at the firm and Sam's onscreen best friend. "Morning."

"Morning," Eliza replied, a faint smile curving her lips as she attempted to hold still for the makeup team. "Ready to get shot?"

Piper grumbled in response, because yeah, she was going to spend the morning getting knocked on her ass and drenched in stage blood when Sam got shot by the disgruntled ex-husband of one of her clients. She'd spent several hours yesterday rehearsing the stunt, falling backward onto an airbag, and consequently, she was already sore.

"Morning, Piper," her makeup artist, Ariana, said as she stepped up to Piper's chair.

"Morning," she replied, smiling at her in the mirror.

An hour later, she was on her way back to her dressing room to put on one of Sam's signature power suits. Usually, Sam wore skirt suits, but for the sake of today's stunt, she would wear pants. Piper surveyed herself in the mirror as she buttoned her blazer. Her auburn hair cascaded over her shoulders in long, loose waves that she could never manage to recreate on her own, and yes, she'd tried.

Sam's hair had become almost as iconic as her badass attitude, so much so that it had been written into Piper's contract that she couldn't alter it in any significant way for the duration of her work on the show. She didn't mind, except that her hair had become her most recognizable feature. If she went out in public without covering it, she was almost certain to be recognized, which was why she'd invested in various wigs and hats to help her go about her daily life anonymously.

A wig wouldn't work on the beach, though. She'd just have to hope she was less recognizable on Grand Cayman. Generally, that had been the case in the past, although she hadn't traveled since last year, and the show had picked up even more momentum in the meantime. It consistently ranked as one of the most-viewed shows on the streaming service that produced it and had racked up an impressive list of awards, including Piper's first Emmy nomination.

As she left her dressing room, she almost bumped head-long into Nate Mauldin, who played Sam's business partner, Tony Reynolds. Nate paused with a smile. He was dressed for their shoot in a gray suit that offset his dark brown skin. She and Nate had a great rapport, both on and off screen, and the rumors about them circulated on both fronts as well, but although the show's producers played up the "will they or won't they" for Sam and Tony, Piper and Nate were definitely just friends.

"Ready to be a stunt queen this morning?" he asked as he fell into step beside her.

"So ready to fall repeatedly on my ass." She rolled her eyes playfully as they walked toward the set that repre-sented the firm's lobby, where they'd be filming this morn-ing. Truly, she didn't mind doing stunt work. It was physically intensive, but not emotionally, which was a nice change of pace from some of the more angsty stuff she'd filmed earlier in the week.

For the first scene of the morning, Piper and Nate would walk down the hallway together, deep in conversation before being confronted by a client's ex-husband in the lobby. They took their marks at the end of the hall while the crew assembled around them. The assistant director rehashed the logistics of the scene with them, a production assistant attached their mics, and soon enough, they were rolling.

She and Nate walked down the hall, discussing the case Sam and Tony had just closed. The actor playing their client's ex-husband—an older man named David Seabrooke—stood facing them in the lobby with a truly terrifying look on his face. Piper flinched. "Mr. Morrow, what are you doing here? I can't speak to you without your counsel present."

He leered at her. "I didn't come here to talk."

He lifted his right hand, brandishing a gun. The cold prickle of fear in the pit of Piper's stomach was real. She was in Sam's head right now, reacting as her character, and that gun was pointed right at her.

Click. Click. Click.

David pulled the trigger three times, but this being a television set, the gun was only a prop. The sound of gunfire would be added in during postproduction.

"Cut," the director, Steve Jackson, called. "And reset."

Immediately, the set filled with a buzz of conversation and activity as the crew began to reset for the next take. This was a simple scene but needed to be shot from multiple angles. In all, it took five takes for Steve to get everything he needed. Piper walked to the craft services table for a drink of water while they set up for the next scene.

"So jealous that you'll be on a beach in the Caymans later today," Nate commented as he followed her.

"I'm counting down the hours," she told him.

"Just you this weekend?"

"Just me," she confirmed as she twisted the cap off a bottle of water and took a long drink.

"Who knows, maybe you'll meet someone while you're there," he teased. "Hot weekend fling in paradise?"

"Highly doubtful," she said. "I just want to relax, honestly."

They walked to the lounge area at the back of the sound-stage and sat, chatting while they waited to be called back onto the set for Piper's stunt scene. Ten minutes later, they reentered the firm's lobby, where a lime-green airbag had been placed just behind Piper's mark for her to fall onto after Samantha was shot. The airbag would be edited out of the shot during postproduction.

The assistant director approached to recap the logistics with her while various assistants hovered, touching up her hair and makeup and checking her mic. She'd rehearsed her fall dozens of times yesterday. She was ready.

"You got this, Stunt Queen," Nate said as he took his place beside her.

"Easy for you to say. You get to stay on your feet." She glanced down to ensure her toes were on the red tape that served as her mark.

"Quiet on set," Steve called. "Camera ready?"

"Ready," the camera operator replied.

"Sound?"

"Sound speed," called the sound mixer.

The assistant director nodded. "Mark it."

A production assistant held the clapboard in front of the camera, marking the scene and take.

"And...rolling."

Piper fell backward, smacking into the airbag. The impact was jarring despite the cushion of air, and her back stung where it met the mat.

"Cut," Steve called. "That was great, Piper. Next time see if you can get a little more momentum in your fall. I don't want to see any hesitation when you go down."

She nodded as she crawled off the airbag and stood,

straightening her clothes. The hair and makeup team rushed in to touch her up. Then she fell again, and again, and again, until she was breathless and sore from head to toe. Finally, they had the shot.

Piper only had one more scene this morning, and it involved an unfortunate amount of stage blood. She unbuttoned her shirt and stood patiently while someone from the special effects department applied a fake gunshot wound above her right breast. Then she stretched out on the floor as if this was where she'd landed after being shot.

She lay there while the special effects team artfully applied stage blood all over her chest before buttoning her back up. They inserted a blood pack beneath her back that, when activated, would slowly spread a red pool across the tiles to illustrate Sam's blood loss.

Eliza—who would be joining them for this scene—stood over Piper while they worked. Between bouts of hysterical laughter, she told Piper about the extra who had farted loudly while they were filming her first scene of the morning.

"That'll go on the blooper reel," Piper said, accepting a red capsule from one of the techs.

"Places, everyone," the AD called, and Piper popped the capsule into her mouth. Nate came to stand beside her, and Eliza went through a door to her right, ready to rush into the lobby when she heard the gunfire. "Quiet on set."

The various departments made their calls and marked the scene.

"And we're rolling."

Piper bit down on the capsule, and her mouth filled with a disgustingly sweet syrup. She lay motionless, staring at the ceiling as a camera on a boom arced across her vision overhead. She heard a shout and a thump as Nate tackled the shooter.

On cue, Piper gasped, allowing a trickle of blood to escape her mouth. It dripped over her cheek as she wheezed for breath. Beneath her, the blood pack activated, and a sticky wetness began to seep through her jacket. This was going to be a mess to clean up later.

She heard footsteps, and then Eliza was leaning over her, eyes wild with panic. "Sam! Sam, oh my God."

Piper stared at her, imagining a searing pain in her chest, her pulse weakening as the pool of blood beneath her spread. She opened her mouth, releasing more stage blood.

Eliza whipped out her cell phone and called for an ambulance before ripping open Piper's blouse. "Stay with me," she urged, tears glistening in her eyes as she pressed one of her hands over the gunshot wound. "You can't leave me, Sam, not like this."

Piper lifted her hand to clutch at Eliza as she struggled to breathe. She wasn't looking at what she was doing—the scene called for her to stare at Eliza's face—so it took her a moment to realize she'd missed the lapel of Eliza's jacket and palmed her breast instead.

Oops.

Neither of them reacted, and since Steve didn't call cut, they kept going with the scene. Eliza slid her free hand over Piper's chest, checking her for additional injuries. Somehow this had felt more technical and less...sexual during yesterday's rehearsal. But with the cameras rolling and Eliza hovering over her, bottom lip pinched between her teeth and both hands on Piper's bare chest, she already knew what the fans would say.

"Cut!" Steve called. "I know that was an accidental fumble, Piper, but I think it works. Let's keep it."

Seriously, they wanted her to purposefully grope Eliza for the next take?

"Sorry," she whispered to her friend, but Eliza just shrugged, looking unconcerned.

This scene—like the others—had to be filmed from multiple angles, so Piper stayed where she was. She sat up so the crew could clean up the pool of blood beneath her. The makeup team removed the blood from her face and retouched her makeup. All in all, it was an uncomfortable and time-consuming process. After four grope-filled takes, the scene was complete, and Piper was a blood-soaked mess.

"That's a wrap for you today, Piper," Steve called. "Great job."

"Thank you," Piper told him as she stood, accepting the towel a tech held toward her to wipe excess blood from her skin. By now, her hair was sticky and wet, and her clothes were soaked through. She headed for her dressing room. According to the clock, she had thirty minutes to shower and get ready before the car arrived to take her to the airport. She bumped into *In Her Defense*'s showrunner, Benny Peters, in the hallway.

"Fantastic work today, as always," he told her. "That last scene was particularly intense."

"Thanks. Is it me, or are you playing up the Sam and Claire angle this season?"

"The fans go wild every time you two are on screen together," he said with a shrug. "We have to give them what they want, right?"

"Yes, but unless you plan to actually explore a romance between Sam and Claire, that's queerbaiting, and they won't be happy about it."

His bushy brow furrowed. "I'm not familiar with the

term, but I don't see how this is any different from the way we play up the romantic potential between Sam and Tony."

Piper paused, deciding to forfeit a few minutes of valuable shower time to seize this opportunity to voice her concern, because Benny wasn't on set every day, and she'd been looking for an opening to discuss this with him. He was well intentioned, but he was a straight man, and she was an out bisexual actress playing a character who was dangerously close to becoming a cliché. "Queerbaiting is when a creator teases a same-sex relationship between characters to generate hype but never actually delivers."

"Queerbaiting," Benny muttered, hands on his hips. "That's a new one."

"The LGBTQ community is notoriously underrepresented on mainstream television, and queer viewers jump to support a potential onscreen same-sex relationship, but too many shows have started baiting them with flirtatious characters and situations that never actually turn into something more, to avoid alienating the more conservative audience." She paused. "That's what makes the sexual tension between Sam and Claire different from Sam and Tony."

"Ah, okay," he said. "I see."

"Anyway, trust me when I tell you that *Defense*'s queer fans will be pissed if you keep teasing them with scenes between Claire and Sam like the one we just shot without eventually following through with at least a kiss."

"I'll think about it," Benny told her, patting her shoulder as he continued down the hall.

Piper turned toward her dressing room, hurrying now. Her skin was sticky and wet with stage blood, her clothes clung to her uncomfortably, and she was desperate for a shower. She closed the door to her dressing room behind her and peeled off the ruined suit, tossing it into the bin for the costume department to deal with, but she imagined they'd throw it away. Surely, there was no way to get that much blood—even fake blood—out of the fabric.

Once she was ensconced beneath the shower's hot spray, scrubbing red syrup from her skin, she reflected on her conversation with Benny. Hopefully, she hadn't overstepped, but he was generally a reasonable guy, and he had seemed receptive to her concerns.

Clairantha was the name the fans had created for Claire and Samantha to show that they "shipped" them as a couple. Piper was tagged in an ever-increasing amount of Clairantha fanart and posts on her social media, and she was painfully aware she might be responsible for launching the ship, so to speak. During the show's first season, she'd been helplessly attracted to Eliza, and when she rewatched those early episodes, she saw her own yearning on Sam's face as she gazed at Claire.

Luckily or unluckily, Eliza was straight, so nothing had ever happened between them. Piper had gotten over her attraction years ago, but the fandom's response to Sam and Claire's relationship had taken on a life of its own.

And despite her conversation with Benny, Piper didn't exactly relish the idea of kissing Eliza, just in case it brought those old feelings back to life. They were good friends, and she didn't want to mess that up. But she couldn't let her personal issues get in the way of pushing for better queer rep on television. If she got the chance, she would embrace it and be proud to portray a sapphic romance on *In Her Defense*.

After what felt like forever, Piper finally rinsed the last of the stage blood from her body. She stepped out of the shower and toweled off. Ten minutes remained until the car arrived to drive her to the airport. Anxiety swept over her, heavy and all-consuming, causing her heart to pound and a sick feeling to spread through her stomach. This flight was all that stood between her and a much-needed weekend on the beach.

She scrambled into her clothes and picked up her duffel bag. Then she blew out a breath, squared her shoulders, and walked outside. She had a flight to catch and a life to reclaim.

~

CHLOE PUSHED her rolling suitcase through Hartsfield-Jackson International Airport's food court with one hand as she balanced the tray containing her salad and drink with the other. She looked around for Nisha. They'd touched down here in Atlanta about thirty minutes ago and were going to eat lunch together before Chloe flew on to Grand Cayman and Nisha flew to Boston.

Chloe spotted a familiar purple uniform and Nisha's distinctive glossy black bun up ahead. She weaved between tables until she'd reached her, setting her tray down gratefully. "Mm, that looks good," she said, eyeing Nisha's burger and fries with envy. Nisha was a vegetarian, but veggie burgers were pretty good these days, and Chloe had her friend to thank for that knowledge.

"It's my cheat day," Nisha told her as she dipped a fry in ketchup and popped it into her mouth.

"I'm saving mine for tomorrow," Chloe said. As flight attendants, they both ate a *lot* of meals in airport food courts. Chloe had to make an effort to choose salads and other healthy options most of the time, or else she'd end up eating burgers and pizza every day.

"I'm so jealous you get to spend the weekend in

paradise," Nisha said as she unwrapped her burger. "How did you manage that?"

"I just scheduled my route to end there this week instead of Charlotte. I'll miss seeing my family this weekend, but I only have five weeks left as a flight attendant, so I'm living it up while I can. Soon enough, I'll be home with them full time."

"You've got your priorities right," Nisha said. "I am so glad it all worked out for you the way you wanted."

"You do too, you know," Chloe reminded her. "We're both juggling career and family obligations."

"Well, assuming Mom gets a break after this round of chemo, I think I'm going to follow in your footsteps and take her for a vacation, somewhere relaxing and tropical."

"Oh, you *should*," Chloe said as she poured dressing over her salad and speared a bite of chicken. "You guys would have so much fun."

"You'll have to give me all your island recommendations."

"Definitely," Chloe agreed.

"You never heard from that woman you met in New York last week?" Nisha asked.

Chloe shook her head. "I wasn't really expecting to, to be honest. As much as I liked her—and I'm pretty sure the feeling was mutual—I could tell she wasn't looking to start anything. And it's fine, because she lives in New York, so it couldn't have been anything more than a hookup anyway. Hopefully, I'll meet a nice girl in North Carolina once I'm there permanently."

"I hope you do." Nisha wiped ketchup from her cheek. "Once Mom's well, I want to put some effort on that front too. She's been trying to set me up with one of her friends' sons, but the man is just obnoxious."

"Hopefully, this year will bring romance for both of us," Chloe agreed.

They chatted through the rest of their lunch and parted ways before Chloe boarded the plane train to the international terminal. Once there, she stopped in the ladies' room to brush her teeth and touch up her makeup. She used the facilities so she could avoid the airplane's tiny lavatory, and then she made her way to the gate.

"Hello, Chloe."

She turned to find Tammy, a fellow flight attendant, waving as she wheeled her suitcase toward the gate. As the most senior member of this crew, Tammy would be the purser on their flight into Grand Cayman and work the first-class cabin. Tammy was about ten years older than Chloe and sometimes prone to doling out unsolicited advice, but Chloe flew a lot of international flights with her, and they generally got along fine. "Hey, Tammy."

"Hi, ladies." Zach, the third member of their flight crew, joined them at the gate. He would be working the main cabin with Chloe. They exchanged greetings and boarded the plane together, stowing their luggage at the rear of the aircraft before they began to complete their preflight check.

The pilot came out to brief them on the upcoming flight, letting them know they'd be flying over some inclement weather that might cause in-flight turbulence. Chloe and Zach walked through the economy cabin, ensuring all the safety equipment was in place and working properly. Once everything had been thoroughly checked, the gate crew opened the jet bridge so passengers could begin boarding.

This being a flight to the Caribbean, Chloe greeted numerous passengers in tropical-printed clothes, eagerly anticipating a long-awaited vacation. It made her happy. These were her favorite flights, when the majority of the passengers were beginning their vacation. Their excitement was infectious.

She walked through the main cabin, assisting with overhead bins. Soon, everyone was seated, and she, Zach, and Tammy were completing their last walkthrough while the safety video played. This would be a relatively short flight, about two hours from takeoff to touchdown.

Chloe was already daydreaming about a quiet weekend on the beach, fruity drinks in hand and perhaps a snorkeling trip in the afternoon. Maybe parasailing? She hadn't been parasailing in years. It was amazingly peaceful up there, soaring over the ocean with nothing but the sound of the wind in her ears.

Speaking of soaring, she and Zach strapped themselves into the jump seats at the rear of the plane as it taxied toward the runway. A few minutes later, they lifted off, leaving Atlanta behind. As soon as the plane reached cruising altitude, Chloe and Zach made their way to the galley to begin the in-flight drink service. Tammy was already there, preparing drinks for the first-class passengers.

"There's a celebrity on this flight," she whispered with a delighted smile. This wasn't unusual or something that Chloe generally got very worked up about, especially since she was working the main cabin and the famous face was no doubt in first.

"Who?" Zach asked.

"Piper Sheridan," Tammy told him. "She's on that legal drama...what's it called..."

"*In Her Defense*," Zach said, turning to peer covertly into the cabin. "Oh my God, you're right."

Chloe felt an uncomfortable tug of recognition at the name. She formed a mental image of an attractive redhead in a killer suit, but why did she feel more familiar than that?

Chloe straightened, turning to face the first-class cabin, and found herself staring straight into the equally shocked eyes of her mystery woman.

She was dressed all in black with a knit cap on her head, allowing only a few auburn strands of hair to escape, but Chloe would know that face anywhere...and not from the TV. This was the woman she'd shared an oddly intimate evening with, the woman she'd kissed without ever knowing her name.

Piper Sheridan.

No fucking way. Chloe had had a vague idea that her mystery woman might be a public figure, but okay, she hadn't actually thought she was *this* famous. Piper's expression had changed, surprise morphing into something much more brittle, and Chloe realized she was staring. Gawking was probably more like it.

Real smooth, Chloe.

She gave Piper what she hoped was a reassuring smile, a "your secret is safe with me" kind of smile.

In response, Piper unclipped her seat belt and rose, sliding over the empty seat beside her to reach the aisle. She rushed toward the lavatory, which, unluckily for her, was occupied. She braced one hand against the wall, chest heaving, eyes darting around the cabin, and Chloe realized belatedly that she was panicking. Worse, she was probably panicking *because* of Chloe, because she had gawked at Piper as if she were an animal in the zoo.

Dammit. She approached Piper to apologize, but just as she reached her side, Piper's knees gave out and she slumped toward the floor.

5

The world was spinning. Piper wiggled her toes frantically inside her boots, one hand on the side of the airplane in a desperate attempt to keep herself upright. The light on the door to the lavatory remained frustratingly red. Why hadn't the person inside come out yet?

The plane lurched beneath her feet, and Piper lost her balance entirely. She pitched forward in a dizzying reversal of the stunt she'd performed earlier, bracing herself for a nosedive onto the carpet before warm hands closed over her biceps, steadying her.

"Hey," Chloe's voice said quietly, and Piper wrenched her eyes open, not sure whether to be grateful or horrified that it was Chloe who'd come to her rescue. "I'm sorry if I freaked you out. I was just surprised to see you, that's all."

Piper squeezed her eyes shut again, because everything was still spinning, like her brain had come loose inside her skull. Her heart pounded painfully, and she couldn't seem to draw air into her lungs. The walls were closing in, and she just needed to get inside the bathroom for a moment of privacy so she could pull herself back together.

Oh God, she was making a spectacle. She'd so desperately wanted to go unrecognized, and now the whole plane was probably staring. The plane lurched again, and her stomach dipped. Someone whimpered, and it took her one slow, agonizing breath to realize it was her.

"Come with me," Chloe said, wrapping an arm around Piper's shoulders.

Piper didn't know where they could possibly go, but anywhere had to be better than standing at the front of the plane in full view of the whole cabin while she had a panic attack. She stared at her feet as Chloe guided her forward, resting a hand against Piper's lower back to steady her. When she lifted her gaze, they were in the galley where the flight crew prepared drinks and meals. Directly in front of her were several coffee pots and to either side, she saw a confusing assortment of drawers and compartments.

Chloe stood behind her, effectively trapping her in the narrow space, but as Piper braced her hands against the walls, she was able to draw her first full breath in too many minutes. She stood there, concentrating on her breathing, grounding herself in her shoes, until the pressure in her chest eased. Gradually, the world stopped spinning.

She became aware of the scent of coffee, the vibration of the floor beneath her feet, and Chloe's warm presence behind her. *Chloe.* What were the chances she'd be on this flight? Slowly, Piper turned to face her.

Chloe wore a purple pencil skirt and matching jacket buttoned snugly over a white blouse. Her blonde hair was tied back, accentuating her cheekbones. She looked professional yet undeniably sexy in her uniform. The way her skirt hugged the curve of her hips ought to be illegal, but that was probably Piper's hormones talking. After all, she'd done entirely too much fantasizing about Chloe since their evening together in Brooklyn.

Now she knows who I am.

Piper sucked in a breath, heart rate again spiking.

"Okay?" Chloe asked.

"Fine," Piper muttered, suddenly desperate to get back to her seat, or maybe to the bathroom after all, where not even Chloe could see her.

"I'm sorry for staring," Chloe said quietly. "I didn't mean to upset you."

"It's not...that's not why."

"The pilot turned on the fasten seat belt sign because of turbulence," Chloe told her. "Beverage service will be delayed, but do you want something while we're in here? Water? Something stronger?"

"Water would be good." She accepted the bottle Chloe held toward her. "Thank you."

"No problem."

They stared at each other for a few moments of awkward silence, and Piper was still too unbalanced to manage whatever this was. She just wanted to close her eyes and wake up in the Caymans. "I guess I should get back to my seat, then."

"If you're ready," Chloe said.

"I'm ready."

Chloe extended a hand, holding something toward Piper, and as she squinted at it, she realized it was her hat. *Fuck.* She was suddenly aware of her hair cascading over her shoulders. She desperately wanted to know how much of a scene she'd made out there, but she couldn't bring herself to ask, could hardly even bring herself to meet Chloe's eyes. Instead, she accepted the hat with a mumbled thanks, tucking her hair carefully beneath it.

Then she walked past Chloe into the aisle, keeping her gaze firmly on the ground as she made her way back to her seat. She sank into it gratefully, fastened her seat belt, and reached into her bag for her noise canceling headphones, which she slipped over her ears. She started her relaxation playlist and leaned her head against the side of the jet, closing her eyes so that she was enveloped in the haunting beauty of Adele's voice.

She could only hope and pray that none of the other passengers had filmed her meltdown. Not only would it be embarrassing, but she didn't want anyone to know she was in the Caymans until after she'd left.

And then there was Chloe.

What would she do now that she knew Piper's identity? Secure in her anonymity, Piper had told her things that weren't public knowledge. She'd been vulnerable with Chloe in a way she rarely allowed herself to be with anyone, let alone a perfect stranger. And now that stranger knew her secrets.

But she couldn't think about that right now. For the moment, she needed to concentrate on her breathing. Her hands shook, and that jittery feeling in the pit of her stomach still hadn't dissipated. If she wasn't careful, she'd spiral right back into panic. She shouldn't think about Chloe or wonder if she was watching Piper right now. She definitely shouldn't think about Chloe's ass in that skirt. This flight would have been infinitely easier if Chloe wasn't on it.

So she wasn't sure why she was disappointed when she looked up sometime later to find that the flight attendant taking her drink order wasn't Chloe at all. It was an older woman with an eager sort of smile that told Piper she knew exactly who she was and couldn't wait to tell everyone she knew that Piper Sheridan had been on her flight.

~

CHLOE STEPPED into the terminal in Grand Cayman, hoping desperately that Piper might be waiting for her as she exited the aircraft. She'd rushed through her postflight checklist on the off chance she might get to see Piper again, to talk to her, something, *anything*. But Piper wasn't here.

Chloe hadn't gotten to speak to her again during the flight. When she passed her seat, Piper wore noise-canceling headphones, face carefully averted from the aisle, and since Chloe was assigned to the main cabin, she had no reason to approach Piper other than a personal one, which didn't feel right under the circumstances.

Now, Chloe was in Grand Cayman, and Piper was long gone. So that was that, then. She knew the identity of her mystery woman, for all the difference it made, because she'd probably never see Piper again. Chloe was staying at a budget hotel a few blocks from the beach, so there was no chance they were staying at the same place.

"Have a great weekend," Zach called with a wave.

"You too."

Chloe bit back her disappointment as she strode through the terminal bustling with eager tourists. As a flight attendant, she didn't have to wait in line with them at customs, though. She went through the expedited lane reserved for flight crew and was soon in a taxi on the way to her hotel. It was an older building, but she'd stayed here before and knew it to be clean and comfortable.

She checked into her room and headed up, sighing as she pulled the door shut behind her. There was a double bed at the center of the room and a table in the corner. Her window overlooked the small pool in back, gleaming brightly and filled with happy vacationers. She couldn't see the beach from here, but she could walk to it. In fact, she decided to do just that. She rolled her suitcase to the bed and pulled out a light cotton dress and sandals, quickly changing out of her uniform.

She'd go for a walk on the beach and then find someplace to have dinner and a drink. Actually, she probably deserved several drinks after a long work week and her eventful flight with Piper fucking Sheridan. She gave her head a slight shake. Now that she knew Piper's identity, she wondered how she hadn't recognized her before. She wasn't a loyal viewer of *In Her Defense*, but she'd seen enough episodes to know who Piper was. She'd even seen Piper in a TV movie a few years ago.

Chloe had been impressed with her performance, even if she hadn't been paying close enough attention to really call herself a fan. She didn't remember hearing about the incident Piper had described in the subway, so she suspected Piper's presence wasn't public knowledge, and she was glad for that.

Once she'd changed, Chloe grabbed her purse and left her room. She was tired enough that if she paused, if she sat down on her bed, she'd never make it out, and she really did want to see the beach tonight. Besides, this wasn't the kind of hotel that had room service, even if that was what she'd wanted, and she was starving.

The sidewalk outside bustled with tourists. Most of them seemed to be American, based on the accents she heard as she walked. Two girls about Cait's age raced by with ice-cream cones, putting Chloe in the mood for something sweet after dinner. This weekend was a vacation, after all. It was her last vacation before she settled down in North Carolina and started the next chapter in her life, and she was going to live it up.

She located the public beach access between two towering hotels, amber lights illuminating the sand. She could smell the ocean now and hear the rhythmic roar of the waves. The tension of a long day drained from her shoulders as she kicked off her sandals and sank her toes into the cool sand.

Bliss.

For someone born and raised in the mountains, the ocean had always held a special place in her heart. She loved it here. The beach was fairly crowded considering that the sun had gone down hours ago. Groups of friends and families had gathered on blankets and chairs, laughing and drinking, and lots of people were out for an evening stroll.

Chloe walked down to the surf, crossing the line where the sand changed from soft and dry to hard-packed and wet. She paused there, waiting for the next wave to come and get her. It didn't take long. A gentle wave rolled in, splashing against her feet. The water was colder than she'd expected, and she took an involuntary step back.

She looked up, spying a full moon overhead. It gleamed between puffy silver clouds, reflected on the ocean below. So pretty. But when she lifted her phone and tried to snap a photo, she got nothing but an unimpressive white blob on an otherwise black screen, which was a bummer. She had wanted to send a photo to Cait, but she'd have to wait and send her one tomorrow in the sunshine.

Her phone chimed in her hand, indicating she'd received a text message. She'd barely registered that it was from an unknown number when her gaze caught on the preview.

Hi, it's Piper...

Chloe felt a ping in her stomach, adrenaline rushing through her system. It gave her such a jolt, she almost dropped her phone on the wet sand in the process of calling up the rest of the text.

Hi, it's Piper aka your mystery date from last week.

Chloe drew in a breath. Why was Piper texting her now, after ignoring her for over a week and rushing off the plane without speaking to her? She stared at the message for a moment, unsure how to respond.

Her fingers hovered over the screen as she debated whether to apologize again for her behavior on the plane or ask how long Piper was going to be on the island. Finally, Chloe decided to go for playful and let Piper set the tone for their interaction.

So you didn't delete my number after all! It was good to see you today.

She hit Send and then stood there, waves washing over her feet as she waited for Piper's response. Almost immediately, the little dots at the bottom of the text box began to bounce.

Are you still on the island?

Yes, Chloe replied.

Can we meet?

By now, Chloe's heart was racing, butterflies flapping in her stomach, a swirling whirl of indecision, because she wanted to see Piper *so* badly. She liked her, she was hella attracted to her, and she felt a bit protective of her after witnessing her panic attack on the airplane.

But on the flip side, Chloe couldn't help feeling hurt that Piper hadn't texted earlier, that she'd done her best to avoid Chloe during the flight. It made her wonder why Piper was texting her now and maybe even a little cynical about her intentions. Ultimately, though, Chloe was too desperately curious not to find out.

Sure, she replied.

Where are you?

Seven Mile Beach, Chloe told her.

Send me an address, and I'll come to you, came Piper's reply.

Chloe hesitated. It was pretty crowded here. Surely it was quieter wherever Piper was, but she couldn't exactly invite herself over. She spun to face the hotel behind her and googled its address, which she sent to Piper.

And then, having spied a beach bar behind the hotel that didn't seem too crowded, she headed that way. She slid onto an empty stool and ordered a ridiculously expensive strawberry daquiri, texting Piper again to let her know where to find her. She sat back, content to listen to the hum of conversation around her, the happy notes of the music playing at the bar, and the ever-present roar of the ocean.

Yep, this was paradise. And Piper was on her way. Chloe glanced at her simple cotton dress, wishing she'd chosen something sexier or at least put on some jewelry. Hell, she wasn't even sure what her hair or makeup looked like at this point. She'd pretty much stripped out of her uniform and walked straight to the beach.

Chloe wasn't generally vain about her appearance, but that tingle in her belly said she liked Piper a lot, maybe even more than she'd realized, and also, she was a bit intimidated now that she knew Piper was a celebrity. She was probably used to hanging out with people a lot more glamorous than Chloe, but then again, she was on her way over, wasn't she?

God, she hoped Piper hadn't asked to see her just to make Chloe sign a nondisclosure agreement or something now that her identity had been unveiled. That thought cooled the embers that had been burning in her stomach.

Her daquiri arrived, and she took a grateful sip. Mm, it was delicious, sweet and slushy. It froze her tongue but filled her stomach with the warmth of rum. She sipped again, giving herself a brain freeze in the process. She slapped a hand against her forehead, grimacing as she waited for the pain to ease.

"Are you okay?" a familiar voice asked from behind her.

Chloe opened her eyes, turning to find Piper standing there in a pink tank top and white shorts, her hair piled in a messy knot on her head. She wore minimal makeup, which did nothing to diminish her natural beauty, but it did lend her a casual beachy vibe that in no way identified her as a celebrity. "Brain freeze," Chloe whispered, rubbing at her temple.

"Those are a bitch," Piper said, taking a hesitant step closer.

"The daquiri's good, though," Chloe said. "Want one?"

Piper eyed the plastic cup in front of Chloe. "Can we walk on the beach with those?"

"Yeah, I think so." Chloe had seen lots of people with cups like these on the beach earlier.

"Want to take them to go?" Piper asked.

"Sure."

Piper stepped up to the bar beside her and gave the drink menu a quick scan before ordering a mango daquiri. The scent of her perfume reached Chloe, something soft and feminine that brought to mind memories of their night in Brooklyn. Piper didn't say much as she waited for her drink, one hip leaned against a stool, gaze locked on the waves visible in the distance.

Chloe toyed with her drink, not wanting to finish it

before Piper got hers, but also not wanting it to melt. Not to mention, she could use a little liquid courage right now. They settled their bar tab while they waited, and Chloe insisted on paying for their drinks this time, despite Piper's offer to cover it.

When Piper's daquiri arrived, Chloe slid off her stool, and they walked toward the ocean together, but the silence was starting to feel awkward, at least to Chloe. She wasn't naturally a quiet person, and she and Piper certainly hadn't been this hesitant with each other the last time they'd shared drinks together.

"How long are you here for?" she asked, to get the conversation started.

"Sunday," Piper told her.

"Me too."

"Really?" Piper slid a glance in her direction. "Do you often get weekends off in tropical places?"

"Sometimes," Chloe told her. "I became a flight attendant to see the world, after all."

"I'm sorry," Piper said quietly, which was such a non sequitur that Chloe just stared at her. "I didn't think I'd ever see you again, and then I panicked when I saw you on the plane. I...I came here tonight to ask you to please keep the things I told you that night in Brooklyn to yourself, but now that I'm here, I don't feel like I need to say it."

"You don't." Chloe sucked on her daquiri, letting it freeze over the sting of disappointment. Piper really had asked to see her just to tell Chloe to keep quiet about their night together, and that sucked. "I wouldn't say anything, whether you're famous or not."

"Thank you." Piper sipped her own drink, and they walked a few more steps in silence. They reached the edge of the water, and Piper looked down at her toes as a wave washed over them. "Pretty big coincidence, us both being here this weekend."

"It is," Chloe agreed. "But I'm guessing you're here because I raved about the Caymans, and while it's true that I love it here, part of the reason it was on my mind that night was because I was looking forward to this weekend."

"Ah," Piper said before taking another sip of her daquiri. "You planted the seed for me."

"I guess I did." Chloe sucked down the last of her drink. "Sorry for freaking you out on the plane."

Piper shook her head. "It wasn't you. It was me."

"Got any plans this weekend, or are you just here to relax?"

"Playing it by ear." Piper lifted one shoulder in a half-hearted shrug. "After that night at Dragonfly, I wanted to keep pushing myself, and God, I really needed a vacation."

"Sounds like it," Chloe agreed.

"You were on my mind," Piper said quietly. "I thought about texting you, but I didn't know what to say, and I...I still don't. I mean, we live five hundred miles apart."

"Well, we're both here tonight," Chloe said, emboldened by Piper's words. "And we seem to be pretty good at sharing random fun evenings together."

Piper gave her a shy smile. "Yeah, we do."

A wave splashed against them, bigger than its predecessors. It sprayed the hem of Chloe's dress, and she let out a little yelp as the cold water met her warm skin. She jumped backward, bumping into Piper in the process. Piper's hand landed on her waist, and when Chloe turned, they were standing way too close.

"We also seem to spend a lot of time kissing on beaches," Piper whispered, right before her lips met Chloe's.

Chloe closed her eyes, absorbing the kiss, the sweet taste

of mango on Piper's lips and the thrill of her tongue as it swept into Chloe's mouth. Piper tilted her head to the side, changing the angle of the kiss as her free hand pressed against Chloe's lower back, and she was lost, swept away by the chemistry that had been building between them from the moment they met.

"You're really good at this," Chloe murmured against her lips.

"I doubt it," Piper responded. "I'm pretty out of practice."

"You can practice on me all you want." Chloe pressed closer, her breasts bumping against Piper's, warmth chasing away the remaining chill from the frozen drink or the rogue wave.

Piper let out a little gasp of pleasure as her left hand—still resting against Chloe's lower back—pulled her closer. Of course, Chloe's stomach chose that moment to growl obnoxiously. She hadn't eaten since her salad in Atlanta with Nisha, a lifetime ago.

Piper chucked softly. "Chloe, would you like to have dinner with me?"

6

Piper settled against the cracked vinyl seat with a sigh. She and Chloe had left the beach, wandering until they found a restaurant that advertised local seafood. Now, they were seated at a booth in back, fresh fruity drinks on the table between them. Across from her, Chloe twirled the paper umbrella in her drink. Her blonde hair, so neatly coiffed on the airplane earlier, was wild and windswept now, and Piper had the irrational urge to run her fingers through it.

"Are you staying near here?" she asked.

Chloe nodded. "A couple of blocks away. I like to be in the heart of the action." She paused, meeting Piper's eyes. "I'm guessing your hotel is someplace quieter."

"Who says I'm staying in a hotel?" Piper picked up her glass and took a hearty sip. The sweetness of tropical fruit blended with the sharper flavor of rum on her tongue.

"One of those fancy condos I passed in the taxi earlier?" Chloe guessed.

"Nope."

"Surely you didn't rent an entire beach house just for

yourself," Chloe said. "I mean, I'm sure you're rich, but I don't get a pretentious vibe."

"No?" Piper took another drink. "I do like my privacy, as you know."

Chloe shook her head as an amused smile tugged at her lips. "I can't believe you're...*you*."

"I'm not *that* famous," Piper said, careful to keep her voice down, although no one was paying them any attention. The restaurant was packed with tourists, talking and laughing so loudly, Piper could barely hear her own words, let alone be overheard. "And I didn't rent a whole beach house for myself. It's more of a...cottage."

Chloe's smile widened. "A cottage is a house. I should know. I just bought one."

"You did?" Piper swirled the straw in her drink, trying not to gulp it down too quickly because she was drinking on an empty stomach, but the crowded restaurant had her buzzing with anxiety. At least their booth provided them with privacy, and so far, that was allowing her to keep it under control.

"Yeah." Chloe reached for her phone. She tapped the screen a few times before passing it across the table to Piper.

She took the phone, which displayed a photo of a brown-paneled cabin surrounded by towering trees. "This is your new house?"

Chloe nodded. "Yep. It's small and kind of a mess inside, but it feels like home."

"Well, you can fix anything you don't like. It's adorable. Congratulations." Piper handed the phone back to Chloe. "So you're really doing it...putting down roots."

Chloe nodded as she looked at the house on her screen, a fond expression on her face. "I'm excited about it."

"Good for you," Piper said, surprised at the little ping of

disappointment she felt at the reminder of how far apart their lives really were.

"Thank you," Chloe said.

"Any leads on a new job there?" she asked.

Chloe shook her head. "I'll probably wait tables or something while I get my résumé out. It'll be enough for me to get by until I've found something more permanent. I just won't be able to travel for a while."

"Good thing you've gotten in plenty of travel these last few years, then," Piper said.

"Exactly." Chloe lifted her drink. "I'll definitely miss it, but I can't say I haven't done my fair share of traveling."

Piper sucked down what remained of her own drink, comfortably tipsy and uncomfortably smitten with the woman sitting across from her. Thankfully, the alcohol—and Chloe—had helped her relax.

"What about you?" Chloe asked. "Are you still working through your list?"

"I guess that's why I'm here," Piper said, staring into her empty glass. "Spending a weekend in paradise felt like a good way to push myself out of my comfort zone while still having control of the situation. I don't have to leave my cottage if I don't want to."

"But you did tonight," Chloe said.

"Yes."

"I could help," Chloe offered. "I mean, if you want to do something together tomorrow, even if it's just sunbathing on the beach. It might be fun."

"Might be?" Piper teased.

Chloe ducked her head in an unsuccessful attempt to hide her smile. "We seem to have fun together, or at least I do."

"I do too," Piper admitted.

Their meals arrived, and they ordered another round of drinks. Piper couldn't remember the last time she'd had three drinks in one evening, and she was definitely feeling it.

As they ate, Chloe shared outrageous tales from her life as a flight attendant, and Piper heard herself giggling. *Giggling.* There were multiple mishaps while passengers attempted to join the mile-high club and even a woman who had sleepwalked down the aisle and tried to open the cabin door at thirty-five thousand feet. But when Chloe told her about the drunk passenger who peed himself in his seat and tried to conceal it with his suit jacket, Piper lost it.

"Never a dull moment, hm?" she managed once she'd stopped laughing, wiping tears from her eyes.

"Never," Chloe told her. "But mostly it's just belligerent passengers not wanting to follow the rules."

"I believe it," Piper said. "The world is full of entirely too many of those people."

"It sure is."

They finished their meals, and Piper insisted on paying the tab, despite Chloe's protests. She'd been the one to invite Chloe to dinner, and she could afford it. Not to mention, she just wanted to buy Chloe dinner.

They walked outside into the balmy, breezy night, and Chloe turned to face her. "This was really nice."

"Yeah," Piper agreed, emboldened by the alcohol in her veins, or maybe it was just the effect Chloe had on her. "Would you like to come over and judge my pretentious rental cottage for yourself?"

Chloe's eyes widened, and she reached up to brush back a lock of hair that the wind had blown into her face. "I'm sure it's not pretentious," she said, sounding almost shy.

"It probably is," Piper countered, trying to ignore the

sting of Chloe's unspoken rejection, "but it's quiet and private, and that's what I like."

"I don't care how pretentious it is, as long as it makes you happy." Chloe stepped forward, cupping Piper's face in her hands as she drew her in for a kiss. "I don't make a habit of going home with people I barely know, but I'd like to make an exception tonight."

Piper felt herself grinning against Chloe's lips. "Really?"

"Mm-hmm." Chloe kissed her more insistently, seemingly fueled by her decision. Her breath fanned over Piper's cheeks as her hands slid from Piper's face to her shoulders.

Piper leaned forward, intent on pressing their bodies together, desperate for the feel of Chloe against her, but she tripped on the curb, slamming into her instead. Chloe stumbled, and they went down in an ungraceful heap. Chloe landed on her ass with Piper sprawled over her, hands braced against the pavement in an effort to stall her fall.

"Oh my God," she gasped, blinking at Chloe in shock and embarrassment. "I'm so sorry. Are you okay?"

"Yep," Chloe said, grinning at her. "Might have an unfortunate bruise later, though."

Piper crawled backward and spun to sit beside Chloe on the curb. "If it makes you feel any better, I'm probably bruised in the same place."

Chloe lifted a skeptical eyebrow. "On your ass?"

"Yep. I had to do a stunt this morning that involved falling repeatedly onto an oversized airbag."

Chloe's mouth gaped slightly, her gaze falling to Piper's ass. "I think it just hit me that you're really a television star."

"I really am, but I'm also just me." She paused because her stumble had knocked some sense into her alcohol and lust-infused brain, causing her to realize the error in her plan. "We have a slight problem, though."

"What's that?" Chloe asked.

"I invited you back to my place, but I'm too tipsy to drive." She sucked in a breath, staring at her hands, which shook slightly. Her panic attack on the plane had taken a lot out of her, and God, she'd been around entirely too many people tonight. She desperately needed the seclusion of her cottage, preferably with Chloe.

"You drove here?" Chloe looked surprised.

Piper nodded. "My cottage isn't in walking distance of any shops or restaurants, so I rented a car."

"Oh." Chloe dragged her teeth over her bottom lip, and Piper felt it low in her belly, an insistent ache that only grew stronger the longer they sat here.

"I'll call a cab."

Chloe rose to her feet, drawing Piper up beside her. "If you don't mind slumming, my hotel's just over there."

Piper hesitated because that meant staying here in the noise and crowds of Seven Mile Beach, but then again, Chloe's hotel room would be quiet. And it was close. "Let's go."

$\sim$

CHLOE WAVED her key card in front of the door, and a green light flashed as the mechanism clicked inside the lock. She pushed it open, leading the way into her room, trying not to overthink the fact that Piper Sheridan was now inside her crummy little hotel room. But Piper was just Piper, after all, a woman Chloe was insanely attracted to, and for tonight, she was doing her best to live in the moment.

She switched on the lamp beside the bed so they wouldn't be fumbling around in the dark and turned to face Piper, who stood with her hands clasped in front of herself as if she were every bit as nervous about this as Chloe. For some reason, Piper's hesitance seemed to counteract Chloe's, and she closed the distance between them, resting her hands on Piper's hips as she drew her in for a kiss.

Piper kissed her back eagerly, leaning forward until their bodies were pressed together. They kissed for several long minutes, their mouths getting progressively sloppier as the temperature between them rose. Chloe reached for the elastic that held Piper's hair in a pile on top of her head, tugging it free so her hair tumbled over her shoulders in a coppery waterfall.

"God," Chloe whispered as she ran her fingers through it. "You have the most gorgeous hair I've ever seen." The night they met, Chloe had wondered what she'd been hiding beneath that wig, and Piper's auburn waves definitely didn't disappoint.

"Thanks." Piper rubbed at her scalp as if it were sore from the pressure of the elastic.

"Shame you can't wear it down more often."

"Too recognizable," Piper said, sweeping it over her shoulders before pressing herself back into Chloe's arms.

"I guess it would be," Chloe agreed.

Piper's fingers slipped beneath the hem of Chloe's dress, brushing against her bare thighs, and her knees almost went out from under her, but she wasn't going to fall on her ass twice in one night. Instead, she let her hands do a little roaming of their own. She slid them beneath the whispery-soft fabric of Piper's top, encountering smooth, warm skin beneath.

Piper exhaled, her eyes sliding shut as her fingernails bit lightly into the backs of Chloe's thighs. Chloe brought her hands around to cup Piper over her bra, feeling the scrape of lace against her fingers.

Piper arched her back, pushing her breasts into Chloe's hands. "Please touch me."

There was an urgency in her tone that had Chloe rushing to pop the clasp resting against Piper's sternum. She took Piper's bare breasts in her hands, circling her nipples until they tightened into firm nubs. Piper whimpered, bringing her hands to grip Chloe's ass. And then it was her turn to whimper, because *God*, that felt good.

A restless ache grew steadily between her thighs as they kissed, but she ignored it for now, focused on the way Piper responded to her touch. Her breasts must be sensitive, because she seemed to unravel a little more with every stroke of Chloe's thumbs. Chloe ducked her head, lifting Piper's top so she could close her mouth over her exposed nipple. She swirled her tongue, grazing the underside of her breast with her teeth, and Piper's head dropped back, a cry of pleasure escaping her lips.

Feeling empowered, Chloe repeated the action on Piper's other breast, rewarded by another cry. She pushed a thigh between Piper's, encouraging Piper to move against her as Chloe continued to lavish her breasts with attention until Piper pulled away abruptly.

"You're going to make me come before you even finish undressing me," she said breathlessly as she reached for Chloe's dress, attempting to tug it over her head.

Chloe raised her arms to help her out. "That's not a bad thing, is it?" she asked, standing before Piper in nothing but a flesh-tone bra and pink cotton panties. She might have felt self-conscious about the status of her underwear if Piper wasn't looking at her like *that*.

"It might be a little embarrassing on my part," Piper said, sucking in a breath as Chloe popped the button on her shorts. She pushed down the zipper and began to ease them over Piper's thighs, revealing a nude thong.

"On the contrary, it might have made me feel a bit like superwoman," Chloe said as she rid Piper of her shorts and turned her attention to her top.

"I think you'll be feeling like superwoman in no time." Piper's breath hitched as Chloe removed her top to expose a matching bra.

"Is that a challenge, Ms. Sheridan? Because it sounded like a challenge." She spun to push Piper onto the bed, but paused at the last moment to tug down the blankets first, because hotel bedspreads...yuck.

"What was that?" Piper asked with an amused smile.

"Look, I'm a flight attendant. I know a few things about hotel rooms, and you don't want to touch the bedspread, especially when you're naked."

"Good to know." Piper yelped as Chloe followed through on her original intention and pressed her onto the exposed sheets, crisp and clean and ready for action.

Chloe climbed on top of her, quickly ridding Piper of her underwear. She took a moment to appreciate the sight of Piper lying naked beneath her, because...wow. She had the most alluring collection of freckles scattered over her pale skin. Chloe trailed her fingers over them before reaching to tuck a lock of hair behind Piper's ear. "You're stunning."

"Thanks," Piper whispered.

Chloe straightened, staring at her red-stained fingers. "Oh my God. You're bleeding."

"What?" Piper's brow wrinkled, and then she laughed under her breath. "No, it's...I got shot this morning."

"Shot?" Chloe squeaked.

Piper shook her head. "It's stage blood. I was drenched

in it, and I had to rush my shower to get to the airport. I must have missed a spot."

"Stage blood," Chloe repeated.

Piper nodded. "Sorry."

Chloe laughed, shaking her head. "It's okay, Miss Television Star. Hang on."

She went into the bathroom to wash her hands and brought a warm damp cloth back to the bed with her to clean the spot behind Piper's ear. "Now, where were we?" Chloe dipped her head to Piper's breasts.

"Right there," Piper confirmed breathlessly.

Chloe slipped a hand between her thighs, thrilled to feel how wet Piper already was.

"Please," Piper gasped, hips bucking against her hand.

Chloe skimmed her fingers over Piper's clit, causing her to arch her back and moan with pleasure. She was so responsive. Chloe could do this all night. She kept moving, lavishing Piper's breasts with her mouth while she worked her with her fingers, and Piper hadn't been exaggerating about how close she was. Within minutes, she was panting, begging, grinding herself against Chloe's palm. And then she cried out as her body clamped down on Chloe's fingers, a tremor racing through her as she came.

"Fuck," she gasped, bringing her hands to her face. With her hair cascading over the pillow, she looked like a goddess from a classic painting.

Getting Piper off really *did* make Chloe feel like Superwoman. She pressed her thighs together, feeling her own wetness. She didn't often experience a connection like this with someone so quickly. There was just something about Piper...

"Wow, I needed that," Piper murmured, her chest heaving for breath, cheeks flushed a most attractive shade of pink. And then, before Chloe could think of a response, Piper slid out from beneath her, rolling on top of Chloe. "And now, it's your turn."

"Okay," Chloe whispered, which wasn't the most brilliant response, but she could barely think with Piper's naked body covering hers, one thigh pressed firmly right where Chloe ached for her. Her last rational thought was that even though her underwear wasn't particularly sexy, at least she'd shaved that morning in anticipation of donning a bikini. Then Piper was stripping away her underwear, and Chloe was reduced to needy whimpers and breathless moans.

Piper seemed to be everywhere at once. Her hair teased Chloe's shoulders as she flicked her tongue over Chloe's nipple and her fingers slid between Chloe's thighs. She started out gently, exploring Chloe's body with leisurely strokes until she was writhing beneath her. Piper's breasts brushed against Chloe's stomach as she moved, her legs threaded with Chloe's, skin against skin.

Just when Chloe thought she couldn't possibly be any more aroused, Piper slid down to envelop Chloe in the delicious heat of her mouth. "Yes," she wheezed, barely recognizing her own voice.

Piper swirled her tongue over Chloe's clit as she pumped two fingers in and out of her body, and just like that, Chloe broke, release rushing through her in a cleansing wave, washing away the stress of a long, busy week and the discovery that her mysterious crush was actually a fancy celebrity.

Piper looked up with a wicked grin as she wiped her mouth with the back of her hand, hair hanging messily over her shoulders, and Chloe felt herself flush at the eroticism of the moment. Then Piper slid up to lie beside her, wrapping an arm around Chloe. "I wasn't exactly thrilled to see you on my flight this afternoon, but I'm awfully glad we're both here now."

"Me too," Chloe said, rolling to face her, her body still tingling with the aftershocks of her orgasm. She nuzzled closer to Piper, eyes sliding shut as the exhaustion of the day caught up with her. When it came down to it, she loved cuddling, and the feel of Piper's arm wrapped snugly around her was absolutely perfect. "Will you stay the night?"

"Yeah," Piper whispered. "I'd like that."

7

Piper blinked into the darkness. Despite a long, exhausting day that had ended in the most unexpectedly pleasurable way, she couldn't sleep. Her muscles were painfully tight, and she was restless and jumpy. This always happened the night after a panic attack, residual anxiety lingering in her system. Combined with the fact that she always had trouble sleeping on vacation, she was screwed. She'd brought medication to help, but of course, it was at her rental cottage.

She closed her eyes and blew out a slow breath. Dammit, if she didn't fall asleep soon, she was going to be miserable tomorrow. Her body was sabotaging what was supposed to be a relaxing, carefree weekend. She really was her own worst enemy sometimes.

The air-conditioning unit mounted in the wall rumbled to life, and she jumped at the sound. She pressed a hand over her heart, willing it to stop racing, willing herself to relax, willing the bone-deep fatigue inside her to lull her to sleep. The white noise from the air conditioner was soothing, though. Maybe it would help. She counted beats in her head as she breathed, five in, six out, slow and steady.

Sleep had just begun to soften the edges of her consciousness when the air conditioner shut off, startling her again. She heaved a quiet sigh. Now she had to pee, but she didn't want to stumble around the hotel room in the dark and wake Chloe. This might be a long, miserable night. Briefly, she considered just getting dressed and leaving, but she didn't want to do that either. She liked Chloe, and it would be inexcusably rude to sneak off in the night. Stifling a groan, she rolled over, attempting to get comfortable.

"Can't sleep?" Chloe mumbled, wrapping an arm around Piper and drawing her against the warmth of her body.

"Sorry if I woke you."

"Mm, it's okay," Chloe said. "Got nowhere to be in the morning."

"Still, it's your vacation, and you should sleep."

"So should you," Chloe murmured into her hair.

"I don't sleep well when I'm traveling...or the night after a panic attack. I don't want to keep you up."

"Anything I can do?" Chloe asked, fingers trailing up and down Piper's back, and *God*, that felt good.

"Not really." Piper's voice was swallowed by the air conditioner as it groaned back to life.

"Can you take something to help you sleep?"

"I have a prescription, but it's at my rental." She rolled to face Chloe. "It's fine, honestly. I'll fall asleep eventually."

Chloe rose up on one elbow, peering over Piper at the clock. "It's only one o'clock. We could go to your place and sleep there if you want?"

"That's silly," Piper deflected.

"No, it's not," Chloe responded. "How far is it from

here?"

"Maybe fifteen minutes."

"See? You could be in your own bed sleeping peacefully in half an hour or so." Chloe sat up, drawing Piper's attention to her breasts, visible in the pale light that filtered into the room from the streetlamp outside. "I can even drive if you're too tired."

Piper dragged herself upright, wrapping her arms around her knees. She was exhausted and anxious and wishing her own bed actually was fifteen minutes away, not the bed in a rental cottage she'd barely seen, let alone slept in.

"I mean, unless you want to just go," Chloe said quietly, apparently having misinterpreted Piper's silence.

"No," Piper said, because this was the one thing she was sure of. "I want to spend the night with you. In fact, I'd like to spend the whole weekend with you, if that's not too forward of me to ask."

"I'd like that too," Chloe said. "A lot."

"You're sure you don't mind heading over to my cottage in the middle of the night?"

"The night's still young for a lot of the party people out there, I'm sure," Chloe said as she slipped out of bed and started getting dressed. "I'm used to getting up and heading out at all hours when I'm on call, so this is no big deal for me, I promise. I can sleep anywhere, anytime. It's one of the benefits of a nomadic lifestyle like mine, I guess."

Piper rubbed her hands over her face, feeling like a disheveled mess by comparison. She was so tired, she couldn't imagine getting up and driving across the island, but ultimately, it would be good for them to relocate to her rental, since she had a bigger space and more amenities than this hotel room. So she dragged herself out of bed.

"Are you sure about the whole weekend?" Chloe asked, gesturing to her suitcase. "Because I hadn't even started to unpack, so I could just bring this with me and not even come back to the hotel."

"Yes," Piper told her. "I'm sure."

~

CHLOE SAT in the passenger seat of Piper's rental car. Despite Piper's obvious fatigue, she'd insisted on driving, and now they were on their way to her cottage in West Bay. This was a quieter part of the island, away from the hustle and bustle that surrounded the high-rise hotels at Seven Mile Beach.

Piper drove them down a narrow residential road lined with houses with names like Coconut Cottage and Deja Blue. She pulled the car up to a wrought iron gate and punched a number into a keypad. And Chloe felt herself shrink in her seat—just a bit—to realize Piper was staying in a house so fancy, it needed a gate. But on second glance, this appeared to be a gated community, not a private mansion for a television queen.

Piper turned onto a narrow, winding driveway thick with palm trees and other vegetation, eventually crunching to a stop behind a light-colored cottage. Chloe couldn't quite tell what color it was. It shone almost silver in the moonlight.

As they stepped out of the car, she caught a glimpse of a turquoise pool gleaming through the trees, and she could hear the rhythmic roar of the ocean. "This place is amazing."

"It's very relaxing, that's for sure," Piper agreed. "Or at least, I think it will be. I was only here a few minutes before I left to meet you earlier."

"I can't wait to see it tomorrow in the daylight."

Piper gave her a small smile as she pushed her key into the lock and let them inside. "The master bedroom's through here." Her shoes clicked over the tile floor as she led the way.

Chloe followed, rolling her suitcase alongside her. There wasn't much to see with the lights off, but the cottage didn't seem overly extravagant. It was definitely outside Chloe's means, but not superstar-level fancy. She walked into the bedroom behind Piper, who immediately went to the suitcase lying open beside the bed. She pulled out a pill bottle, flicked a small white tablet onto her palm, and left the room, presumably in search of water.

Chloe followed, realizing she was thirsty too. She met Piper in the moonlit kitchen, where they both poured glasses of water. Then they changed and washed up before climbing into bed together.

"Much more comfortable," Chloe said as she settled into Piper's bed.

"Mm." Piper lay facing her, eyes already drooping. "Thanks for coming."

"That's what she said," Chloe whispered, and Piper grinned.

Outside, waves crashed rhythmically against the shore, lulling Chloe toward sleep. She'd intended to stay awake this time, to watch Piper fall asleep first so Chloe knew she was okay, but she couldn't seem to hold her eyes open. The next thing she knew, sunlight streamed through the windows, and Piper slept beside her, peaceful and gorgeous with her fiery hair fanned over the pillow behind her.

Chloe lay still, not wanting to disturb her, content to watch the rise and fall of Piper's breasts beneath her barely-there cotton gown. It was a pale seafoam green, edged in lace that dipped into her cleavage. Chloe remembered how sensitive Piper's breasts had been last night when she kissed her there, and a warm ache grew between her thighs.

As much as she wanted to lie here and watch Piper sleep, though, she'd drunk a glass of water right before climbing into bed, and now her bladder was complaining fairly urgently. Carefully, she scooted backward out of bed, relieved when Piper didn't stir. Instead of going into the en suite bathroom, Chloe left the master bedroom and walked through the living room, searching for a guest bath where she wouldn't disturb Piper by flushing the toilet.

The main living space was light and bright with off-white tile floors and white walls except for an accent wall painted a warm coral. The kitchen had shiny quartz countertops and a tile backsplash that brought in the coral hues from the living room. Chloe was immediately enchanted with the décor. It had a relaxed, happy vibe that was exactly her aesthetic.

She located a bathroom in the guest room and used it before padding back into the living room. The walls were adorned with several large and brightly colored abstract paintings. Chloe appreciated that the owner hadn't gone for a clichéd beach theme. Not that there was anything wrong with that, but it was refreshing to see a unique take on traditional beach décor.

She'd always been fascinated with interior design and found herself imagining what she'd change as she strolled through the cottage. Hopefully soon, this would be her job, the start of a new career. Hopefully, it would be enough to fulfill her. Certainly, it would be a major change of pace. But even if it wasn't as exciting as her life as a flight attendant, it would let her have a home of her own, a home where she could watch Cait grow and be a part of her daily life. And Chloe wouldn't trade that for the world.

"Morning."

Chloe turned as Piper walked into the living room, her hair loose over her shoulders. She crossed the room to place a gentle kiss against Chloe's lips.

"Morning," Chloe murmured. "I didn't wake you, did I?"

"Nope, but it's past ten, so I'd say we got our beauty sleep."

"Good," Chloe said.

Indeed, Piper looked rested and refreshed, more relaxed than Chloe had ever seen her. This was Piper at home, Piper who didn't have to wear a disguise or fear being recognized. In fact, this was the first time Chloe had seen her in the light of day. They'd spent two unusual and intimate evenings together, but the unfamiliar sight of Piper barefoot in a nightgown was a stark reminder that they were barely more than strangers.

"What do you want to do today?" Piper asked, walking past Chloe to turn on the coffee machine.

"I'm game for pretty much anything," Chloe told her, "but let's start with breakfast."

"I stopped at the grocery store on my way here from the airport, and even though I was only shopping for one at the time, I think we can get by, at least for breakfast." Piper walked to one of the cabinets and pulled out a box of cereal. "This okay with you? There's also bread if you want to make toast."

"Cereal's fine," Chloe told her.

Together, they fixed cups of coffee and bowls of cereal and carried their breakfast outside to eat on the patio. Chloe settled in a chair, sipping coffee as she took in her surroundings. The cottage was surrounded by trees for privacy, with a path leading from the patio to the beach, which was just visible through the foliage. She spied a strip of golden sand

and what appeared to be a rocky shoreline before the perfect turquoise expanse of the ocean beyond.

"Can you swim on that beach?" Chloe asked.

"I don't think so," Piper said, "but the rental company provided water shoes and snorkel equipment. Supposedly, you can walk out past the rocks and do some snorkeling."

"Sounds fun," Chloe offered as she started on her cereal.

"Do you want to?" Piper asked, sliding a glance in Chloe's direction. "Go snorkeling?"

"Sure. I mean, as long as it sounds fun to you too." This was the potentially awkward part of spending the weekend with someone she barely knew. She had no idea what Piper liked or when she was pushing her too far outside of her comfort zone.

"Yeah, I'd like to snorkel," Piper said. "I need to be careful that I don't burn since I have to be on set Monday, but I'd hate to waste my one full day here without doing something islandy."

On set. Chloe grinned into her coffee cup. "When we met that night at Dragonfly, you told me you were trying to get a handle on your panic attacks so you could apply for a job, and I was envisioning something, I don't know...in an office."

"It's a movie," Piper told her. "A Hollywood romcom, not the made-for-TV movies I usually get offered."

"Wow," Chloe said. "That's a big deal. I mean, isn't it?"

Piper nodded, lips curving as she sipped her coffee. "And I want it *so much*, but I'll need to be able to roll with what-ever they throw at me, and I already know there are several pivotal scenes on a subway platform."

"Oh," Chloe said. "Damn."

"Right," Piper said with a brisk nod. "So I have to get my shit together."

"How long do you have?"

"Well, my audition's in two weeks, but filming doesn't start until the beginning of June, so if I can just make it through the audition, I'll buy myself some time."

"You can do it." Chloe reached over to give her hand a quick squeeze. "I haven't known you long, but you seem like the kind of person who doesn't back down when she wants something. You're going to nail that audition and get your life back while you're at it."

"I hope so," Piper said quietly, gaze locked on the sliver of beach visible at the end of the path. "Because I *need* my life back. I didn't fully realize how much I was missing until I met you."

"I'd love to take credit for this." Chloe gestured around them. "But you set this in motion when you walked into that bar last week, and then you kept your momentum going when you decided to book this trip."

"Maybe a little of both, then." Piper set her empty cereal bowl on the table.

They finished their coffee and went inside to change into swimsuits. Chloe went into the bathroom to brush her teeth, and when she came back out, Piper was standing by the bed in a bikini the color of the ocean outside, a perfect contrast with her fair skin and red hair.

"Wow," Chloe said as she took her in, the swell of her breasts contained beneath the aqua fabric and the thin band stretched over her hips. And then there were freckles, like a copper-tinted constellation scattered over her chest and shoulders, just begging for Chloe to map it with her fingers...or her tongue. Apparently, she had a thing for freckles. Who knew? "You look amazing."

"Thanks," Piper said as she piled her hair on top of her head and tied it there. She turned and picked up a bottle of sunblock from the table beside the bed. "Can you help with my back?"

"Sure," Chloe said, thrilled for the excuse to touch her.

"Don't be shy," Piper told her as she handed over the bottle. "Really slather it on me. I'm pale as a freaking ghost, and I really can't go to work on Monday with a sunburn."

"I'm on it." Chloe started with Piper's neck and shoulders, familiarizing herself with those freckles as she smoothed cream over them. Slowly, she worked her way down, covering Piper's back and sides. She loved the way Piper's breath hitched when Chloe's hands skimmed the undersides of her breasts before she moved on to Piper's lower back. She dipped her fingers just inside the band of Piper's suit, careful not to leave any of her skin uncovered. "Oh my God."

"What?" Piper asked, looking over her shoulder.

"You really do have bruises on your ass from your stunt yesterday." Piper's pale skin was marred by several dark spots.

"I'm not surprised," she said. "It's sore as hell."

"Maybe I can kiss it and make it better," Chloe teased as she rubbed cream over Piper's hips. Briefly, she considered pushing Piper against the wall and doing just that, but something held her back, her own insecurities probably. She hadn't even known Piper's name for a full twenty-four hours and had no idea what her real life in New York was like.

Piper turned, taking the bottle of sunblock from Chloe, and she saw the same hesitation in the sky-blue depths of Piper's eyes. "Later," she said, giving Chloe a coy smile before she walked to the bed to finish applying her sunblock.

8

Piper felt like she was swimming in an aquarium. She floated facedown in the ocean, watching as a school of yellow-and-black-striped fish darted beneath her, more relaxed than she had been in weeks, maybe months. Part of that was due to the woman beside her, unreasonably adorable in her pink-and-white-polka-dot bikini with the most distracting little ruffle between her breasts.

Not only had Chloe given her a mind-blowing orgasm last night, she also made Piper laugh. She pushed her out of her comfort zone, but in a good way. When she was with Chloe, Piper remembered what life had been like before she became a prisoner to her panic attacks, and she worked harder to get that life back.

A ray glided by to her left, and Piper spluttered into her snorkel. She grabbed Chloe's hand, pointing at it, and Chloe's eyes widened behind her mask. They were in maybe ten feet of water, having swum to a cluster of coral on the seafloor that teemed with colorful fish.

It was peaceful, floating here like this, buoyed by the

water, just drifting with the waves. Piper didn't fear the wildlife when she could see it. This felt infinitely less scary than standing in the surf, oblivious to an approaching shark. But then again, Chloe had told her there weren't many sharks in the Caymans. This really was the perfect place.

She'd expected it to be silent underwater, but she could hear the gentle splash of the water against her body, the whoosh of her breath through the snorkel, and also a strange staticky sound, almost like something under the water was fizzing. She couldn't imagine what that was, but it wasn't alarming.

The ray disappeared into the midnight abyss of the open ocean, and Piper returned her attention to the reef beneath her. As long as she and Chloe stayed over this patch of coral, they didn't have to worry that they were drifting out to sea, because there was definitely a current here. They had to kick their fins from time to time to keep from being pushed away by the waves.

After floating for a while, Chloe tapped Piper's arm before rolling to her back, sticking her head out of the water. Piper followed suit, treading water as she spit the snorkel out of her mouth and pushed her mask up her forehead.

"Almost ready to head back?" Chloe asked.

Piper glanced toward the shore several hundred feet away. Truthfully, she could float here all day, watching the fish, but she should probably get out of the sun for a bit, before she wound up with a sunburn on her back and ass. "Sure."

"Can you believe we saw a ray?" Chloe said with a smile, treading water beside Piper. "That was so cool."

"It was amazing," Piper agreed. "What's that fizzing sound, do you know?"

Chloe nodded. "That's the fish munching on the coral."

"Wow," Piper said. "That's wild. Okay, I want to listen to it again now that I know what it is, and then we can swim back."

"Sounds like a plan."

They put their masks back on, and Piper relaxed as she stuck her face into the water. It was tiring to tread water and fight the waves. Floating with the snorkel was so much easier and more peaceful. Immediately, she was enveloped back into the underwater world, fish darting around the coral, delighting her with their antics.

And now that she knew what she was listening to, she heard crunching instead of fizzing. Actually, she saw the parrotfish nibbling on the coral with their elongated faces and dramatic lips, perpetually looking like they were about to give someone a smooch. Piper smiled around her snorkel.

She watched the fish for a few more minutes, and then she took Chloe's hand as she began to kick toward shore. They swam hand in hand so they could watch the fish instead of having to look for each other. When the water got shallow enough to stand, they put their feet down and removed their masks and snorkels.

Piper rubbed at her forehead, sore from the pressure of the mask. "That was without a doubt one of the coolest things I've ever done."

Chloe beamed at her. "I'm glad."

"And now I'm starving. Ready for lunch?"

"Sure," Chloe agreed as they sloshed their way toward the shore.

The waves were relatively small and gentle here, broken by a larger reef in the distance, but the bottom was rocky the closer they got to shore, and Piper was glad for the water shoes to protect her feet. She and Chloe held on to each other as they picked their way carefully over the rocks, which were slippery with seaweed. The waves slapping at their legs made things more challenging.

They made it safely onto the sand, and Piper drew her in for a quick kiss, grinning against Chloe's lips. It was hard to believe they'd only *really* known each other for twenty-four hours. Piper didn't usually experience this kind of instant connection with someone. It wasn't just physical either. Sure, she and Chloe had great chemistry, but Piper felt comfortable with her. They shared an easy rapport that usually took Piper months to settle into.

Some people just clicked.

"What do you want to do for lunch?" Chloe asked as she stepped onto the path ahead of Piper, drawing her attention to that polka dot bikini and the way it perfectly cupped Chloe's ass.

"I grabbed a Caribbean red bean salad and some fruit at the store yesterday, if that sounds good to you. Not sure if I've mentioned it, but I'm a vegetarian."

"Oh, my friend Nisha is a vegetarian too. Her family's from India, near Mumbai, and a lot of people from that region don't eat meat, so she's already introduced me to a lot of great veggie stuff." Chloe paused to rinse her feet at the faucet before she climbed the steps onto the patio. She turned to face Piper, one hand on her hip. "This is just a question, not a judgment. Do you want to stay here at the cottage all weekend, or do you want to go out at all?"

Piper ducked her head, using the moment to put down her snorkel equipment and rinse her own feet. A warm, prickly feeling spread across her chest as Chloe's words struck home. It was true. Piper had already been thinking ahead to a quiet afternoon by the pool and dinner here at the cottage, but she hadn't flown to the Caymans to be a hermit here too. "Let's go somewhere after lunch."

"Are you sure?"

"Yes. Got any suggestions?"

"Hm." Chloe tapped a finger against her lips. Sunlight glistened in her wet hair and shimmered in the water droplets on her eyelashes. "How do you feel about parasailing?"

Piper felt herself nodding almost immediately. "Sounds fun."

"Really?" Chloe asked. "Because if it doesn't, you can tell me."

"It does, truly," Piper said as she wrapped a towel around herself. "My anxiety disorder isn't related to thrill-seeking behaviors or anything like that. It's just good old-fashioned social anxiety, and more specifically, a fear of being recognized, so the part that might be stressful is the boat ride, not going up in a parachute."

"Why the fear of being recognized?" Chloe asked as she walked into the living room.

"Shower before lunch?" Piper deflected, because the air-conditioning instantly made her cold, and so did Chloe's question. Also, she felt sandy and gritty and gross now that she was out of the water.

"Sure," Chloe agreed.

Piper led the way into the master bedroom and turned on the shower, getting it nice and hot before she stripped out of her suit. Chloe did the same, stepping into the shower beside her.

Why the fear of being recognized?

It was a reasonable question, and only Dr. Jorgensen knew the answer. But maybe it was time to raise that number to two. Piper closed her eyes, letting the hot water course over her face as she tried to tug the elastic out of her hair, groaning as she realized it was hopelessly knotted.

The band from the mask had made quite a mess of her hair.

"Let me," Chloe offered. She squirted a handful of conditioner into her hands and began massaging it into Piper's hair, smoothing out the tangles.

Piper exhaled into her touch, relaxing so that her back rested against Chloe's chest. "Thank you." She closed her eyes. "There's something I didn't tell you before about that day on the subway platform."

"Oh," Chloe murmured as her fingers gently combed through Piper's hair, smoothing it out bit by bit, a perfect metaphor for the way she handled Piper in general.

Piper's eyes were still closed, her senses distilled to the shower's hot spray against her skin and Chloe's wonderful hands. Her body pressed into Piper's from behind, enveloping her in a warm, safe cocoon. In her mind's eye, she saw the woman on the platform, clear as day. She'd worn her brown hair in a high ponytail, hands shoved into the pockets of her jacket, posture tense but not alarmingly so. "She recognized me."

Chloe inhaled sharply. "Oh, Piper..."

"She looked at me and said, 'You're Piper Sheridan,' and I just smiled at her, sort of hoping she wasn't about to make a scene on the subway platform, because I was just trying to get home, and I had a headache, and I didn't really want to pose for a bunch of pictures." She'd been over it a million times, wondering if she should have noticed something, a sign, a warning.

Chloe was quiet, letting her tell the story at her own pace, hands still working through Piper's hair, rinsing away salt and sand, so fucking soothing she never wanted it to end.

"I looked down at my phone, hoping she wouldn't say

anything else, and when the subway pulled into the station, she just...jumped." Piper squeezed her eyes more tightly shut, wishing she could block out the mental image, the shock, the horror, the screams of the other passengers on the platform.

"Jesus," Chloe whispered.

"It's why I panicked yesterday on the plane," Piper told her. "You recognized me. It's sort of a trigger for me lately."

"Well, I can understand why," Chloe said, spinning Piper to face her.

The shower beat down on her back and her hair. "I can't help wondering, if I'd just talked to her, posed for a selfie or whatever, would she have still jumped?"

"You can't hold yourself responsible for her actions," Chloe told her. "There's no way you could have known."

"I know." Piper settled closer in Chloe's arms. "I've been through it in therapy, but I guess it just illustrated for me how much of an impact we can have on another person without even realizing."

"That's true," Chloe agreed.

"It's not my fault she jumped, but it's still possible that I could have stopped her if I'd been friendlier. Who knows how many people you've helped through a tough moment during a flight with one of your smiles?"

"Oh, I don't know about that," Chloe said.

"You certainly have a calming effect on me."

∼

CHLOE SAT beside Piper on the boat, hands clasped together. Piper wore a navy bikini with a gauzy coral coverup, and the color combination was a definite win. Her hair was in a thick braid down her back, a floppy hat on her head, presumably to shield her face from the sun, but it also protected her from the prying eyes of the other guests on the boat.

Chloe had noticed a few questioning glances in their direction, but no one had said anything, maybe because Chloe had leaned forward to block Piper from anyone she caught looking. It was rude to stare, dammit. Piper wasn't a tourist attraction.

The boat bounced over turquoise waves, rainbow-striped parachute soaring overhead as another couple went up. Chloe glanced at Piper, who was smiling as she watched them go. She'd seemed relaxed and happy all day, except for her confession in the shower, and Chloe was helplessly smitten with her.

When their turn came, they were harnessed together, holding hands as the winch began to turn, letting out the line that tethered them to the boat. The parachute lifted, and their feet left the deck. Piper gave Chloe an excited grin. At first, the noise of the winch was too loud to hear anything else, but as they got higher up, it faded away, along with the engine noise from the boat, leaving them with nothing but the whisper of the ocean breeze in their ears.

"It's so beautiful up here." Piper swung her feet through the air.

"It really is," Chloe agreed. A gust of wind caught their parachute, and her stomach dipped like she'd just gone over the summit of a roller coaster. Below them, the ocean glistened in the sunlight. It started out a light turquoise near the beach and plunged to a sapphire blue so dark it almost appeared black where the water deepened beyond the reef.

She could see the high-rise hotels along Seven Mile Beach and the little dots that represented people swimming in the shallows. In the distance, a plane touched down at the airport. From here, it looked light as a feather, absent the roar of the jets and the jolt of the wheels making contact with the runway.

"Oh look," Piper exclaimed, tugging at Chloe's hand as she pointed behind them. "Is that the place where you feed stingrays?"

Chloe followed her gaze to a light patch of water where several small boats were clustered, people wading between dark, round shapes that glided over the sand. "Looks like it."

"Maybe if I ever come back, I'll try it," Piper said. She'd left her hat on the boat so it didn't blow away, and her braid bounced behind her in the sea breeze.

"Same," Chloe said. "That ray we saw this morning didn't look as intimidating as I was expecting."

Piper laughed softly. "I'm not afraid of sea creatures as long as I can see them."

"That sounds like a good life policy in general," Chloe said, nudging her shoulder against Piper's. "The threats we can see are less scary than the ones we can't."

"Yep." Piper swung her feet again, and their harness rocked. "Ever wonder what would happen if this rope snapped and we just drifted away?"

"Uh...no?" Chloe said with a laugh.

"I like being up here, floating over the real world. It's nice." There was something wistful in her tone.

"Yeah." She gave Piper's hand a squeeze.

"See that place over there?" Piper pointed toward one of the high-rise hotels, a particularly tall and shiny one, reflecting the afternoon sun back at them. "Let's have dinner there, at one of those tables in the sand. I've always wanted to do that."

Chloe dropped her gaze to the tables artfully arranged on the beach behind the hotel. Each one was shielded with a canopy of palm fronds. It looked romantic and fancy and expensive. But when in the Caymans... "I'd love to."

They drifted along, taking in the sights, until the line jerked beneath them as the ride operator began to reel them back in. Piper sighed. "Too bad we couldn't stay up here forever."

"This was really fun." But everything they'd done so far had been fun. Surely, dinner on the beach would continue the streak.

They descended to the boat, landing awkwardly on the platform as a gust of wind caught the chute. One of the ride operators extended his hands, expertly steadying them both while another employee began to undo their harnesses.

Chloe felt windblown as she made her way over to the bench where she and Piper had left their belongings. She smoothed a hand over her hair as she toed into her flip-flops. Piper sat beside her, slipping her hat back onto her head. They'd been the last ones to go up, so the parachute was quickly packed away, and the boat headed for shore.

An employee passed out plastic cups of lemonade as they sped toward the dock. Fifteen minutes later, she and Piper stepped off the boat together. Chloe took Piper's hand as they walked down the dock.

"Excuse me." One of the other passengers on the boat, a woman about their age, stepped in front of them with a hesitant smile. "I didn't want to bother you while you were parasailing, but...are you Piper Sheridan?"

Beside Chloe, Piper went deathly still.

9

P iper couldn't hear past the static buzzing in her ears. She couldn't breathe. The dock seemed to sway beneath her feet, a combination of her altered equilibrium from the boat and her impending panic attack. The woman in front of her took a step back, her expression contrite.

Chloe took Piper's hand and squeezed, and she focused on the sensation of Chloe's fingers threaded through hers, the gentle press of her fingernails against Piper's palm. Her chest loosened, and she sucked in a ragged breath.

"I'm sorry," the woman said, taking another step back. "I didn't mean to bother you."

"No, it's okay," Piper managed, forcing a smile. She drew in another breath, steadying herself. She'd done this hundreds of times before that day on the subway platform. She could do it again. She *would*. "And yes, I am Piper Sheridan."

The woman's expression brightened. "I just wanted to say I'm a huge fan. Sam Whitaker is my hero, and it's super cool that we went parasailing together today." She laughed nervously. "I mean, well...you know what I mean."

Piper's smile softened into something that felt more natural. "I do, and thank you. I'm pretty fond of Sam myself."

"Do you mind?" The woman reached into her bag and pulled out her cell phone. "I mean, I totally understand if you don't like to pose for pictures when you're on vacation."

"It's fine," Piper told her, "as long as you don't mind waiting a few days before you post it online."

"Definitely," the woman agreed.

"Want me to take it for you?" Chloe offered, and the woman handed her phone to her.

Piper stepped next to her and posed for a photo, hoping the woman couldn't feel the way Piper's hand shook as it rested on her shoulder. Chloe handed the phone back, and with a quick thanks, the woman was on her way, rejoining a group of women further down the dock.

Piper exhaled slowly, rolling her shoulders.

"You okay?" Chloe asked.

"Yeah."

"That felt like a big deal," Chloe said quietly. "Don't you think?"

"I'm still standing this time, so yeah." She rubbed a hand over the back of her neck, attempting to loosen the painfully tense muscles there.

Chloe turned to face her. "Sometimes I feel like we've known each other forever, and then I remember I barely know you, because...are you out? I'd really like to kiss you right now."

Piper answered that question by pressing her lips against Chloe's. "I'm definitely out, but you should know that there's always a chance photos of us will wind up posted online somewhere. Everyone is an amateur paparazzo with their cell phones these days."

Chloe grinned against her lips, wrapping her arms around Piper. "I don't care if you don't."

"I don't." Piper straightened, glancing around. She spotted an empty bench farther down the dock. "Do you mind if we sit for a minute?"

"Course not," Chloe said.

They walked to the bench and sat. Piper leaned back, closing her eyes. Sweat dampened her skin, and her heart was still racing, but she'd managed to ward off a full panic attack, and as Chloe had pointed out, that was a pretty big deal.

"What happens if she posts the picture today anyway?" Chloe asked.

Piper shrugged, rolling her shoulders again. "Nothing really, but I'd rather if word that I'm here didn't get out until after I'm gone."

"It's still kind of surreal to me that you're a celebrity, to be honest," Chloe said, giving her head a slight shake. "I mean, I didn't know who you were when we met, and I've been with you pretty much since I found out you're Piper Sheridan, so I haven't even had a chance to google you."

Piper laughed while Chloe's cheeks darkened.

"I mean...not to be creepy," Chloe clarified. "But just out of curiosity."

"It's not creepy," Piper told her. "That's what Wikipedia is for. Do you even watch the show?"

"I've seen a few episodes," Chloe said, cheeks still pink. "It's hard to keep up with TV when I'm always traveling."

"Understandable," Piper said. "Ready for dinner?"

"I am, but I have no idea what time it is." Chloe pulled out her phone to check, and Piper saw that her lock screen photo was a picture of Chloe with a little girl who looked so much like her, it was hard to imagine her being anything other than Chloe's daughter. She hadn't mentioned a child, but...

"Who's that?" Piper asked, gesturing toward the phone, vaguely unsettled by the idea of Chloe having a daughter she hadn't known about.

"My niece, Cait," Chloe told her.

"Wow," Piper said. "She could be your daughter."

"Genetically, she might as well be," Chloe said, smiling at Piper's confusion. "She's my identical twin sister's daughter."

"You have an identical twin?" Piper wasn't sure she'd met an identical twin before. The concept was sort of mind boggling to her, another person who looked exactly like you.

"Had." Chloe's smile fell flat.

Oh, *fuck*. "Jesus, Chloe. I'm sorry."

Chloe looked away. "She died in a car crash about eight years ago."

"I'm so sorry," Piper said. Losing a sibling had to be hell, but losing an identical twin? She wrapped her arms around Chloe, and they held on to each other for a few seconds.

When Chloe pulled free, her eyes were glossy. "Remember how I told you that I'd been in therapy for a while too? That's why."

"Makes sense," Piper said. "I hope it's helped."

"It has." Chloe blew out a breath, much as Piper had done earlier. "Anyway, it's five thirty. Early dinner?"

"Yeah," Piper agreed.

"Then maybe we can check out the pool afterward?" Chloe suggested.

"There's also a hot tub," Piper told her. "Although I share both with the other three cabins on the property."

They walked together to the car, swapping their coverups for sundresses, which they put on over their bikinis. Chloe's dress was sky blue with little white daisies all over it, while Piper's was gray-and-white striped. From there, they headed to the restaurant, where luck was apparently on their side—or more likely, the early hour—and they were seated immediately.

They sat at a table for two on the beach, with the ocean as their backdrop. Their table was draped in a white tablecloth with a candle flickering next to a small vase of tropical flowers between them, and the canopy of palm fronds provided a fair amount of privacy without detracting from the view. Piper relaxed into her seat, digging her toes into the sand to ground herself. She was still jittery, but she was definitely making progress, taking her life back just as she'd hoped.

They ordered tropical drinks while they perused the menu, and Piper began to realize she wasn't the only one still processing her emotions. Chloe had been unusually quiet since telling Piper about her sister. It wasn't an uncomfortable silence, though. On the contrary, the emotional truths they'd shared seemed to bring them closer together.

Once they had their drinks in hand, they clinked their glasses together.

"To our last night in the Caymans," Chloe said.

"It's been a great weekend." Piper lifted her glass and sipped, letting the warmth of the rum mask her mixed feelings over their upcoming departure.

"It has." Chloe met her eyes across the table. "So what happens after we go home?"

"For us, you mean?" Piper asked.

Chloe nodded, sucking her bottom lip between her teeth.

"I don't know," Piper told her honestly. "I like you a lot, and I'd really like to see you again. I don't know what we could pull off, relationship-wise, with you living in North Carolina and me in New York, but I'm willing to try if you are."

"At the very least, I'd like to stay in touch as friends," Chloe said.

"Definitely," Piper agreed.

"And for the next month, I'll be flying through New York once a week."

"Why don't we start there and see what happens?" Piper suggested.

Chloe smiled. "I'd like that."

～

CHLOE SANK into the swirling depths of the hot tub, watching as Piper slid in beside her. The lights beneath the water cast a flickering blue reflection across her face that was mesmerizing to watch. Then again, Chloe always seemed to find Piper mesmerizing to watch. They'd enjoyed a lovely dinner together on the beach and now were back at Piper's rental to enjoy an evening beneath the stars.

"You told me that you had always wanted to travel, but how did you decide to become a flight attendant to achieve that instead of, I don't know, working on a cruise ship or something?" Piper asked. The reflection of the water danced over the swell of her breasts, which was highly distracting.

"It was Cassie's idea, actually," Chloe told her. "My sister. We were watching TV one night. I have no idea what show it was, but there was a scene on a plane. Cassie made an offhand comment that we should become flight attendants together when we grew up so that we could fly around the world, and somehow, the idea just stuck."

"So she was a flight attendant too?" Piper asked.

Chloe shook her head. "She got pregnant her freshman year of college and dropped out. After Cait was born, she needed to stick closer to home, but she insisted that I follow through with it so she could live vicariously through me."

"Was that what you wanted?" Piper asked.

Chloe shrugged. "I didn't *not* want it. If Cassie hadn't been so set on me becoming a flight attendant, maybe I would have done something else, but I don't have any regrets. It's been an amazing opportunity."

"What's it like, having a twin?" Piper asked. "Or is it painful to talk about?"

"It's painful, but I still like to talk about her." Chloe sank deeper into the tub, watching the steam that rose from the water, evaporating into the night. "She was my best friend, but it was more than that, you know? We shared a bedroom for nineteen years. Even at college, we were roommates. After she died, I realized I didn't have many other friends."

"That must have been devastating," Piper said quietly.

"I had always been half of a pair. Sometimes I think I'm still learning how to be my own person."

Piper scooted closer, her toes bumping Chloe's beneath the swirling water. "I can't even imagine what that's like, but from what I've seen, you're doing just fine on your own."

"I hope so. Do you have siblings?"

Piper smiled. "I have a brother, but we're ten years apart. He's only nineteen, so we don't exactly have much in common at the moment."

"That's a big age gap," Chloe agreed.

"I assume he was an 'oops,' but my parents would never say."

"Are you close with your family?" Chloe realized she'd never heard Piper talk about them.

"I mean, there's no bad blood or anything," Piper said with a shrug. "We get along fine, but we aren't super close. We see each other on holidays and keep in touch on social media, mostly."

"Where do they live?"

"Massachusetts, just outside Boston."

"So that's where you grew up?"

Piper nodded. "I love it there, but I love New York more."

Chloe rested her head against the back of the tub, watching the stars pop out overhead. She wished she could hear the ocean, but it was drowned out by the steady hum of the jets. "We should go for a walk on the beach later," she suggested. "I love walking on the beach after dark."

"Definitely," Piper agreed. "What are the chances we're on the same flight home too?"

"High if you're on the same airline, because we only have two flights off the island tomorrow."

Piper nodded. "I'm on the one o'clock flight."

"Same flight," Chloe confirmed. "But I'm working coach again, so you won't see much of me."

"How do you decide who gets to work first class?"

"Seniority. I don't think you have Tammy this time, though," Chloe told her as she ducked her head to hide her smile.

"Good." Piper laughed quietly. "She was...not my favorite."

"Yeah, well, you didn't hear it from me, but she's not mine either."

"I thought she was going to ask for my autograph," Piper said. "Or start taking sneaky pictures on her cell phone."

"I wouldn't put it past her," Chloe said. "Although we aren't allowed to do either."

"Okay, I don't know about you, but I'm starting to boil," Piper said, waving her hands dramatically in front of her face.

"Same."

They climbed out of the hot tub and went inside to get dressed before heading out for a moonlit stroll on the beach. It was dark on this part of the island, away from the high-rise hotels. Chloe visited a lot of beaches in her travels, but she almost always stayed in the most touristy area, right in the heart of the action.

This was different. Their beach was only accessible to people staying inside the gated community, which meant it was nearly deserted even in the middle of the day. Tonight, they had it to themselves, for the moment, at least. Chloe had never minded crowds, but this seemed somehow more mature, like she was on an adult vacation instead of spring break. And it was romantic as hell.

A cool breeze gusted against her exposed skin, making her shiver. They walked to the water line and stood, watching the silvery reflection of the moon as it swirled over the waves.

"Look up," Piper whispered, giving Chloe's hand a squeeze.

She did, smiling as she saw the stars twinkling overhead, so thick the whole sky seemed to glitter. "It's one of my favorite things in the world."

"Living in the city, I never get to see them like this," Piper said, sounding awestruck.

"You can see them in the mountains where I live, as long as the trees aren't obstructing your view."

"I filmed a few scenes for a movie in the North Carolina

mountains once, but I was working such long hours, I never got a chance to look up at the stars." Piper's voice was hushed by the night.

"You should come," Chloe said impulsively. "Once I've moved into my new house and you've wrapped filming for the season, come visit me and see the mountains."

"I'd like that."

"This weekend has been magical," Chloe whispered. "It's totally crazy that I didn't even know your name two days ago, at least not in any sort of personal context."

"I'm awfully glad you planted the seed for this trip in my head that night in Brooklyn."

"Me too," Chloe agreed.

They turned toward each other. The ocean breeze whipped Piper's hair over her shoulders so that it tickled the exposed skin on Chloe's chest. She reached out, tracing the contours of Piper's face with her fingers, wanting to memorize every gorgeous curve, just in case they never saw each other again. No matter what they said tonight on this beach, tomorrow they would return to their real lives, and who knew what would happen?

Piper was a TV star, for crying out loud. She lived in New York and was about to audition for a movie that might totally launch her career, while Chloe prepared to settle down in North Carolina. It seemed like an impossible equation to start a relationship, but she couldn't help being glad —ridiculously glad—that they were at least going to try.

Her fingers skimmed Piper's lips, coming away sticky with her lip gloss. Impulsively, Chloe brought her fingers to her mouth, tasting the sweet cherry flavor she'd come to associate with Piper.

It had been hard for Chloe to maintain relationships with her jet-setting lifestyle. That was another thing she hoped to change once she moved into her new house. She craved the kind of closeness and intimacy she felt with Piper right now. She felt like she could stand here all night, satisfied by the simple fact of being together.

"I..." Piper's voice drifted away, evaporating into the night.

"I know," Chloe whispered, hoping they were feeling the same thing.

They leaned toward each other, lips meeting in a gentle kiss. Chloe's hands were still on Piper's face. Her thumbs stroked Piper's perfect cheekbones as Piper's hands settled on the dip of Chloe's waist. They kissed like they had all the time in the world, like time had no meaning, like they were one with the night around them.

The ocean provided their soundtrack, the steady push and pull of the waves matching the movement of their bodies as they settled closer against each other. Water rushed over Chloe's feet, grounding her in the moment. She slid her hands into Piper's hair, soft and cool from the night air.

To Chloe's right, lights from the cottages filtered through the trees, appearing to flicker as the palm fronds swayed around them. To her left, the ocean glistened endlessly, dotted here and there with the light from a passing ship. All around them, the wind gusted, whispering through the trees.

Piper exhaled against her lips, sounding at peace with the world. A steady thrum of desire built inside Chloe, centered in the ache between her thighs, but she felt it from her scalp to her toes, as if every cell in her body had been infused with the power of the ocean or maybe it was just the power of her connection with Piper.

"I'm awfully glad you sat beside me that night at the

bar," Piper whispered.

"So am I."

Another wave rushed over Chloe's toes, and she giggled, pressing closer in Piper's arms. Piper's fingers slid under Chloe's skirt, cupping her over her underwear, and her giggle evaporated into a gasp.

"Piper..."

"Shh, no one could see, even if there was anyone else on this beach," she whispered.

"Oh," Chloe breathed as Piper's fingers danced over the front of her underwear. She'd never been one for sex in public, but somehow this felt safe, despite the relative risk. Piper was right. No one would be able to see what they were doing, even if they walked right past them. They were standing up, fully clothed.

She brought a hand down to touch Piper the way she was touching Chloe, finding her already wet beneath the soft lace of her thong. They moved quietly, touching and stroking as the ocean swirled around them. The occasional cold splash of a wave against Chloe's legs provided a stark contrast to the heat building inside her, centered beneath Piper's talented fingers.

Their gasps and whimpers joined with the rhythmic hiss and splash of the sea. Piper dropped her face against Chloe's shoulder, muffling her cry as she came. Chloe followed a few seconds later, release rushing through her just as the next wave crested, wetting them to their thighs.

Piper let out a breathless laugh as she held Chloe tighter, and they stood like that for a long minute, just breathing as the stars gleamed overhead and the ocean surged against their legs. It was beautiful, peaceful, a moment Chloe would never forget, no matter what happened after they went home tomorrow.

10

Piper unlocked the door to her apartment, pushing her suitcase ahead of her as she walked inside. Thankfully, the flight home had been uneventful. Chloe had walked through the first class cabin a few times on her way to and from the galley, giving Piper secret smiles. Those little smiles had kept Piper's mood light and flirty all the way home, or at least until her layover in Atlanta, where they parted ways.

Tomorrow, she'd be back at work, but her weekend in the Caymans had been good for her on so many fronts. She'd pushed herself out of her comfort zone. She'd made definite progress with her panic attacks. And she'd shared the most magical weekend with Chloe.

Piper rolled her suitcase into the bedroom and changed into her pajamas before going into the bathroom to wash her face. This was going to be a "study tomorrow's script while eating a frozen meal on the couch" kind of evening. Clad in a soft blue tee and her favorite lounge pants, she walked barefoot to the shelf where Master's tank sat.

The fish stared at her, fluffing his crimson tail as if to

admonish her for leaving him alone all weekend, even though he'd been perfectly fine without her. He swam closer to the glass, his little front fins fluttering frantically while his tail glided gracefully behind him. Bettas were so fun to watch.

"Here you go, dude," she said as she picked up the container of freeze-dried bloodworms and dropped a couple of them onto the surface of his water.

Immediately, he lunged at the surface, grabbing a worm.

While he ate, she walked to the kitchen to warm up her own dinner. Once her squash ravioli was ready, she sat on the couch to review tomorrow's schedule. Since Sam would be in the hospital, recovering from her gunshot wound, Piper didn't have many lines to learn. Mostly, she'd spend the day in a hospital bed with her eyes closed. Maybe she could even sneak in a nap.

That was a nice thought, but it wouldn't happen. The set was loud, and they'd constantly be resetting the scene, take after take until they'd captured every detail from every angle. Still, the hospital bed would be a welcome respite after her stunt work on Friday.

Her phone dinged with an incoming text message.

Missing the beach. And you. It was from Chloe.

Same, Piper replied. *Are you home?*

Nope. I'm in St. Louis tonight.

When will you be in NY? Piper couldn't help asking.

Thursday night. Want to grab dinner?

It's a date.

Piper set down her phone with a smile. This long-distance thing might not always be fun, but for tonight it was. She was already looking forward to Thursday.

The next morning, she was up at dawn and in the car on her way to the set. For the last six months, she'd used a car service for her commute. Soon, she'd try the subway again, but not this week. She arrived with enough time to grab a yogurt parfait from the craft services table before she reported to hair and makeup.

"Hey! How was your weekend?" Eliza asked as she dropped into the chair beside Piper.

"Amazing," Piper told her. "Just what I needed."

"You look rested," Eliza commented. "Ariana's going to have her work cut out for her, covering that rosy glow in your cheeks so you look like an unconscious gunshot victim."

Piper touched her cheek self-consciously, glancing at herself in the mirror. "I used up almost a whole bottle of sunblock."

"Not to worry," Ariana said as she approached Piper's chair. "I'll have you pale as a ghost in no time."

And indeed she did. Piper left her chair thirty minutes later with a sickly pallor, her eyes shadowed like she hadn't slept in a week. Once she'd changed into today's costume— a blue-checked hospital gown—she definitely looked the part. She took her place in the hospital bed that had been set up in the multipurpose set, making herself comfortable as she prepared for a long day.

Soon Eliza joined her, sitting in the chair beside the bed. She wore a crisp black suit that would have definitely gotten Piper's blood pumping a few years ago. Today, she just wanted to close her eyes and daydream about Chloe. The rest of the crew assembled around them, adjusting lighting and positions. One of the assistants fitted Piper with an oxygen tube for her nose.

Eliza leaned back in her chair, squeezing drops into her eyes to make them watery. She slipped the bottle into her pocket as the crew called their marks. Piper pushed out a deep breath and closed her eyes. She heard the snap of the clapboard, and then the director called, "And we're rolling."

Eliza's hand gripped Piper's, her fingers cold and damp from the bottle of eyedrops. "I know you can hear me, Sam. I'm here, and I'm not leaving until you wake up."

The door opened, and Piper heard Nate's heavy footsteps as he approached the bed. "Any change?" he asked, his voice deep and somber.

"Nothing," Eliza told him.

While they talked, Piper drifted between paying attention and thinking about her weekend with Chloe. Usually, she'd never let her mind wander during a scene. She stayed in Sam's mindset whenever the camera was rolling. But there weren't any cues for her to miss in this scene. There wasn't anything for Sam to react to. All Piper had to do was lie here.

She remembered the way it felt to soar over the ocean beneath a parachute, her sunset dinner on the sand with Chloe, and their moonlit encounter on the beach. Okay, maybe she shouldn't think about *that* while she was pretending to be unconscious, because she could already feel her cheeks growing warm beneath her sickbed makeup.

Somehow, lying in a hospital bed all day was unreasonably exhausting, or maybe it was just residual fatigue from her busy weekend, because by the time she made it home that night, she was ready to crawl straight into bed. She wasn't going to, though. She'd made a lot of progress over the weekend, and she had to keep it going.

So she tucked her hair under a baseball cap and went for a walk around her neighborhood, just to blow off some steam. And then she stopped in the deli on the corner and bought a sandwich for dinner. Satisfied that she'd been social enough for the day, she went home. She curled up on the couch, queued up an episode of *Grace and Frankie* on her TV, and settled in to enjoy a quiet evening. She was halfway through her sandwich when Chloe texted.

Guess what I'm watching tonight?

The accompanying image was a screencap of Piper dressed as Sam in a scene from the first season of *In Her Defense*. She blushed involuntarily at the idea of Chloe sitting in a hotel room somewhere, watching her. In the attached image, Piper was gazing rather heatedly at Eliza. Would Chloe be able to see Piper's feelings for her, or would she just assume that was Sam looking at Claire?

Interesting choice, Piper texted back with a winking emoji.

Sam's pretty hot, I have to say.

Yeah? Piper was grinning like an idiot now.

Oh yeah. Mega hot. Chloe inserted a flame emoji. *Also, the show is really good. I'm hooked.*

It's possible you're biased.

Entirely possible, Chloe typed.

There was a lull in their conversation as Piper finished her supper and Chloe apparently watched more *Defense*. Piper found it highly distracting to sit on her couch and think about Chloe, hundreds of miles away, watching Piper on her tablet. On her own screen, Grace and Frankie were bickering about a lost toilet. This was one of Piper's favorite episodes, but tonight, she found her gaze flicking to her phone every few minutes, anxious to hear from Chloe again, to know if she was still watching and what she thought.

Holy shit! Chloe's text popped up on her screen about an hour later. *That thing where you used your high heel to take down the asshole hassling your client? I did not see that coming.*

It took me like 20 takes to get that right, Piper responded. *And I broke a heel.*

Sexy.

It wasn't. But this conversation was. Piper pressed a hand against her flushed cheek.

Maybe you can reenact it for me when I see you on Thursday.

~

CHLOE ENTERED the restaurant with a bounce in her step, heart racing in anticipation of seeing Piper again. She'd binged the first season of *In Her Defense* this week, and she was halfway smitten with Sam Whitaker and one hundred percent smitten with the woman who brought her to life. She didn't care that Piper was a celebrity, but it was surreal and exciting watching her on TV now that they were tentatively dating.

Tonight, Chloe hoped to merge the Piper she knew with the Piper she'd seen on TV. She needed to know what her life here in New York looked like and if Chloe could fit into it. Could she handle having a famous girlfriend? She really, *really* hoped so.

She glimpsed red in a booth to her left, a waterfall of hair that sent a warm shiver down Chloe's spine. Piper turned, and their eyes locked. Chloe's stomach began to fizz like she'd just guzzled a bottle of champagne, drunk off the sight of her.

Piper rose to greet her, pressing her lips against Chloe's for a kiss that increased all the fizzing inside her. Yep, she was smitten all right.

"You're not incognito tonight," she murmured against Piper's lips.

"Nope."

Chloe drew back to look at her, taking in Piper's makeup, her shimmery eyeshadow, lips pink and glossy from a combination of her lipstick and their kiss. Her hair cascaded down her back in rich auburn waves, more polished than it had been in the Caymans and heavy with styling product. This was Sam Whitaker's hair. Chloe's throat went dry at the realization.

"It's good to see you," Piper said, giving her another quick kiss before she reclaimed her seat at the table.

Chloe eyed the bench seat across from her and then, making a snap decision, she slid in next to Piper. Not only did this bring them closer, but it also allowed Chloe to shield Piper from any prying eyes in the restaurant. She didn't necessarily want to share Piper tonight, or to put her in a situation that might cause her anxiety. "I'm so happy I'm here."

"I'm glad you are too," Piper said.

They sat close to each other, closer than the seat required. Chloe's thigh pressed against Piper's, allowing warmth to pass between them.

"Did you check in to your hotel room?" Piper asked, no doubt having noticed Chloe's black jeans and pink patterned top, a far cry from her airline uniform.

"I did, but I kept my suitcase packed...just in case."

"Good, because we're going to go get it after dinner and bring it back to my apartment."

"I pay for a lot of hotel rooms that I don't use when I'm with you," Chloe teased. "Although the airline is paying for this one, so it's no loss for me."

"I hate to waste money, though," Piper said. "If we're going to make a go of this, we should plan better."

"Okay," Chloe agreed, slightly giddy at the way their evening had started. She'd halfway convinced herself that Piper would lose interest in her once they left the Caymans.

Surely she met more exciting people through her work than Chloe.

But Piper was exactly the same as she had been on the island, only with more makeup. It was Chloe who had changed. She'd gone home and googled Piper. She'd swooned over red carpet photos of her in stunning couture gowns and binge watched her TV show, and now she was slightly intimidated by the knowledge she'd gained.

"How was your week?" Piper leaned an elbow on the table, blue eyes fixed on Chloe's.

"Good but crazy. I flew all over the place, went home and spent time with my parents and Cait, and took out a mortgage on my new house. It's been sitting vacant for a while, so they want to move quickly on the closing. I should have the keys later this month."

"That's exciting," Piper said.

"It is," Chloe agreed. "It needs a lot of work, but I'm going to have plenty of time on my hands when I quit my job, so this will keep me busy while I look for something new."

"And you want to work in interior design?"

"Yeah. I can practice with my own house first, right? It'll be fun fixing it up."

The waiter arrived at their table, and they ordered a bottle of cabernet to share and an artichoke dip as an appetizer. Chloe had always enjoyed going to new restaurants all over the world and ordering fancy things she might not have in her own small town, not that artichoke dip was particularly fancy, but at a restaurant like this, it was sure to be good.

"What's your personal decorating style?" Piper asked, relaxing into the seat beside her. "Do you know yet?"

"Hm," Chloe said, reaching for the glass of water in front

of her. She sipped, thinking. "Somewhere between boho and modern, I think. I like lots of color and funky, eclectic things, but I also enjoy the clean lines and minimalistic vibe of a modern look."

"Sounds interesting to try to marry the two," Piper commented.

"Well, hopefully you'll get a chance to see how it turns out," she said as the waiter returned with their wine.

Perhaps having recognized Piper, he offered her a sample to approve before he poured their glasses and took their dinner orders. Piper ordered wild mushroom risotto, and Chloe went with the ahi tuna salad.

Chloe sipped her wine, savoring its rich flavor on her tongue. "And how was *your* week? Do any fancy TV-star stuff?"

Piper rolled her eyes playfully as she sipped her own wine. "I spent most of it lying in a hospital bed."

"Oh no." Chloe blinked, pressing a hand against her chest. "I'm invested in Sam's life now, Piper. Please tell me she's going to be okay. Wait...don't tell me. I've only just started season two."

"And we're about to wrap season five, so I'm not telling you anything." Piper gave her a nudge. "But I *can* tell you that I'm contracted through season seven, so..."

"Okay, that sounds promising," Chloe agreed. "It's really good too, by the way. You're so different as Sam. You're like really badass."

Piper grinned. "I'll take that as a compliment, even though you're implying that I'm *not* badass in real life."

"Oh, you definitely are," Chloe told her, "but in a different way. Sam is badass in a 'wear a thousand-dollar suit and make men trip with a single look' kind of way."

"That she is," Piper agreed.

"And *you* are badass in an 'out actress in an industry where it could still hurt you and facing your fears on a daily basis' kind of way."

"Hm." Piper sipped her wine, staring into its ruby depths. "Trying to, anyway."

"And you're succeeding," Chloe told her. "I can already see how much progress you've made since we met."

"I guess, somewhere over the last week or so, I realized I have to let go of the fear of panicking in public. It's going to happen. It *has* happened, and it wasn't the end of the world. Hopefully it will get easier over time, but nothing was ever going to get better if I just hid in my apartment forever."

"Exactly," Chloe agreed. "Like you said, it's already happened, and you handled it like a pro. You're doing this."

Their meals arrived, and they fell to lighter topics while they ate, discussing Piper's movie audition and Chloe's upcoming flight schedule.

"Usually I'm only in New York overnight, but there's a possibility week after next that I could push out my flight and spend Friday here too," she told Piper.

"I'll have to work on Friday." Piper glanced at her as she chewed. "But maybe you want to come with me?"

"Uh, I would *love* that," Chloe told her.

"You could have a look around and see me in action."

"Please." Chloe was nodding like crazy. "But don't be embarrassed if I geek out a little bit."

"I'm sure you'll be adorable," Piper told her.

Chloe scrunched her nose. "We'll see about that."

They finished their meal and called an Uber to take them to Chloe's hotel for her suitcase and then on to Piper's apartment. The car turned onto a quiet street lined with brick-fronted row houses, all neatly tended, some with flower boxes outside. Chloe couldn't wait to see them tomorrow in the sunlight.

"God, the architecture," she said, admiring the intricate stonework on Piper's building as the car pulled to a stop. "This is stunning."

"I love the architecture here in the city, but damn, Europe really puts us to shame."

"It's true," Chloe agreed. "I haven't gotten to explore Europe as much as I'd like, but I've seen enough to be starry-eyed forever."

"Don't you get to fly to Europe much?" Piper asked after they'd thanked the driver and left the car with Chloe's suitcase in tow.

She shook her head. "I don't speak a second language, so I'm generally limited to flights to English-speaking countries."

"Ah," Piper said, nodding. "Makes sense."

"You told me you lived in an apartment," Chloe said as they walked up the front steps. "I'd call this a house." And it must cost a fortune.

"My apartment is on the third floor," Piper told her. "I'm not *that* rich, you know?"

"We'll see about that." Chloe stood back, holding on to the handle of her suitcase as Piper unlocked the door and let them inside. They stepped into a fairly nondescript entryway with hardwood floors and off-white walls.

Piper gestured to the stairs ahead. "Need help with the suitcase?"

"Nope," Chloe told her. "I'm used to hauling it all over, and it's pretty light anyway."

She lifted it and followed Piper up two flights of stairs, stopping in front of a black-painted door. Piper unlocked it and pushed it open, holding it for Chloe, who wheeled her suitcase over the hardwood floors with a clatter of wheels.

"Home sweet home," Piper said as she flicked a switch.

A lamp blazed to life, illuminating the main area of the apartment in its slightly amber glow. Chloe saw a black microfiber couch and a matching chair. The walls were painted a cool gray, except for the one in back, which featured a built-in bookcase filled with photos and knickknacks.

"Do you mind?" Chloe asked, gesturing toward it. Maybe it was the interior designer in her, but she loved seeing what people put on their shelves.

"Not at all," Piper told her.

Chloe walked over, scanning photos of Piper with her friends and family. Piper pointed out her younger brother and her parents, plus various friends, some of whom Chloe recognized.

She pointed to a photo obviously taken on set. "It's you and Tony and Claire!"

"It's me and Nate and Eliza, yes," Piper confirmed, laughter in her voice.

Chloe made a face at her. "So you mean if I visit you on set in a few weeks, I should call them by their real names?"

"Suit yourself," Piper said, eyes twinkling. "I'm sure they'd get a laugh out of it."

"I'll remember their real names when I meet them, I promise." Chloe gave her head a slight shake as the reality of visiting Piper on set began to sink in. She'd have to get all her excitement out ahead of time so she didn't make a fool of herself.

Interspersed with Piper's photos were various decorative items, a little turquoise vase filled with a spray of fake flowers, a candle inlaid with dried flowers, and a copper-plated giraffe. The top shelf was filled with books. "What do you like to read?" Chloe asked, squinting at them.

"Mostly romance or sci-fi," Piper said from behind her. "I like to escape reality when I read."

"Lesbian romance?" Chloe asked. "Is that a thing? I don't find enough time to read lately, I guess."

"I read lesbian romance, yes," Piper said. "It's definitely a thing, but I read straight romance too. You know I'm bisexual, right?"

"I guess I did," Chloe said. "I mean, I googled you after we got home from the Caymans and found pictures of you with both men and women." She gave Piper a sheepish look.

"It's fine. That's what Google is for."

"Anyway, I'm not too hung up on labels," Chloe told her. "I'm a lesbian, but I couldn't care less what genders you're attracted to, as long as women are on the list."

"Definitely on the list," Piper said as she stepped up behind Chloe, pressing a hot, openmouthed kiss against her neck. "In fact, when you're around, you are the *only* person on my list."

11

Chloe woke to the buzz of an unfamiliar alarm. She blinked into the gray-toned landscape of Piper's bedroom, smiling as she remembered where she was and why she was here.

"Sorry," Piper mumbled from behind her. There was a bump, and the buzzing stopped.

"Don't be. I have to be up this morning too, remember?" She scooted backward as Piper's arm came around her waist, basking in the warmth of her body.

"Where are you jetting off to today?" Piper asked, her voice scratchy with sleep.

"New York to Chicago to LA and back to Charlotte, then I'll drive home and spend a few days with my family."

"Sounds exhausting," Piper said.

"It's definitely exhausting." Chloe traced her fingers over Piper's where they rested on her stomach. "But there's also something exhilarating about traveling thousands of miles in a day and getting paid to do it."

"Sounds like you picked the right career, then."

Chloe blinked the sleep from her eyes as she looked

around Piper's bedroom. It had been dark when they made it in here last night, and they'd been preoccupied with undressing each other. She spotted an aquarium on the dresser with a red betta fish inside. "Oh, you have a fish!"

"His name is Master."

"Master the betta." Chloe gasped with laughter as she realized what she'd just said. *Master Betta.* "Oh my God, Piper."

"I guess I was drowning in my own weird sense of humor when I named him," Piper said sheepishly. "And maybe a bit lonely...and horny."

Chloe laughed as she rolled to face her. "It's hilarious, but how do you explain his name to your family?"

"They've never asked his name," she said with a shrug. "If they did, I'd probably either tell them he doesn't have one or make one up."

Still giggling, Chloe slid out of bed, because her job didn't allow her the luxury of running late. She and Piper moved around the bedroom together as they washed up and got dressed.

"Hungry?" Piper asked as she led the way out of the bedroom.

"Sure, if you have something easy. Otherwise I'll just grab something at the airport."

"Cereal?"

"Sounds good." Chloe followed her to the kitchen. She probably hadn't eaten cereal since high school, or she hadn't until her weekend in the Caymans. It seemed to be Piper's breakfast of choice, and Chloe was developing a new affinity for it. Well, cereal, and pretty much everything Piper-related.

They ate together, and Chloe repacked her suitcase as they prepared to head out to their respective workdays,

Piper to a soundstage here in Brooklyn and Chloe to the airport.

Piper gave her an appreciative look as they stepped onto the sidewalk. "You're really hot in your uniform, you know that?"

"Am I?" Chloe smoothed a hand over her jacket, cheeks warming at Piper's compliment. Today, Chloe was wearing pants. She alternated between her uniform skirt, dress, and pants depending on her mood, but when she had a particularly long day of flying ahead, pants were just more comfortable. "Speaking of work clothes, will you send me a picture of you in one of Sam's power suits? Talk about hot." She fanned her cheeks.

"I can do that," Piper told her with a smile. She gestured toward a black sedan at the curb. "That's my car."

They walked to it, and Chloe put her suitcase in the trunk. Last night, they'd arranged for Piper's driver to drop Chloe off at her hotel so she could catch the airline's shuttle to the airport. It was a short drive, and all too soon, the car pulled to a stop in front of the hotel.

Piper leaned in for a quick kiss. "I'll text you."

Chloe nodded. "Hopefully we can do this again next week."

"Count on it," Piper said.

After one last kiss, Chloe got out of the car, retrieved her suitcase, and walked to the shuttle waiting outside the hotel. From there, she rode to JFK and checked in for her first flight of the day. By mid-afternoon, she was blinking out the window into the bright LA sunshine. She snapped a quick picture and sent it to Piper with the caption. *Hello from Hollywood!*

Piper didn't respond, which meant she was probably filming. Chloe imagined her all done up in one of Sam's sleek suits, and her pulse raced. Shaking her head at herself, she pushed her suitcase through the terminal in search of a late lunch before she boarded her last flight of the day back to Charlotte.

"Hey stranger!"

Chloe turned at the sound of Nisha's voice, smiling to see her friend walking down the terminal behind her. "I was hoping to bump into you. Have you eaten yet?"

"Nope." Nisha fell into step beside her. She and Chloe often worked flights into Charlotte together, since they were both based out of that airport. "How was your weekend in the Caymans? Any update on your new house? I feel so out of the loop."

Chloe laughed softly. "I have a *lot* to catch you up on."

"I like the sound of that, assuming they're good things," Nisha said.

"They are," Chloe confirmed. She and Nisha separated at the food court to buy their lunches and then sat together at a little table where Chloe started on her barbeque chicken wrap while Nisha dug into her curry bowl. "I found out who my Mystery Woman is, and we're kind of dating now."

Nisha paused with her fork halfway to her mouth, eyes going wide. "Oh my God, tell me everything."

Chloe paused for a moment, considering whether she should share Piper's identity with her friend. But Piper hadn't asked her to keep it a secret, and besides, Nisha would never betray Chloe's trust. She needed to share this with someone. "She's Piper Sheridan."

Nisha promptly choked on her rice, coughing and sputtering as she attempted to form words. "Piper Sheridan, as in Sam Whitaker on *In Her Defense*?"

Chloe nodded. "Yep."

"Um, did you forget that's my favorite TV show?" Nisha asked, still coughing as she reached for her water. "Oh my God, Chloe!"

Chloe blinked. "Apparently, I did forget. Remind me."

"I've been watching it since the first season, partly because of my crush on Nate Mauldin, who plays Sam's partner Tony, but also because the show is so freaking good. It's well written, diverse, and full of strong, competent women. In fact, I'm pretty sure I hassled you to watch it with me a few years ago."

Chloe looked at her friend. "You're right. I had totally forgotten you were the one who told me to watch it."

"So, um, let's get to the part where you're dating Piper Sheridan, because holy shit. She's your Mystery Woman?" Nisha was practically bouncing in her seat.

"Yep. She was wearing a wig that night, so I didn't recognize her, but she was on my flight to the Caymans last Friday without a disguise, so I realized who she was. Actually, Tammy pointed her out to me, because apparently I'm hopeless where recognizing celebrities is concerned."

Nisha gaped at her, motioning with her hands for Chloe to continue.

"Anyway, we met up on the island and ended up spending the whole weekend together," Chloe told her. "And it was so great, Nisha. Like, I can't remember the last time I connected with someone so quickly. I spent last night at her apartment in Brooklyn."

Nisha chewed and swallowed a bite of curry. "That is... wow. I am so happy for you, Chloe. You deserve this, and if you ever introduce her to me, I promise I'll do my best to keep my fangirling to a minimum."

Chloe laughed as she took another bite of her sandwich.

"I'll definitely introduce you to her if I get the chance, just to see you turn into a giggling fangirl."

"Don't laugh, because that's exactly what will happen." Nisha gave her a mock-serious look.

"Anyway, it feels like a lot because of how quickly things happened for us, and obviously it's complicated because of the long-distance thing, so we're just taking it one day at a time."

Nisha nodded. "Who knows how things will play out? You're about to give up this jet-setting life, so if things with you and Piper get serious, maybe you'll land in New York instead of North Carolina."

Chloe frowned. "I also bought a house...in North Carolina."

"Oh," Nisha said. "Well, that does complicate things."

"I wouldn't have moved to New York anyway, though. My family needs me in Hendersonville."

"Do they?" Nisha countered, looking up from her meal.

"Yes. Cait starts middle school next year, and my parents aren't getting any younger, you know? If she's half the handful Cassie and I were, they're going to need my help. Plus, I just want to be there for her. I feel like I haven't been around enough."

"I get that. Believe me, I do. Just don't lose sight of what you want because you think you owe it to your family to stick close to home, okay?"

"Home is where I want to be," Chloe assured her, even as she felt a little twinge of sadness at leaving this life behind, new places, new faces, the opportunity to see Piper more often. "Anyway, enough about me. How's your mom?"

Nisha's brown eyes warmed. "She had her last treatment yesterday. If her numbers stay where they're supposed to, we might be out of the woods, at least for now."

"Oh my God, Nisha." Chloe reached across the table to press a hand over her friend's. "That is the best news. I'm so glad."

"Me too," Nisha said. "If her numbers hold, I'm definitely going to take your advice and book a weekend getaway for us, somewhere warm and beachy."

"Yes," Chloe agreed. "You deserve it. You both do."

"Now what are the chances Nate Mauldin will be on my flight?" Nisha teased. "Because I want a celebrity romance of my own."

≈

PIPER STOOD in front of the mirror in her dressing room. It was almost eight, and she'd just wrapped filming for the day. She was exhausted, starving, and more than ready to get out of this suit and the heels that had been torturing her all day, but first...

She lifted her phone and snapped a mirror selfie, giving her iciest Sam Whitaker stare. Then she took another, smiling as herself. She sent them both to Chloe, then set down her phone and changed into the knit pants and tee she'd worn to the set that morning. Sighing in relief to be back in comfortable clothes, she reached into her mini fridge for a bottle of water before sinking into her chair. She had about ten minutes before the car would arrive to take her home.

Hottttttttttt, came Chloe's reply to her mirror selfies.

Your turn, Piper typed.

You already saw mine, but here you go anyway.

A photo of Chloe in her uniform appeared on Piper's screen, and warmth spread through her chest. *Worth seeing again. How was LA?*

Looked pretty out the window. I'm back in Charlotte now, just landed. Headed home!

Drive safely. xx.

Piper packed up and walked outside, relieved to see her car turning onto the street behind the lot. She missed the freedom of riding the subway, leaving when she wanted instead of at a scheduled time. Today, she'd gotten her timing right, but on those rare days when she wrapped early, she'd be stuck here anyway, waiting for her ride.

She'd tackle the subway soon. Not today, but soon.

When she got home, she ordered takeout from the Himalayan restaurant down the street and stepped into a hot shower. She'd worked a twelve-hour day, and she was ready to crash. She ate dinner and curled up in bed to read until she fell asleep. Her phone dinged with a new text.

I can't decide which selfie I like better – you or Sam.

Piper smiled. *Don't tell me I need to be jealous of my character.*

Nothing to worry about on that front.

Good.

They texted back and forth for a few more minutes, and Piper fell asleep that night feeling relaxed and happy.

The next week seemed to fly by. She was so busy on set, she could barely keep up. Every year, the last month of filming was the most grueling. The days often ran long— even longer than usual—as they tried to pack it all in before they wrapped for the season.

And Piper was tired, so friggin' tired. She wasn't complaining, because she loved this show and what it had done for her career, but she was more than ready for a few weeks off after the season wrapped.

Even with her long hours, she kept pushing herself to leave her apartment. On Saturday, she enjoyed a cappuccino at her favorite coffee shop after her therapy appointment. She was making her way down her checklist, one goal at the time, and Dr. Jorgensen was pleased with her progress...and with her new relationship with Chloe.

She and Chloe spent another night together the following Thursday. They made pasta and spent a quiet evening at Piper's apartment. When they weren't together, they called or FaceTimed each other every night before bed. Chloe's hours were as long as Piper's right now, so neither of them had time to miss each other as much as they might have otherwise. Their long-distance relationship was off to a seamless start. Piper felt happier than she had in years, and she knew she had Chloe to thank for it.

She couldn't wait to see what would happen for her and Chloe once she was on hiatus from the show and had more free time on her hands. Hopefully, it would bring them closer. Hopefully, she'd get a chance to fly out and visit Chloe in North Carolina. Hopefully, she had a lot of good things to look forward to, both personally and professionally.

On Sunday, she boarded a flight to LA for her big Hollywood audition. Anticipating the paparazzi that always lurked around LAX, she wore her black wig to avoid drawing attention to herself. Still, she was a nervous mess for the entire six hours she was in the air. At one point, she locked herself in the lavatory just to have a chance to breathe without anyone looking at her. Not that anyone was looking at her. The disguise worked. But she *felt* like they were looking at her.

By the time she'd gotten settled in her hotel room, she was exhausted, the kind of bone-deep fatigue caused by the combination of a long day of travel and hours of anxiety. It was only seven here in LA, but that meant it was ten at home, and as she picked at the salad she'd ordered from room service, she was ready to drop.

But first, she needed to hear Chloe's voice, if she could catch her. Sipping from the glass of wine she'd ordered with her salad, she picked up her phone and dialed. The line rang, unanswered, as Piper tried to remember where Chloe was tonight. Just as she thought it was going to go through to voicemail, there was a click.

"Hey!" Chloe answered, sounding vaguely out of breath.

"Hi." Piper's eyes slid shut, and she exhaled, instantly relaxed by the sound of Chloe's voice. "Where are you tonight?"

"Ottawa," Chloe answered. "Walking to the airline shuttle now. How was your flight to LA?"

"Stressful but uneventful." For whatever reason, she never felt the need to hide her anxiety from Chloe the way she often did with her family and coworkers. Maybe because Chloe never made a fuss about it, which was calming in and of itself.

"I'm glad," Chloe said. "I'll be crossing all my fingers for you tomorrow."

"Don't do that while you're working," Piper teased. "Your passengers might look at you funny."

"I'll be discreet," Chloe told her. "Call me after? Even if I'm in the air, leave me a voicemail and let me know how it went."

"I will."

"I tried to shuffle things around so I could fly through LA tomorrow, but it didn't work out," Chloe said. The hollow sound of her heels echoed over the line as she walked through the terminal.

"That's too bad," Piper said. "It would have been fun to bump into you at the airport. I'm flying out right after my audition, and I have to be on set pretty much the minute I land. They're holding my scenes until later in the afternoon to accommodate me."

"I'm glad they could be flexible, but ugh, I'm sorry you have to go straight to work when you land. You're going to be exhausted tomorrow night."

"I will be, but for good reason. And filming for season five wraps next month, so I can catch up on my sleep then."

"Yes," Chloe agreed. "Hey, speaking of schedules, I got approved for that day off next week that I told you about, so I'll be in New York from Thursday night until Saturday morning. I know you have to work on Friday, but if you were serious about letting me tag along with you on set..."

"I was," Piper told her, heart soaring at the thought. "Let's plan on it, then."

"Perfect," Chloe said brightly. "I can't wait."

"I can't either."

Piper held on to that thought long after the call had ended and she'd taken a sleeping pill to keep herself from tossing restlessly all night. She fell asleep thinking about Chloe, and she woke the next morning with the image of Chloe's smiling face behind her eyelids, a remnant from a blissful dream.

Unfortunately, that peaceful image faded fast as Piper's nerves kicked in. Auditions had always been stressful for her, and this would be her first since the panic attacks started. If she panicked during the audition...

Groaning, she rolled over to silence her alarm. It was only six here on the West Coast, but at least to her body, it felt like nine, which meant she was fairly well rested going into what would be yet another long and exhausting day. She got up, showered, and spent extra time in front of the mirror polishing her hair and makeup. Then she sat on the bed and picked up her script, running through the scenes she'd been asked to prepare.

She already knew them backward and forward, but last-minute repetition never hurt, and it helped to keep her from spiraling into anxious thought patterns. She was auditioning to play Tara Quinn, a free-spirited artist. In the movie, Tara would navigate the road from friends to lovers with the buttoned-up businessman who'd been her best friend since childhood.

It was standard fare as far as Hollywood romcoms went, but the script was surprisingly heartfelt and funny, and the role would bring invaluable exposure for Piper, not to mention a sweet paycheck. She was determined not to fuck this up, no matter how frantically her heart pounded as she prepared to leave her hotel room. This was Hollywood, after all. There would likely be eyes—and cameras—on her from the moment she left this room.

She packed her suitcase since she'd be heading straight to the airport after her audition, and then she did several of the breathing exercises Dr. Jorgensen had taught her. Pushing her suitcase ahead of her, Piper stepped into the hall and walked to the elevator bank. Her foot tapped restlessly as she waited for one to arrive.

When it did, she wedged herself into the back corner, keeping her gaze firmly on her suitcase and praying no one would recognize her. The elevator glided from floor to floor, seeming to stop at each one as more people squeezed in. Piper glanced up, only to find herself staring into her own slightly dazed face on the mirrored wall.

A tall man in a business suit pressed in beside her, and sweat began to trickle down her back. He was too close. Everyone in this damn elevator was standing too close. Her pulse roared in her ears, muffling the hum of conversation around her. The doors opened again, and yet more people stuffed themselves inside.

Piper turned toward the wall. She pressed a hand against the heaviness in her chest, squeezing her eyes shut. Her fingernails bit into her palms, and she focused on the sensation, attempting to block out the stifling press of bodies around her. She could feel her hair sticking to her damp cheeks.

Even if she made it out of this elevator without causing a scene, she was going to arrive at her audition a sweaty, frazzled mess. A baby started to cry on the other side of the space, and Piper could relate. Tears burned behind her eyelids, and her knees started to shake. A quick glance at the control panel told her they had only made it to the fifteenth floor. Her chest seized, and spots danced across her vision.

She wasn't going to make it.

12

*G*ood luck!! Whatever happens, I know you're going to nail this audition.

Chloe stared at the text she'd sent Piper earlier that morning, the text that was still unread. Maybe she'd sent it after Piper had already gone into her audition, except Chloe was an expert on time zones, and she knew she'd sent it early enough. Maybe Piper had been too nervous this morning to check her phone. Chloe closed her eyes and sent up as much good energy as she could muster that Piper hadn't had a panic attack this morning of all mornings.

Chloe boarded the plane, greeting her fellow crew members for the journey from Ottawa to Chicago. With one last regretful look at her phone, she stowed her luggage at the rear of the plane and began running through the preflight check.

There was an unfamiliar heaviness in the pit of her stomach as she buckled into her jump seat for takeoff. Somehow, Piper had rooted herself more deeply into Chloe's psyche than she'd anticipated, so deeply that she could hardly concentrate on her job that morning. She needed to make sure Piper was okay and be there for her if she wasn't.

How had she gotten this attached to Piper so quickly? They hadn't even known each other a month yet. Chloe had never felt anything like this before. She'd never been in love, not that she was in love with Piper...not yet. But the ache in her chest as she worried about Piper's audition suggested she might be headed in that direction.

Chloe hadn't dated much in high school. She and Cassie had been inseparable, and neither of them had been thinking about girls...or boys, in Cassie's case. Even in college, Chloe had been a late bloomer, probably at least in part because she was still coming to terms with her sexuality. She and Cassie had always shared *everything*, so when Cassie started dating boy after boy, Chloe had been slow to realize why the concept held no appeal for her.

She'd gone on a few boring dates with boys on campus, but it wasn't until she met Aimee during her junior year that Chloe felt the spark Cassie was always talking about. Chloe spent an entire semester pining over Aimee without ever working up the courage to ask her out. Then, Cassie died, and Chloe's life shifted on its axis. Left adrift without her twin, Chloe joined an LGBT group on campus and finally had her first girlfriend senior year.

She'd dated a lot that last year of college, but all of her relationships had been casual. As soon as she graduated, she enrolled in flight attendant training and started flying. There hadn't been time to fall in love. She'd been too busy flying all over the world, trying desperately to figure out who she was without Cassie.

Sometimes, she wasn't sure she ever would. Tears sprang to her eyes without warning. It still hit her like this sometimes, how much she missed her sister. She would have given anything right then to talk to Cassie, to get her advice on her relationship with Piper.

When Chloe landed in Chicago, she forced herself not to be impatient as she said goodbye to the passengers disembarking the plane. She completed her post-flight tasks, and then *finally*, she grabbed her bag and switched her phone off airplane mode. As always, it took a minute to connect to the network, so she held it in her palm as she pushed her suitcase down the jetway into O'Hare International Airport.

With a ding, a string of texts from Piper appeared on the screen.

OMG I had a panic attack in the elevator at the hotel this morning, and I almost missed my audition. BUT...

It went well!

<gif of a woman collapsing on the floor>

I mean, I was a mess beforehand, but I pulled myself together in the car on the way to the studio.

Who knows what will happen, but I can say I gave it my best.

You must be flying, and by the time you land, I'll be flying LOL.

I'll be on set until late, but I'll try to catch up with you before bed.

Thanks so much for being my cheerleader on this. It really helped xx.

Chloe finished reading with a huge smile on her face. Oh, her stomach had dipped when she read about Piper's panic attack, but she was so relieved the audition had gone well.

Sooooo glad to hear this, she replied before adding a string of happy and relieved emojis.

I really wish I could hug you right now and that I could have been with you in that elevator. She inserted a silly gif of a woman tackle-hugging another woman.

I'm in Chicago at the moment, about to fly to Charlotte. Call me when you get home, no matter how late!

Feeling significantly lighter on her feet, Chloe headed to the food court for lunch. In honor of her newly improved mood, she treated herself to a cheeseburger and a chocolate milkshake.

Her flight from O'Hare to Charlotte was uneventful, and soon she was in her RAV4 on her way home. As much as she loved her parents and her niece, she couldn't wait to get the keys to her new house. It would be the first time she'd ever had her own place, and that felt like an important next step to figuring out who she was as her own person.

Not Cassie's twin or Cait's aunt or Piper's girlfriend.

She had dinner with her family, played with Cait and her hamster until the girl's bedtime, and then retreated to her third-floor bedroom to watch *In Her Defense* while she waited for Piper to call. She was nearing the end of season three now, and she was totally invested in these characters. She'd made it through an episode and a half when her phone rang.

"Hi," she answered breathlessly, heart racing and butterflies dancing in her belly.

"Hi," Piper answered. "I didn't wake you, did I?"

Chloe glanced at the clock. It was almost midnight, but she was off tomorrow, so she could sleep in. "Nope. I was just lying in bed watching *In Her Defense.*"

"Oh geez," Piper said with a laugh.

"I have some questions for you about that, but first, tell me all about your audition."

"Well," Piper said, exhaling as if she'd just stretched out

in bed. Chloe pictured her under her gray striped quilt, maybe wearing that little blue nightgown she'd worn the last time Chloe visited. "I read opposite Landon Wilkes, which was pretty exciting in and of itself."

"Oh my God," Chloe breathed, imagining Piper starring in a movie with the blond heartthrob all the straight girls seemed to be lusting over. He was handsome. Even she could see that, and he seemed charming too. "That is so cool. What's he like in person?"

"He was really great. He's already got the part, obviously. They just brought him in to do a chemistry test with me."

"What's that?" Chloe asked, not quite liking the mental image it conjured.

"Just reading a scene together to see if we mesh on camera."

"Oh good," Chloe said with a little laugh.

"Well, if I get the part, I'll have to kiss him and film a sex scene."

"Ew." Chloe scrunched her face. "I mean, I know it's your job, but…"

Piper laughed. "Sex scenes are the opposite of sexy, trust me. Anyway, I read a scene on my own and one with Landon, and then I sat with the director and producer. It all seemed to go really well, but I don't know how many other actresses auditioned, so I don't want to get too excited."

"I doubt they'd bring Landon in unless they were pretty sure," Chloe said.

"I think you're right, and my agent agrees. So keep those fingers crossed."

"I will." Chloe crossed the fingers on her free hand. "I'm so proud of you, Piper. This is going to be so amazing for your career."

"Don't say that yet," Piper admonished. "You'll jinx me.

But I'm proud of myself for getting through the audition, especially after I had such a shitty start to my morning. Now I've got to get on the subway."

"I'll ride it with you when I'm in town this week if you want," she offered. "If you think it would help to have me there."

"Yeah," Piper said quietly. "It would. Thanks."

"Okay. It's a subway date," she joked, keeping the tone light. "Did you really just get home from the set?"

"Yeah." Piper sighed again, but she didn't sound upset about it, just tired. "It was a long day, but a good one overall."

"I'm glad. Okay, now that I'm almost finished with season three, tell me what's going on with Sam and Claire. Am I just imagining a queer vibe there?"

"You're not, or at least you're far from the only one who sees it," Piper said. "Do you want spoilers?"

"I guess not."

"Well, it didn't start intentionally. The showrunner has always envisioned Sam ending up with Tony, but you know how they love to milk the 'will they or won't they' storylines," Piper told her. "While they were dragging out the Sam and Tony angle, our online fans started shipping Sam with Claire, and it's become quite a thing."

"Shipping?" Chloe asked.

"It's what the fans call it when they want two characters to be in a relationship. Anyway, we've attracted a huge queer following who want Sam and Claire to wind up together."

"I'm not surprised," Chloe said. "You and the actress who plays Claire have great chemistry together, and I'd imagine since you're a queer actress, you probably have a lot of fans who are too."

"All true," Piper confirmed.

"Even the chemistry part?" Chloe teased, but it was something that had been nagging at her, because the way Sam gazed at Claire was *not* platonic, and if the showrunner wasn't pushing that angle, then was it Piper herself?

"Even the chemistry, or so I'm told anyway." Piper laughed, but there was something awkward in her tone that hadn't been there before.

"Did you guys ever date?"

"God, no," Piper said with another laugh. "Eliza's straight."

"Oh," Chloe said.

Piper sighed. "I was attracted to her when we first started filming the show, which was super awkward, but I think it's what launched the ship, so to speak."

"Oh," Chloe repeated. "But you're not attracted to her anymore?"

"No," Piper said, and she sounded sincere, at least as far as Chloe could tell without being able to see her face. "It was unrequited obviously, and I got over it years ago. Eliza and I are good friends."

"I'm glad," Chloe said. "I mean, that you guys are friends."

"Anyway, I have more thoughts on the Sam and Claire thing, but I'll wait to share them with you until you've caught up on the show."

"Deal," Chloe agreed. "And while I'm not wild about the idea of you kissing your former crush, I kind of hope Sam and Claire do get together. It would be so awesome to see another sapphic relationship on TV. The pickings have been slim lately."

"I agree, and just so you know, I'm pushing for it too, so we'll see what happens."

"Okay."

A loud yawn carried over the line. "Much as I love talking to you, I'm beat. Mind if we call it a night?"

"Nope, I'm pretty tired too," Chloe agreed. "Congratulations again on the audition. I'll chat with you tomorrow."

"Count on it. Good night, Chloe."

Chloe put down her phone and clicked Play on the episode of *In Her Defense* that she'd paused when Piper called. It was a scene with Sam and Claire, but suddenly, Chloe wasn't in the mood to watch Piper stare longingly at her costar, not after what Piper had just told her. Annoyed with herself, Chloe turned it off and went to bed.

∼

PIPER'S WEEK passed in a blur of filming on the *Defense* set. The last few episodes had been extremely Sam-centric, which was a great thing for Piper, but it made for long days. She was excited about Sam's trajectory, though. America's favorite fictional lawyer had gone a bit dark after recovering from her gunshot wound and had a one-night stand with a man she met in a bar while flirting shamelessly with Claire at the office.

Piper had talked to Benny, their showrunner, again about the importance of following through with Sam and Claire's relationship, now that the sexual tension between them had become such a focus of season five, but she hadn't yet seen the script for the finale, so she didn't know if he'd taken her advice.

By Thursday, she was beyond eager to see Chloe again. She'd left a key hidden in the ornamental planter outside her building so Chloe could let herself in after she landed, because she was certain to arrive before Piper finished filming. Just past five o'clock, Chloe texted a selfie of herself sitting in Piper's living room.

Consequently, Piper was extremely distracted during her last scene of the day, imagining Chloe in her apartment and wishing she was there with her. By seven, she was finally on her way home. After texting with Chloe, Piper placed an order from the Mediterranean restaurant near her apartment since it was getting late and they were both starving.

When the car pulled up in front of her building, Piper jogged up both flights of stairs and unlocked the door to reveal Chloe on the couch, tablet in hand, reading. She looked up with one of those effervescent smiles that had the power to make Piper's heart lose its rhythm.

Chloe stood, and they walked into each other's arms. "Hi," she whispered against Piper's lips.

"Hi yourself." Piper wrapped her arms around her. "I've been waiting for this all week."

"Same."

They sat on the couch together, alternately kissing and catching up, because despite their nightly FaceTime sessions, they never seemed to run out of things to talk about. When the food arrived, they opened a bottle of wine and enjoyed a quiet dinner together.

"Have you ever read fan fiction?" Chloe asked as she bit into a stuffed grape leaf.

"No," Piper told her. "Why? Have you?"

"Well..." Chloe's cheeks flushed a deep pink. "My friend Nisha is a huge fan of the show, and she sent me a link this afternoon. She's straight, but she thought I might like this one because it's about Sam and Claire."

"Oh." Piper felt herself grinning. "Did you read it?"

"Well, I started it while I was waiting for you to get

home. It's really long, like book length, but it's surprisingly good. And *hot*."

"Interesting." For some reason, it turned Piper on to think about Chloe reading smutty Clairantha fanfic.

"Want the link?"

"Might be weird," she deflected, even though a part of her was oddly curious.

"I'm sending it to you anyway," Chloe said with a wink.

It was after eight by the time they finished eating. It would be so easy to call it a night, to take Chloe into the bedroom and spend the rest of the evening there with her, but they'd stayed in the last time Chloe was in New York. In fact, Piper hadn't been out since her cappuccino excursion almost two weeks ago. She was falling back into her old ways.

"Want to go out for a drink?" she suggested. "We could stop by the bar where we met."

"I'm up for it if you are," Chloe said. "That place was really nice."

Piper nodded. "And...let's take the subway."

Chloe straightened. "Are you sure?"

"It's the last thing on my list. I have to do it sooner than later, and I'm not ashamed to say I'd like to have you beside me for moral support when I do."

Chloe beamed at her. "Okay. Let's ride the subway, and then we'll celebrate your success with a drink."

Decision made, Piper stood and walked into the bedroom to change into something nicer than the sweatpants she'd worn home from the set. Chloe followed, unzipping her suitcase to do the same. "I'm going to wear my wig for this," Piper told her.

"Good idea," Chloe agreed. "One thing at the time. First,

get on the subway without having to worry about anyone recognizing you."

"Exactly." She dressed in skinny jeans and a black tunic, then went into the bathroom to tuck her hair beneath the wig. Already, her heart was racing, and her skin was damp as she broke into a nervous sweat.

"Weird," Chloe said quietly, watching her from the doorway.

"What?"

Chloe gave her head a shake. "You look like my Mystery Woman again. I had almost forgotten about her."

"I'll take it off to go in the bar."

"Are you sure?" Chloe asked. "I don't want you to be uncomfortable."

"I'm sure," Piper told her. "I need to keep pushing myself, and it's easier to do when you're here."

Chloe's face lit as if Piper had just given her the biggest compliment. "You're plenty brave on your own, but I love being here to watch you in action."

"Speaking of watching me in action," Piper said, step-ping closer. "You're coming with me to the set tomorrow, right?"

Chloe nodded. "And I'm super excited about it."

"Me too." Piper reached out to smooth down a flyaway strand of Chloe's hair, letting her fingers linger there for an extra moment. There was something so soothing about being this close to her, touching her, breathing in her scent. The knot of nervous energy in Piper's stomach loosened.

"Would it be completely inappropriate for me to get an autograph while I'm there?"

"From who?" Piper asked. She hadn't imagined Chloe to be the fangirl type.

"Nisha—the friend who sent me that fan fiction—is a huge fan of the actor who plays Tony. In fact, as she reminded me last week, she's the one who originally got me to watch the show. I thought it would be fun to surprise her with an autograph."

"That's so sweet. I'm sure Nate would be happy to sign something for her."

They finished getting ready and walked outside into the crisp April evening. This was her favorite weather, just cool enough for a light jacket. The sun had set, staining the sky a deep indigo overhead. A light breeze ruffled Piper's wig. She brushed black hair out of her eyes, annoyed to realize her hands were shaking.

Determined not to lose her nerve, she led the way toward the entrance to the subway. It was a two-block walk, which was about two blocks too far right now. Her muscles were painfully stiff, and an uncomfortable crawling sensation spread over her skin.

Chloe's hand slid into hers, giving her a reassuring squeeze. "You got this. I won't say it'll be easy, but it will be worth it."

Piper nodded, her throat too tight for words. She paused at the top of the steps leading to the subway, fumbling in her purse for the MetroCard she'd reactivated last week. She hadn't used it in almost seven months. Beside her, Chloe produced a similar card.

Hand in hand, they started down the steps. Piper's pulse seemed to grow louder with each step, until all she could hear was the roar of blood in her ears. Her hand trembled as she swiped her card, and the machine beeped, displaying a red X on the display. A card read error.

For fuck's sake.

Now she looked like a tourist, while Chloe—who actually *was* a tourist—swiped through on her first try. Piper's chest constricted. Beep. Another error. She closed her eyes, dragging in a desperate breath before she tried again. The green light flashed, and she pushed through the turnstile onto the platform.

There were probably twenty other people already waiting for the train, most of them clustered near the edge of the platform along the yellow-painted safety line. So close to the tracks. *Too* close.

"Okay?" Chloe asked, again taking Piper's hand.

She nodded. That fateful day, she had stood with her toes on the yellow line, watching the marquee that announced the next incoming train, impatient to get home. Tonight, she stood behind the crowd, staring at her feet, not daring to look at the tracks or make eye contact with anyone, even Chloe.

The air in the station—as always—was hot and stale, and it only seemed to increase the heaviness in her chest. She closed her eyes, wiggling her toes inside her boots, attempting to take slow, deep breaths when she wanted to scream, to cry, to shove her way back through that turnstile and run until she'd reached the fresh air awaiting her on the street overhead.

But her feet were rooted to the ground on legs as heavy and useless as her chest. She tightened her grip on Chloe's hand, receiving a reassuring squeeze in return. There was a metallic squeal, and the air around her began to stir, pushed ahead of the approaching train. Piper opened her eyes to see the other passengers pressing forward, vying to be the first to board.

Nausea rose in her stomach. They were so close to the tracks, so vulnerable if anyone tripped or...

With a screech of metal and a puff of hot air, the train swept into the station. The sound of the wheels whining against metal rails was a scream in her ears. Piper gasped, taking an involuntary step back. And then Chloe was in front of her, filling Piper's field of vision with her bright hazel eyes and warm smile, blonde hair gusting around her face.

"All good," she said calmly. "We'll let the eager commuters board first."

Piper nodded yet again. It seemed to be the only method of communication left to her. Chloe kept her hands on Piper's, steadying her until it was time for them to board. Then she turned, leading Piper toward the train. They stepped into the nearest car to find the seats already occupied, but that was okay because Piper was too stiff to sit anyway.

She reached for the pole in front of her as the train lurched forward, knocking her hip into Chloe's. Chloe placed her hand beneath Piper's on the pole, keeping her body close, so close Piper could smell the fruity scent of her shampoo.

Piper closed her eyes, sucking in a deep breath. She looked down at her shoes, surprised to see black hair hanging around her face. She'd almost forgotten she was wearing the wig, but thank goodness for it. If someone recognized her right now, she might actually scream. A tremor ran through her, shaking her from her scalp to her toes, and that prickly, crawling sensation on her skin hadn't gone away.

The train pulled to a stop, and she and Chloe took a step back to allow other passengers to exit. Chloe tugged at her hand, guiding Piper toward a pair of seats that had opened up. They sat, Piper's hand clutched between Chloe's in the warmth of her lap.

"One more stop," Chloe said quietly.

Piper leaned closer so her shoulder pressed against Chloe's. She was on the subway. In five minutes, she'd be able to say she had successfully ridden it for the first time since the incident that derailed her life. She wouldn't go so far as to say she'd conquered her fear tonight, but she'd taken an important first step toward managing it.

With a hiss, the doors closed, and they were off again. Piper breathed, five beats in, six beats out, slow and steady. This time, instead of wiggling her toes, she squeezed Chloe's fingers, focusing on the smooth warmth of her skin and the way Chloe's thumb traced back and forth over Piper's palm, so soft it almost tickled.

The train rattled down the track, its creaks and groans as familiar to Piper as her own breath. She'd been riding the New York City subway since she was a teenager. It had been a comfortable place for her once, a part of her daily life, and it would be again.

Soon the train began to slow as it pulled into the next station. She and Chloe stood, exiting with a stream of other passengers. Back on the platform, Piper pushed forward, moving blindly as she shoved herself through the turnstile and bolted for the safety of the street above.

13

———

C hloe burst onto the street behind Piper, both of them breathless after their dash up the stairs. She hadn't realized how stuffy the subway was until she was out of it, sucking in fresh air as she tugged Piper against her for a hug. "You did it."

"I did," Piper gasped, the first words she'd spoken since before they descended to the platform over fifteen minutes ago.

"How do you feel?"

"Shaky," Piper said quietly.

"And emotionally?"

"I'm okay." Piper nodded against Chloe's cheek. "I just need a minute."

"Take as long as you need." Chloe could stand here with her all night, arms wrapped snugly around Piper, bursting with pride at the way she'd pushed through her fear to get on that train.

After a few minutes, Piper's gasping breaths slowed, and she rested her forehead against Chloe's shoulder. Beneath her fingers, Chloe felt the tension drain out of Piper, muscles that had been bunched tight gradually softening. Chloe rubbed a hand up and down her back, and Piper burrowed closer against her, letting out a sigh that sounded like relief.

"I'm so proud of you," Chloe whispered.

Piper raised her head, giving Chloe a hesitant smile. "It's not over for me, but it'll be easier next time, I think."

"Yes. So that was really the last thing on your list?"

"It was. Now I just have to *keep* doing these things until the fear is gone."

"That's badass, Piper." Chloe dipped her head, pressing her lips to Piper's. Their kiss was gentle and tender, seeking comfort, not heat. Later, they'd share a different kind of kiss, the kind Chloe had been dreaming about all week, but not here on a public street after Piper had just ridden the subway for the first time in months to bring them to the bar where they'd met.

They had some celebrating to do before they got naked.

Piper stepped back, reaching up to tug the wig from her head. She rolled it into a ball and shoved it into her purse before fluffing her hair. Chloe reached out to smooth down a wayward strand that had gone rogue under the wig. And before her eyes, the Mystery Woman became her Piper.

Her Piper. Where did that come from?

"Come on," Piper said. "I'm ready for that drink."

"Me too." Actually, she was parched after their subway ride, and Piper had to be too.

They walked leisurely down the street, but Chloe felt the tremor in Piper's hand. No doubt, she was experiencing aftereffects from her anxiety and all the adrenaline it had released into her body. Chloe had done a little research about panic attacks after meeting Piper, just to better understand what she was dealing with and how to help. She had a *lot* of ideas to help relax her once they got back to the apartment...

After walking a few blocks, they arrived at Dragonfly, the adorable little gay bar where they'd met exactly four weeks ago. Chloe could hardly wrap her mind around all the ways her life had changed since then. The bar's lavender logo gleamed like a welcome beacon, the promise of a safe place for them to enjoy a drink without any peripheral worry about being harassed or judged for being together. Chloe had liked this place a lot the first time she visited. She was glad to be back.

They stepped inside, enveloped in the chill of air-conditioning and the soft strains of jazz music. Overhead, strands of twinkling fairy lights added to the ambiance. She followed Piper to a table for two in back, a more private—and romantic—location than the bar.

She slid onto a bar-height stool across from Piper. "Want me to go order our drinks?"

"Actually, I don't think you'll have to." She nodded toward the pink-haired bartender, who was making her way toward them.

"Oh," Chloe said. "I thought we'd have to order at the bar."

"Sometimes you do," the bartender told her with a smile. "But it's not too busy tonight—yet, anyway—so I can come to you." She narrowed her eyes at Chloe. "I think I remember you. Were you in here a few weeks ago?"

"Yep," Chloe told her. "Good memory."

The bartender beamed. "Remembering faces is part of my job description. I'm Josie, by the way."

"Chloe," Chloe told her. "I'm a flight attendant, so I'm here in the city sporadically."

"Oh, how cool!" Josie said. "I'd love to hear more about

that, but let me get your drinks first." She glanced across the table at Piper, who'd been watching the conversation quietly. Josie's eyes widened in recognition.

Chloe felt a sudden urge to protect Piper, to drag her out of here before the bartender caused her unnecessary stress, because Piper was still raw from her subway ride. "Remind me which drink I had last time," Chloe said, hoping to distract Josie's attention. "It had lemon and mint in it?"

"The Midnight in Manhattan," Josie said, eyes flicking back to Chloe. She'd definitely recognized Piper but seemed to have gotten the memo that Piper didn't want her identity known. Maybe she was cool after all. She set a lavender bar menu on the table between them. "It's one of the house drinks."

"Yes, that's it," Chloe said. "I'll have another one of those."

"And for you?" Josie asked, looking at Piper.

"I'll try the Broadway Bubbles," Piper said. "And could I also get a glass of water?"

"Make that two," Chloe added.

"Absolutely. I'll be right back with those," Josie told them before heading toward the bar.

"Phew," Chloe said, reaching across the table to squeeze Piper's hand. "For a minute there, I thought she was going to make a scene."

"I don't think she would," Piper said. "She's married to Eve Marlow."

"Eve Marlow." Chloe tapped her lips, trying to place the name.

"She hosts *Do Over*. It's a business makeover show on the *Life & Leisure* channel."

"Oh, right." Chloe was pretty sure she'd caught an

episode or two. She had a vague mental image of a pretty brunette. "How do you know she's married to Josie?"

"Because she told me so the last time I was here. She saw me watching Eve at the bar and thought I was interested in her, when really I was just worried Eve was going to recognize me."

"Interesting," Chloe said. "So you know Eve?"

Piper lifted one shoulder. "Not exactly. I mean, we've been at some of the same events. We've probably said hello."

"God, you must know so many celebrities," Chloe said, remembering all the glamorous photos she'd seen of Piper on the red carpet. Sometimes it was hard to remember that was the same woman she was sitting here with. Maybe it would feel more real after she'd spent the day on set with her tomorrow.

"I guess I do," Piper said, giving her an amused smile.

"Sorry, I'm a dork sometimes."

Piper winked. "An adorable dork."

"Well, thank goodness for that." Chloe mimed wiping her brow, thankful for the teasing vibe between them because it meant Piper was in good spirits.

Josie returned to their table with two glasses of water. She set them down and doubled back for their drinks. The glass she placed in front of Chloe contained a clear liquid with a slight milkiness to the color, like a cloud swirling inside. Piper's was orange and fizzy. Josie gave her a discerning look. "You were here that night too, with Chloe, but you were wearing a wig."

"You really *do* have a good memory for faces," Piper said, sounding impressed.

Josie smiled. "I try to, and don't worry, your identity is safe with me."

"Thanks. I appreciate that," Piper told her.

"So you live here in the city?" Josie asked.

Piper nodded as she lifted her water glass and took several big swallows.

"And you're a flight attendant." Josie turned to Chloe. "I'm so tied to this place that I almost never get to travel, so I'm a little jealous. What's your favorite place to visit?"

"It changes all the time once I fly somewhere new," Chloe told her. "But right now, I'd have to say the Caymans. It's sort of where Piper and I met."

"Sort of?" Josie asked, glancing between them.

"We actually met here at Dragonfly," Piper told her, "the night I was wearing a wig, but I didn't tell her my name."

"Okay, color me fascinated." Eyes sparkling, Josie rested her palms on their table. "So how did you get from an anonymous date at my bar to the Caymans? And if I'm being too nosy, just tell me."

Chloe laughed as she lifted her drink and sipped. Josie's personality was infectious, and Chloe liked her a lot, but she'd let Piper take the lead for how much she wanted to share with her.

"She was working on my flight into Grand Cayman, and she recognized me," Piper told Josie. "Long story short, we spent the weekend together on the island, and here we are."

"Now *that* is a story," Josie said, smacking a palm against their table. "God, I might love it even more than the story of how Eve and I met."

"How did you meet?" Chloe asked.

"She brought me a litter of kittens she'd found in a trash can," Josie told her. "I run a kitten rescue, and at the time, I was about to lose the bar. I had even applied to be on her show, so when she showed up here, I took it as a sign and begged her to save my bar on *Do Over*. She said no."

Piper snorted with laughter as she sipped her drink.

"Oh, it was definitely not love at first sight for us," Josie said.

"That's hilarious, and also, I had no idea you owned this place," Chloe said.

"Yep. This bar has been in my family for three generations. I inherited it three years ago after my dad died. It used to be called Swansons, and it was more of a place to get a beer after work, but it was kind of a dinosaur. It almost went under, but after Eve turned me down, I accidentally went over her head and charmed her boss into giving me a spot on the show. So Eve turned my dive bar into a funky gay bar, and then I married her."

"That's quite a story," Piper said. "And I remember that episode, now that you mention it. I didn't realize this was the same bar."

"It's hardly recognizable from the way it looked during filming," Josie told her.

"Well, it looks great now," Piper said.

"Thank you. Hey, feel free to say no, but I'd love to add your photo to our wall of fame in the back hall." Josie gestured toward the back hallway. "You could either let me snap a picture before you leave tonight or send us a head shot later, and like I said, totally no pressure. But as the owner, I have to at least ask."

Piper nodded. "If I'm not up for a photo before I leave, I'll send you a head shot."

"I really appreciate it," Josie told her. "And believe it or not, it was a lot harder to get Eve to agree to be on the wall. Now I'll get out of your hair and let you two enjoy your evening. Just grab my attention if you need anything." With a wave, she was on her way back to the bar.

"She seems fun," Piper commented, sipping her drink.

"Yeah," Chloe agreed, taking a sip of her own drink. She

stared into its opaque depths, remembering the rumor on the drink menu about how anyone who drank one at midnight would fall in love before the end of the year. Had it been midnight the last time they were here? Was it midnight now?

She glanced at her phone, discovering it was only nine thirty, but her heart had already discovered something else. While the idea of falling in love this year had seemed unlikely to the point of absurd last month, it didn't feel that way now. In fact, she had a feeling she was well on her way.

"You're awfully quiet over there," Piper commented.

Chloe looked up. The fairy lights overhead gleamed in Piper's auburn hair and reflected off her eye shadow, shimmering every time she blinked. "Got lost in my thoughts for a minute."

"Good thoughts?" Piper asked.

"So good," Chloe confirmed.

"My thoughts are pretty good right now too," Piper said. She lifted her glass and gave it a swirl. "Still slightly manic from the subway, but tonight's been a good one."

"I'm so glad," Chloe told her. "Also, it's kind of boggling my mind that the last time we were here, I didn't even know your name."

"What was your guess? Did you think of me as something that night?"

"I didn't have a guess about your name, but I definitely thought you were closeted, being incognito in a gay bar."

Piper's eyebrows rose. "Actually, that was probably a more likely scenario than me being a B list celebrity afraid of having a panic attack if someone recognized me."

Chloe grinned at her. "You're A list to me."

∽

PIPER RESTED her elbows on the table, so relaxed she felt like she might slide right off her stool onto the floor. Well, her third round of Broadway Bubbles might be to blame for her current inclination to fall on the floor, but she just felt so... mellow. Sometimes, anxiety like she'd experienced on the subway left her jumpy and irritable afterward, and sometimes it just left her tired.

Tonight, buoyed by Chloe's endless smile and several cocktails, she was definitely feeling the latter. She lifted her glass and polished off the drink, setting it down a bit more firmly than she'd intended. Okay, she might be more drunk than tipsy, which wasn't her smartest decision since she had to work tomorrow, but at least it was Friday.

"You okay over there?" Chloe asked.

Piper looked at her, fascinated with the way the light played over Chloe's green top, making the fabric seem to shimmer. "Yep."

"Ready to get out of here? We have to be up early tomorrow, right?"

"At six, yeah, and I'm ready. I just need to stop at the ladies' room first."

"I'll come with you," Chloe said.

Piper slid off her stool, leading the way down the hall that she presumed led to the restrooms. She found two doors labeled as all-gender bathrooms, and she and Chloe each entered one. When she came back out, she paused to examine the wall Josie had mentioned while she waited for Chloe.

A placard running the length of the hall documented the history of the bar, with black-and-white photos of Josie's grandparents followed by a younger couple and then a little girl with blonde pigtails doing her homework behind the bar while a man who had to be Josie's father mixed drinks.

The photos went on to illustrate Swansons' transformation into Dragonfly, and yeah, Piper definitely remembered this episode of *Do Over*.

There was a collection of framed photos above the placard, a mixture of snapshots of celebrities enjoying a drink at the bar and signed headshots, as Josie had mentioned. Piper saw pop superstar Katherine Hayes, Josie's wife Eve Marlow, and signed headshots of two Broadway actresses next to a playbill for the musical *It's in Her Kiss*. Piper had been meaning to see that one, since it featured a lesbian romance. Maybe she'd take Chloe the next time she was in New York.

"Going to add your photo to the wall?" Chloe asked, coming to stand beside her.

"Sure."

"It doesn't bother you?"

"Nah," Piper said. "I'm used to being asked, and not always as nicely as Josie did. I like this place, and I don't mind having my photo on the wall."

"Want me to get Josie, then?"

Piper nodded. She returned to their table while Chloe walked to the bar to get Josie's attention. The pink-haired woman nodded excitedly as Chloe talked to her, and then they were heading toward Piper. Josie directed them toward the back wall, where a framed black-and-white photo of a dragonfly tattoo hung beneath a strand of white lights. Chloe took the photo with Josie's phone, while Josie and Piper posed together against the wall.

Josie thanked her profusely, and with a hug, Piper and Chloe were on their way. They stepped outside, and Piper was surprised to find the pavement glistening from recent rain. It was almost eleven, and her apartment was a thirty-minute walk from here. She'd rather use that time getting naked with Chloe, since she had to be up for work all too soon. "I'll call an Uber."

"Okay," Chloe said.

Their car arrived a few minutes later and had them home in ten. Chloe followed her up the stairs. They set down their purses and went into the kitchen for a glass of water. Piper was parched after the adrenaline of the evening followed by several stiff drinks. She gulped down a glass and turned to Chloe.

Wordlessly, they came together, stepping into each other's space as their mouths met for a deep, drunken kiss. Chloe's tongue was cold from the water, sending a delicious shiver through Piper. She ought to be thinking about sleep after working a twelve-hour day with another on tap tomorrow, especially after the stress of her subway ride, but sleep was the last thing on her mind as Chloe sucked at the pulse point on her neck.

She needed this. Tonight, she needed Chloe more than anything. Piper reached back to grip the countertop, goose bumps erupting on her skin as Chloe nipped at a sensitive spot below her ear.

"Been waiting to do this since I landed in New York," Chloe murmured as she kissed her way down Piper's neck, unbuttoning her blouse so she could transfer the attention of her mouth to the sensitive skin between Piper's breasts.

She whimpered, clinging to the counter behind her as she surrendered to the exquisite pleasure of Chloe's mouth. Chloe pushed Piper's bra to the side, swiping her tongue over her nipple as she slipped a hand between her thighs, teasing her over her jeans. Piper moaned in pleasure as a warm, liquid ache built inside her, desire sweeping through her veins.

Her pulse thumped in her ears for the second time that

evening, but this time, her body hummed with pleasure, not fear. Chloe tugged at Piper's blouse, and she helped her slide it over her head, followed by her bra. Now Piper stood with her back against the countertop, naked from the waist up while Chloe lavished her breasts with attention. She kissed and sucked and nipped until Piper was on fire for her.

She shifted her hips restlessly. Her knees shook as Chloe skimmed her teeth across the underside of Piper's breast. Chloe lifted her head, looking up at Piper through wayward blonde strands, her eyes gleaming with intention. Piper stared right back, breathless.

Chloe popped the button on her jeans, pushing them down Piper's legs in one smooth movement. Piper wobbled as she kicked off her shoes and stepped out of her jeans, having the vague thought that they should move this to the bedroom but seemingly unable to form words.

Chloe dropped to her knees and kissed Piper through her panties, nearly sending her over the edge with that simple contact. She gasped, gripping the counter to keep herself upright. Chloe stripped away the lace thong, baring Piper to her completely.

"Hop up here," Chloe said, patting a hand against the counter, and if Piper could speak, maybe she would have protested, because she'd never been a fan of those kitchen sex scenes in romance novels. It sounded uncomfortable and unhygienic, but in this exact moment, it sounded like the best idea Chloe had ever had.

Piper slid onto the counter, hissing as the cold marble met her overheated skin. Chloe's eyes met hers as she pressed her lips against Piper's inner thigh, kissing and licking her way toward where Piper was throbbing for her.

She nipped at Piper's tender skin, hard enough to leave a mark, making her whimper with pleasure.

She reached down, sinking her fingers in Chloe's blonde tresses to steady herself as Chloe moved to place her tongue directly against Piper's clit. Chloe flicked her tongue swiftly back and forth, and Piper was done for. She braced her hands behind herself, eyes slamming shut, astonished to discover that the combination of the cold granite beneath her ass and the heat of Chloe's mouth was unequivocally the best thing she'd ever felt.

Chloe increased the intensity of her actions, sucking hard, and that was all it took to send Piper flying. She heard herself gasping and moaning as release ignited in her core, pulsing beneath Chloe's tongue and rushing through her veins. She fell back onto her elbows, thighs shaking as she panted for breath.

"Beautiful," Chloe whispered, gazing up at her.

Piper just lay there for a long moment, reveling in the sparks of pleasure still ricocheting through her body, cleansing her of the last remnants of her anxiety. Finally, she sat up, reaching for Chloe. "Now you'd better scrape me off this countertop so I can return the favor."

14

C hloe stood against the back wall of the soundstage where *In Her Defense* was filmed. It was a large open space, almost like a warehouse, filled with various sets that represented the primary locations seen on the show. The set on the far left—Sam's apartment— currently buzzed with activity as the crew set up for the first scene of the day.

Of course, Sam's apartment was actually a set with three walls and no ceiling. A dizzying array of lights and equipment hung overhead, and at least a half dozen camera operators were clustered in front of the missing wall, ready to capture Piper from every possible angle as she delivered her lines.

At the far end of the soundstage was the craft services table, filled with fruit and pastries, yogurt parfaits and breakfast sandwiches, enough food to keep the cast and crew fueled for a long day. Currently, Piper was having her hair and makeup done, and Chloe was poking around on her own, trying not to get in the way or look like she didn't belong.

"Piper's girlfriend, right?" a woman with short brown hair asked. She wore all black and carried a paper bag bulging with unknown contents, obviously a member of the crew.

Chloe nodded. "I'm Chloe."

"Monica," the woman said with a friendly smile. "Want to take a peek before they get started?" She jerked her head in the direction of the set.

"Please." Chloe had been trying to decide if that would be too nosy, but she was dying to see all the sets in person that she'd seen on the show.

"What do you do for work, Chloe?" Monica asked as she and Chloe weaved their way through the crush of crew members.

"Right now, I'm a flight attendant, but I've only got a few weeks left before I'm going to settle down and put my interior design degree to use." Chloe felt her eyes grow wide as they entered the Reynolds, Whitaker & Associates boardroom. Like Sam's apartment, it had only three walls and a canopy of lights and rigging where the ceiling should be.

The impressive mahogany table in the center of the room was currently bare, but Monica opened her bag and began placing stacks of paper onto it, followed by red folders filled with yet more paper.

"What do you do for *In Her Defense*?" Chloe asked.

"I'm the prop master," Monica told her as she bustled around the table, arranging paperwork. "I run the props department, and my set dresser is out sick today, so I'm doing some of the grunt work, which I'm secretly thrilled about because I love the chance to dress a set. It's how I got started in this business."

Chloe watched in amazement as Monica arranged the

documents the cast would use during filming. "Dressing the set...is that like being a set decorator?"

"It sure is," Monica told her. "I'm responsible for everything you see onscreen: furniture, artwork, and all the little details that make each set and scene feel real. Right now, I'm laying out briefs the cast will use when they film here later this morning. Then I'll move over to our multipurpose set, the one that changes each week based on what we're shooting. This week, it's going to be Tony's new girlfriend's living room."

"Tony has a new girlfriend?" Chloe repeated, then waved a hand in front of herself. "No, don't tell me. I'm still in season three."

"I guess you haven't been leaning on Piper for spoilers, then," Monica said, looking amused.

"Nope."

"Good for you. Want to give me a hand?" Monica asked. "Feel free to say no if you just want to wander around and explore."

"Actually, I'd love to help."

Monica showed her what to do, and they chatted while they worked. Monica was full of fascinating stories from the various productions she'd worked on over the last twenty years, and Chloe shared a few of her own more interesting anecdotes from her time as a flight attendant. By the time they had the boardroom set up just right, Chloe had a huge smile on her face. They'd transformed an empty table into one scattered with folders and paper, coffee cups and cell phones. It looked like they'd stepped into the middle of a board meeting, minus the lawyers.

"Wow," Chloe said as she admired their work. "That turned out well."

"It's satisfying, right?" Monica said with a brisk nod.

"The next set will be even more interesting, since it's a new one. My favorite part of dressing sets is finding all the right accents and details to turn the space into that specific character's home."

"That sounds so fun. Can I help?"

"Sure. I thought it might appeal to the interior designer in you," Monica said as she led the way toward a set in back. "I've already bought everything we need. I had way too much fun shopping for Letitia."

"Who's Letitia?"

"Tony's new girlfriend, but shh, you didn't hear it from me," Monica told her.

"Right. I guess he and Sam aren't hooking up this season, then."

Monica laughed. "You know they have to keep the fans wondering for as long as possible."

"What about Sam and Claire?"

"Ah." Monica's eyebrows rose. "That would be interesting, wouldn't it?"

"I'm rooting for them," Chloe told her. "They have great onscreen chemistry."

"They sure do, not that the showrunner has any clue," Monica said. "Okay, here we are."

She and Chloe stepped into the open-sided living room. It was currently furnished with a crisp beige couch and side chair. The table between them was done in an antique style that looked almost like a treasure chest. The rest of the set contained more furniture in the same vein but no decorations, none of the little mementos that made a room feel like a home.

"Letitia is a prosecutor and a single mom. She has a five-year-old daughter who won't be in this scene, but her existence should still be present in the room, photos, toys, that kind of thing." Monica continued describing Letitia as they walked to a room in back that was stuffed with props and decorations.

"I had no idea so much detail went into this," she said as Monica showed her the painting she'd ordered, which depicted the Chicago skyline, Letitia's hometown.

"Oh yeah," Monica told her, pride evident in her tone. "Set dressing is an art, and it's one I've spent many years perfecting."

"Well, consider me fascinated," Chloe told her as she followed Monica back to the undressed living room.

"They're starting to shoot." Monica gestured toward the far end of the soundstage, where the lights had suddenly intensified.

Chloe gaped in that direction. "Oh, wow."

"Go see your girlfriend in action," Monica said, waving her off.

"Okay," Chloe agreed, "but I'll check back later to see if you need any help."

"I don't need the help, but I do enjoy the company," Monica told her.

Chloe hurried toward the other end of the soundstage where Piper was filming. To keep herself out of the way, Chloe stood well back from the crew. People bustled this way and that, carrying tablets and props and cameras. The lights overhead were blinding.

Inside Sam's living room, Piper sat on a black leather couch in one of Sam's flawless skirt suits, the kind that made Chloe's heart race every time she watched the show. Today, Piper's suit was ice blue, and Chloe knew that if she were close enough to see, it would flatter Piper's eyes amazingly. The contrast of her auburn hair against the pale blue fabric was equally stunning.

Maybe Chloe needed to meet the on-set stylist while she was here, because clearly they were was amazing at their job. Eliza, the actress who played Claire, knocked on the door to Sam's apartment, and Piper crossed the room to answer it. "Hi," she said, motioning for Eliza to come in.

"Sorry to drop by unannounced," Eliza said, giving Piper a sheepish smile.

"It's fine," Piper said, but she didn't sound quite like Piper. Sam's voice was a little more formal than Piper's, like her clothes and the sleek, expensive apartment.

Now that Chloe had spent time with Monica, she found herself scanning Sam's shelves, or at least trying to. It was hard to see from her position in back. She spotted a photo of Sam in her cap and gown, receiving her diploma. Law school, probably. Beside that was a photo of her with an older couple who were probably supposed to be her parents.

The bottom shelf was filled with heavy black volumes of something. Law books? Encyclopedias? This was a TV set, after all, so maybe they were just blank books. Chloe made a mental note to either ask Monica later or snoop through Sam's apartment herself. Sam had a variety of modern knickknacks on her shelves, a light blue vase with white flowers, several silver figurines, and a little replica of the Eiffel tower that, knowing Monica, had to have significance to Sam's life, although Chloe couldn't remember what.

On the set, Piper and Eliza were seated side by side on the couch, their bodies angled slightly toward each other. Two glasses of red wine—or maybe a wine substitute, another thing Chloe would ask about later—sat on the table in front of them.

"I was a little worried about how we left things earlier," Eliza said, her expression tense.

"No need to be," Piper said, giving a small wave that was just so *Sam* before she reached for her wine. "I'm sorry I got upset, but I didn't mean to direct it at you. I'm just so...frustrated with everything lately." The angst in Piper's voice was palpable. She sipped her wine and leaned back on the couch.

"Like Tony and Letitia?"

Piper straightened, dropping her gaze to the wineglass in her hand. "Not just that."

"But it bothers you," Eliza pressed.

"It shouldn't." Piper swirled her wine and took another sip. "We're just friends. Partners. Colleagues. He can date whoever he wants."

"Come on, Sam. We've all seen the chemistry between you two."

Piper toyed with her hair, avoiding Eliza's gaze. "I'm sure most people who work as closely together as Tony and I do have a spark at some point, right? It doesn't mean anything."

"Maybe," Eliza hedged, leaning subtly closer on the couch. "I mean, have you felt that spark with anyone else you work with, or is it just a 'you and Tony' thing?"

Piper gave her a look dripping with innuendo, and then she stood abruptly and walked to the kitchen. Chloe almost gasped out loud. Surely this didn't mean what she thought it did. After all, when she and Piper had talked about it before, Piper hadn't seemed to think Sam and Claire had any romantic potential. Had something changed, or was Chloe just seeing this scene through a queer lens?

Piper placed her hands on the kitchen counter, and now Chloe was definitely reading things that weren't there, because she was thinking about what they'd done last night in Piper's kitchen, and that was definitely not what this scene was about. "It's mostly a 'me and Tony' thing," she said finally.

"Mostly?" Eliza rose from the couch.

"Mostly." Piper poured more wine into her glass.

"Oh." Eliza brought her own wineglass into the kitchen. She leaned across the counter, her mouth inches from Piper's, and Chloe could barely breathe. She couldn't believe it. Sam and Claire were going to kiss. They were really going to kiss. She was so invested in the moment, she didn't even remember to be bothered that she was about to watch her girlfriend kiss another woman.

They stared at each other across the counter, and Chloe found herself leaning closer, dying to see what happened next. *Damn*, those dramatic TV pauses felt even longer standing here in person, without background music to set the mood. And then, just when Chloe thought she might die from the anticipation, Eliza looked away.

"I should go," she said, so softly, Chloe almost couldn't hear her.

"Okay," Piper said, just as quietly.

Eliza gave her one more searching look, and then she turned and walked out the door. Alone, Piper lifted her glass and drained its contents before slamming it onto the counter.

"Cut!" a male voice boomed. "And reset."

The set erupted with noise and commotion as everyone began to move around, preparing the scene for its second take. Chloe's heart was racing, her throat dry. *Wow*. That was so intense. She couldn't wait to talk to Piper about it, but that would have to wait because Piper was surrounded by people touching up her hair and makeup, while another woman plucked what must have been lint or a stray hair from the shoulder of her jacket.

Chloe was riveted by this peek into her world. Within minutes, they were shooting the scene all over again. And again. And again. Sometimes they focused on only a certain line or portion of the scene, and once they filmed extended close-ups of Piper and Eliza not saying anything at all. In each take, the configuration of the cameras would change. Sometimes a camera operator stood directly behind Piper or Eliza to capture the other actress's reactions.

After completing the scene in Sam's apartment, they moved over to the boardroom to film the scene Chloe and Monica had prepared. This involved a half dozen more takes with a room full of actors. Chloe recognized all the series regulars along with extras who played the unnamed assistants and interns at the firm.

By the time the scene in the boardroom was complete, someone called out that it was time to break for lunch. Piper made her way in Chloe's direction.

"Oh my God, that was so much fun to watch," Chloe gushed. "Although I have to confess, I have no idea how those two scenes fit together."

"That's because we shot them out of order," Piper told her, leading the way toward her dressing room. "The boardroom scene takes place earlier in the day. Later this afternoon, we'll film a scene at my apartment where I get ready for bed after Claire left, but we can't shoot that until last because it's easier for continuity to keep me in the same outfit for as many scenes as possible."

"I'm fascinated by all of this." Chloe followed her into her dressing room, stepping aside so Piper could close the door. A warm tingle grew in the pit of her stomach as she got a good look at Piper up close. Not only were her hair and makeup polished to camera perfection, but she was wearing

Sam's makeup, which made her look subtly different from herself.

And that ice-blue suit...

Chloe ran her fingers over the front of it, toying with one of the buttons. It made Piper's blue eyes pop, just as she'd known it would. "This is...hot."

Piper gave her an amused look. "I'm glad you think so, although I'm finding it hot for an entirely different reason." She fanned her face, drawing Chloe's attention to the sheen of sweat on her brow.

"I have about a million questions for you," Chloe said. "Starting with that very gay scene between you and Claire."

"Well," Piper said as she unbuttoned the jacket and slipped out of it, revealing the white blouse beneath. "I've had a few conversations with the showrunner about Sam's arc, because as much as I love the idea of Sam and Claire, I'm not sure he's willing to commit, and I loathe queerbaiting. But, let's just say...I'm hopeful."

"You mean you don't know?"

Piper shook her head. "Generally I get the scripts for each episode about a week before we start filming so I can prepare, so I don't always know where the season is going beyond the next episode. But like I said, we've talked about it. There's a huge fandom following for Sam and Claire, so I hope it works out."

"I hope so too," Chloe said.

"Do you want me to ask craft services to send some food in here, or do you want to go down to the break room so I can introduce you around?" Piper asked, brushing a strand of copper hair out of her eyes. This close, Chloe could see how heavily it was styled, hairspray holding the whole strand together as Piper moved it from her face.

Chloe reached out to touch it, giggling at how crunchy

Piper's hair was. "Let's eat with the rest of the cast, unless you want to be alone. I'd love to meet them."

"And I'd love to introduce you. Okay, let me just use the bathroom first." She gave Chloe a quick kiss before going into the bathroom.

A few minutes later, they were on their way to the break room. "Nate!" Piper called out, and a tall Black man that Chloe knew as Sam's partner, Tony, turned with a warm smile. He paused to let them catch up with him. "This is my girlfriend, Chloe," Piper told him. "Chloe, this is Nate Mauldin, who I'm sure you recognize from the show."

Nate's gaze settled on Chloe, and his smile widened. He extended a hand. "A pleasure."

"Likewise," Chloe told him as she took his hand and shook. "I confess that I didn't really start watching until after I met Piper, but I'm a fan now. I'm only in season three right now, but I love watching you as Tony. You really kick ass in those courtroom scenes."

He laughed. "Thank you. Those are my favorites to film. You're a flight attendant, right?"

Chloe nodded, secretly thrilled that Piper had talked about her to her castmates. "I live in North Carolina, but my job brings me to New York a lot."

"I bet you have some stories to tell," Nate commented.

"Yeah, for sure," Chloe told him with a laugh.

The three of them walked into a large room filled with round tables, not unlike any other break room Chloe had been in or even the employee lounge at the airport. A long table in back was filled with food, and cast and crew were already gathered there, laughing and chatting as they filled plates.

Chloe, Piper, and Nate joined the line, and Chloe was introduced to several more people by the time they made it to the food. The spread was impressive, with both hot and cold options, a variety of meat and vegetarian dishes. Chloe took a sandwich and some chips, and she noticed similar items on Piper's plate as she muttered about needing to make sure she didn't spill anything on her outfit.

"You guys really get fed like this every day?" Chloe asked as she, Piper, and Nate made their way to an empty table.

"Pretty sweet, right?" Nate asked.

"Yeah. I eat at the food court in the airport entirely too often. This is way better."

"Mind if I join you guys?"

Chloe looked up to see Eliza standing by their table.

Piper nudged the empty seat beside her, and Eliza sat. She had a salad and a wedge of French bread on her plate. "Eliza, this is my girlfriend, Chloe."

"Oh hey!" Eliza said, beaming at her. "It's so great to meet you."

"You too," Chloe told her, but suddenly she was remembering the way Piper had looked at her in earlier seasons with unrequited longing on her face. Piper had confessed to having feelings for Eliza, and after watching them deliver a sexually charged scene together earlier that morning, Chloe felt an uncharacteristic surge of jealousy.

"Piper's told us all about you," Eliza said. "Are you having fun on set?"

"Loving it," Chloe told her.

The four of them fell into easy conversation as they ate. Piper's castmates seemed friendly and down to earth, and she liked them both a lot, despite the way she kept sneaking extra glances at Piper to judge her reactions to Eliza. The brunette was bubbly and engaging and gorgeous as hell. It wasn't hard to see why Piper had been attracted to her. To her relief, though, she detected nothing but friendship between them now.

After lunch, Nate signed a photo for Nisha. Chloe could hardly wait to give it to her friend. Nisha was going to be beyond thrilled. Piper headed off to film her next scene, one in which she and Tony would review a case together in her office. Chloe watched the first take, but when she spotted Monica at the back of the soundstage, Chloe headed over to join her.

Three hours later, Chloe was intimately acquainted with every detail of Letitia's living room. She and Monica had carefully dressed the space, right down to the *Fancy Nancy* books stacked beneath the coffee table. Those had been Chloe's suggestion. They were Cait's favorite books when she was five.

"Don't suppose you're looking for a new job here in New York near your girlfriend, are you?" Monica asked as Chloe set a crystal unicorn bookend on the shelf.

"I wish, but no. My family's in North Carolina, and I just bought a house there," Chloe told her.

"Well, if your situation ever changes, give me a call. We're always looking for help in the props department, and you've got a real eye for it."

"I really appreciate that," Chloe told her. "This has been a lot of fun." And for the first time, Chloe found herself wishing she didn't live in North Carolina, that she might have had the opportunity to take Monica up on her offer, to live and work here with Piper.

15

It was almost seven by the time Piper finished filming her last scene of the day. Now she just needed to find Chloe so they could get out of here and enjoy the rest of their evening. Piper crossed the soundstage without spotting her, so she peeked in her dressing room. No sign of Chloe.

The set was clearing rapidly now that filming had wrapped for the day, because hooray, it was Friday. Piper wished it meant she got to spend the weekend with Chloe, but so far, their chaotic long-distance relationship had worked out pretty damn well, so she wasn't going to complain about spending the weekend alone. She could use the sleep anyway.

Just when she was starting to wonder if she'd have to call Chloe and ask her where she was, Piper finally found her sitting on Sam's bed, poking through the drawers on the bedside table.

"You know, if you want to snoop through my drawers, you should do that in my actual bedroom, not on set, right?"

Piper teased as she stood in the doorway, watching her. The set was bathed in muted light now that the industrial lamps they used during filming were off, casting long shadows over Chloe's face as she looked up with a sheepish smile.

"I'm not trying to snoop through your stuff," Chloe told her. "But I had so much fun helping Monica dress sets today, and it made me curious what kind of details were in Sam's bedroom. Plus, I just wanted to see Sam's apartment up close. It's the coolest thing. I almost feel like I'm on the show."

"You helped dress sets?" Piper hadn't meant for anyone to put Chloe to work today. How had that happened?

"Yeah. It made the interior designer in me very happy."

"I'm glad, but I didn't want you to work today."

"I only did because I wanted to." Chloe stood and crossed the room to kiss her. "It was so cool to see the level of detail that goes into everything, and Monica's really good company. But now I feel like I'm making out with Sam Whitaker in her bedroom, and this feels like some sort of secret fantasy brought to life."

"Yeah?" Piper murmured against her lips. "You have a thing for Sam, huh?"

"Maybe a little," Chloe said, hands sliding around to grip Piper's ass over her skirt. "Especially when she shows her sapphic side."

"Interesting," Piper said, slipping into the slightly more formal way she spoke when she was Sam. "We'll have to investigate that more fully once we're in my dressing room."

"Oh my God," Chloe whispered, an absolutely giddy expression on her face. "You're *her*."

"Of course I am," Piper told her. "Now, if you don't mind, I really am ready to get out of these heels..."

Chloe stepped back, dragging her gaze over Piper's body from head to toe, bottom lip pinched between her teeth. "I'm at your service, Ms. Whitaker."

Piper had been joking about her dressing room before, but it suddenly felt like a very good idea. She did have to change before she went home, after all. "I'm going to need to speak to you privately."

"Whatever you need," Chloe said breathlessly. Her gaze met Piper's for a loaded moment as the air between them snapped and crackled, and then she turned, channeling Sam's brisk stride as she led the way toward her dressing room.

"Oh, there you are."

Piper turned at the familiar yet unexpected voice to find her agent, Jane Fletcher, approaching from the direction of the production office, and the heat inside her cooled. "Jane? This is a surprise."

"Well, I happened to be in town, so I decided to deliver the news in person." Her eyebrows lifted slightly as she caught sight of Chloe standing at Piper's side.

"My girlfriend, Chloe Carson," Piper said. "Chloe, this is my agent, Jane Fletcher. And...what news?"

"Well, darling, I just got off the phone with Sydney Hall, and he's cast you as Tara Quinn in *Tempted*."

Piper felt her mouth drop open. She blinked rapidly, too stunned to form words. Chloe squeezed her hand, letting out a little squeal of excitement beside her.

"I...wow...holy shit." Piper looked from Chloe to Jane and back again. She was going to star in a major studio movie. Nothing was ever guaranteed, least of all in Holly-wood, but this felt like a huge shift in her career. It would open doors for her, *big* doors.

"Holy shit indeed," Jane agreed. "Can I treat the two of you to dinner to celebrate?"

Piper's head was spinning. A moment ago, she'd been rushing toward her dressing room to role play with Chloe, and now...now she was celebrating one of the biggest moments in her career. She looked at Chloe, who was beaming, not looking at all upset that their plans had been interrupted. Turning back to Jane, she nodded. "Yeah, that would be great. I just...wow."

"Perfect," Jane said. "I'll make the arrangements while you get changed." She walked off, phone in hand.

Piper stared after her for a moment, still gathering her wits, and then she grabbed Chloe's hand, tugging her into her dressing room. Chloe kicked the door shut behind them, and then she leaped into Piper's arms.

"Piper! I am so freaking excited for you. This is like beyond amazing."

"Thank you." Piper held on to her, sucking in deep breaths while her body buzzed like she'd just inhaled an obscene amount of caffeine. "I am...apparently still speechless."

Chloe spun her in a dizzying circle. "You're going to be a star. I mean, an even bigger star than you already are. This is seriously the best news."

"It is." Piper grinned as Chloe gave her another twirl. "It really is."

"You're adorable when you're shocked speechless," Chloe said, releasing her. She reached up to tuck a lock of Piper's hair behind her ear. "And I really want to mess up your perfect Samantha hair, but I guess I should wait until after dinner, huh?"

"Yeah, sorry about that." Piper was breathing like she'd

just dashed from one end of the soundstage to the other, adrenaline whirling through her system. It was almost like having a panic attack, except the emotions paralyzing her now were all good, all happy, all *ecstatic*.

"Don't be." Chloe made a dismissive gesture with her hand. "This is *way* better. Are you kidding? We have to celebrate your news!"

"Okay, but we'll revisit this Samantha kink of yours at a later date." Piper drew Chloe against her for a scorching kiss.

"Count on it," Chloe whispered, tugging at Piper's jacket. "And it's going to be *hot*."

"It will." Piper held on to her, grinning like an idiot. "Oh my God."

"I know. Now get dressed so we don't keep your agent waiting." She gave Piper a gentle shove toward the closet.

Luckily, she'd been planning to go out to dinner with Chloe tonight anyway, so she'd brought a black knit dress and strappy sandals with her this morning. Otherwise, she'd have had to go home first to change because—as tempting as it was—she wasn't allowed to raid Sam's very impressive wardrobe for her own personal use.

Chloe wore aqua jeans and a gauzy white top, and she looked so fucking pretty, Piper could hardly stand it. Quickly, she changed and went into the bathroom to freshen up, and together, they left her dressing room to find Jane. That fizzing sensation still hadn't gone away. She couldn't remember the last time she'd felt this light on her feet.

And having Chloe with her tonight to celebrate just felt like the icing on her already overly delicious cake.

~

CHLOE HELD a champagne flute in her right hand, her left clasped with Piper's beneath the table.

"To Piper and *Tempted*," Jane said, and the three of them clinked their glasses together.

Chloe sipped champagne as she gave Piper's fingers a squeeze. This was such a monumental day for her, and now, all her hard work to manage her panic attacks was going to pay off, just the way she'd wanted it to.

"Thank you." Tears glistened in Piper's eyes, the happy kind. She pretty much hadn't stopped smiling all night.

Neither had Chloe. She was so glad she happened to be here to celebrate this milestone with Piper. There would be times when that wasn't the case, a lot of them, probably. Every day that Chloe spent with her, she felt their connection strengthening, but how long could they keep this up?

It was relatively easy right now, while Chloe was flying into New York once a week. But next month, she'd be living full time in North Carolina and trying to find a new job, probably without enough money to travel for the foreseeable future. And Piper would be headed to LA to film her new movie. It seemed frustratingly complicated, but Chloe was trying not to worry too much about it yet.

Jane had brought them to an upscale Asian fusion restaurant in Manhattan, and Chloe was as dazzled by the view outside the window as she was by her current dinner companions. The food was amazing, and Piper had already pointed out two fellow actors at nearby tables. Chloe had officially entered a whole new world.

"There goes my summer, not that I'm complaining," Piper said as she polished off her champagne, a dreamy smile on her face.

"Will you have any time off at all?" Chloe asked, hoping the answer was yes.

Piper nodded. "I'll have about a month after *Defense* wraps before I head to LA, and then about another month after I film *Tempted* before I'm back on set here."

After they'd eaten, Jane insisted they top off the evening with dessert and a second bottle of champagne. "What will you do for work in North Carolina?" she asked Chloe.

"I have a degree in interior design. I'll probably have to start out as an assistant somewhere, especially since I've been out of the industry since I graduated, but I don't mind."

"Oh, that's a great field of work," Jane said with an enthusiastic nod. "People will always need someone to help them decorate. What's your area of focus? Corporate? Residential?"

"Ideally, residential. I love helping people realize their vision for their home, but I won't be picky for an entry-level job, especially out in the mountains. The market is definitely smaller there than here."

"There's no possibility for you to move to New York?" Jane asked, her gaze sliding briefly to Piper.

"I wish, but no," Chloe told her. "I've just bought a house near my family. In fact, I'm closing on it on Monday. My parents are raising my niece, and they could really use an extra set of hands, plus I just really want to be around for her."

"Understandable," Jane said. "Well, I suppose with Piper's new paycheck, you'll be able to afford all the flights you need to see each other."

Chloe dropped her gaze to her champagne flute. She didn't know how much Piper was making for this movie, but it had to be a lot. Millions? Probably. And yet, she didn't feel comfortable letting Piper fly her around the country. That would just be weird. She wasn't looking for a sugar daddy.

All day, people had been asking Chloe if she would move to New York to be with Piper. At first, she had laughed it off. But sitting here in this fancy restaurant, celebrating Piper's new movie role, Chloe felt the distance already yawning between them. Would she ever truly feel like a part of this world if she only got to visit for a weekend here and there? How were she and Piper going to make this work long term?

Beneath the table, Piper gave her hand a squeeze.

After dinner, Jane's driver dropped them off at Piper's apartment. They were quiet as they climbed the steps and Piper let them in.

"Quite a day, huh?" Chloe said.

Piper gave her a weary smile. "It was a *lot*. In a really great way."

"Wish I didn't have to fly out of here tomorrow," Chloe said.

"Do you really?" Piper asked, grabbing one of Chloe's hands and tugging her up against the warmth of her body. "Because you've got a pretty big week coming up."

"Yes and no." She toyed with Piper's hair, still crunchy with too much styling product. "I'll be a homeowner in a few days, which is really friggin' exciting, but I miss you already. I don't know how to figure out our geographical challenges, and it seems like it's only going to get harder from here on out."

"It does, but Jane was right about one thing. I can afford as many flights as we need to see each other. We'll make it work, Chloe. If you want to, that is."

"I do." She stepped forward, nuzzling her face against Piper's neck as her fingers unraveled the perfectly constructed waves in Piper's hair. "It feels kind of daunting right now, but I want to try."

"Good," Piper said, turning her head to bring their lips together. "Because I do too, and I can be really persistent when I want something."

16

Chloe stood in her empty living room, freshly minted key clutched in her hand and Cait at her side. The house was a mess, and it had no furniture, but it was *hers*, a blank slate for her to paint with all the offbeat colors of her personality. She couldn't wait to get started.

"I get to decorate my own bedroom, right?" Cait asked, looking up at her.

Chloe nodded. "But I'm challenging you to make it as grown-up as possible, since it'll be my guest room when you're not here. No hamster bedspreads, right?" She gave her niece a playful nudge.

Cait rolled her eyes in a move more reminiscent of a teenager than a child. "I don't even *want* a hamster bedspread. That would be weird. Can we go shopping after dinner?"

"If there's time. This is a school night, you know?" Chloe was only home for two days, and she had a whole list of things to get done in her new house, but her first priority had been a living room camp out with Cait, even if meant taking her niece on a Monday night. "Hungry?"

Cait nodded before heading toward her bedroom, probably dreaming up girlish ideas for decorating it. Chloe walked to the kitchen and started preheating the oven. She'd gotten them a frozen pizza, and she had s'mores fixings for later. There was a firepit out back, and it seemed like a camping essential...even if they were camping indoors.

She slid the pizza into the oven and went into the living room to inflate the air mattresses. Her parents had sent them over along with sheets and blankets, everything she and Cait needed for their sleepover tonight. Chloe wasn't sure who was more excited about it, her or Cait.

"Aunt Chloe, your backyard is full of fireflies," Cait said as she came back down the hall.

"Sweet." Chloe fist-pumped the air. "I love fireflies. And cicadas...because I can hear those too, and they were what led us to this house, right?"

"Right," Cait agreed.

"Want to give me a hand?"

She and Cait spent the next ten minutes getting their beds set up for the night, and then they sat on the air mattresses and ate pizza and drank soda. This was exactly what Chloe had been longing for, the reason she'd quit her job as a flight attendant. She could hardly wait to be here full time. Just one more week...

"Hey, let's take a sleepover selfie and text it to Piper," she said, reaching for her phone, because despite her giddiness over her new home, she missed her girlfriend a hell of a lot.

Cait moved closer, pressing her cheek against Chloe's as they made funny faces for their selfie. Chloe composed a quick text to go with it.

First sleepover in the new house. Wish you were here!

"I'm not sure there's time to go shopping tonight," she told Cait. "But what do you say if we start a fire and make s'mores instead?"

"Deal," Cait said with a grin. "Then we can tell ghost stories. I know some good ones."

OMG you guys are adorbs! Invite me to the next sleepover?

The text from Piper gleamed on her screen, and Chloe's heart gave a little kick in her chest. Without thinking, she pressed the green icon next to Piper's name and dialed.

"Hey," Piper answered immediately. "You ladies look like you're having fun tonight."

"We are. Wish you were here."

"Is that Piper?" Cait asked. "Put her on speaker."

"I'll do you one better. Hang on, Piper." She pressed the FaceTime icon, and a few moments later, Piper's smiling face appeared on the screen.

"Hi, Cait," Piper said, waving.

"Hi." Cait's voice jumped up an octave in her excitement. "My grandparents let me watch one of your movies last weekend. It was really good. I can't believe my aunt is dating a celebrity."

"Let me guess...*Teen Spy*?" Piper asked.

"Yep," Cait confirmed.

"That was the first movie I ever made," Piper said. "I'm glad you liked it."

"Are you going to come visit and see Aunt Chloe's new house?" Cait asked.

"I'd love to," Piper said. "Chloe and I just have to work out our schedules."

"Why don't you come after you wrap this season of *In Her Defense*?" Chloe suggested. "I'll have furniture by then. Stay as long as you like."

"I'd love that," Piper said.

Chloe squinted at the screen, recognizing the couch in Piper's dressing room. "Are you still at work?"

Piper made a face. "Yep. I was just about to head out when I got your text."

"Well, we won't keep you, then. I'll call you tomorrow, okay?"

Piper nodded. "Have fun at your sleepover. It was great to meet you, Cait."

"You too," Cait said, waving at the screen. "Maybe I can come for a sleepover while you're here."

"Absolutely," Piper said. "Bye!" With a wave, she disappeared from the screen.

"I like her," Cait proclaimed as she hopped up to take their empty pizza plates into the kitchen.

"I'm glad," Chloe said, warmth spreading through her chest at the thought of having Cait and Piper here together in her house. She'd spent the last eight years jetting around the world in search of adventure, but maybe all she really needed was a little house filled with people she loved. She slapped a hand over her mouth. "Oh my God."

"What?" Cait asked as she walked into the living room, arms laden with graham crackers, marshmallows, and a Hershey's chocolate bar.

Chloe blinked at her. *People she loved.* Did Piper fall into that category? "I'm just really happy to be here with you tonight, that's all," she told her niece.

"Me too," Cait said. "I was kind of bummed at first that you were moving out of our house, but now I think this is better, because you'll be living here all the time instead of so much traveling."

"Yeah, I'm pretty happy about that too." She was tired of traveling, tired of sleeping in hotel rooms, tired of eating in airport food courts. But she was going to miss it too, and most of all, she was going to miss her weekly visits to see Piper in New York. Maybe she *was* in love, because her house felt empty without Piper here to share it with her.

Shoving the feeling aside, she stood. "Let's make s'mores."

～

PIPER TUCKED her hair under a hat and grabbed her purse. She was taking the subway home today, her first attempt since she'd ridden it with Chloe last week. FaceTiming with Chloe and her niece had put a smile on her face, but it had also driven home an important point. Watching them interact in Chloe's living room made it somehow more real that Chloe lived in North Carolina, and that adorable, bubbly little girl was the reason Chloe would *always* live there.

Piper sighed as she left the building. She had a ten-minute walk to the subway, which would hopefully help dissipate her nerves. Maybe it would help her shake off this sudden melancholy about her future with Chloe too. Surely Piper could be happy with a long-distance relationship. Her schedule was chaotic, but it often left her with weeks, if not months, off at the time, and she would spend them with Chloe. It could be enough.

She stopped at the entrance to the subway, her body gone cold. Her stomach cramped, her chest tightened, and she wanted to scream. When would this get easier? Why couldn't she just chill out and ride the subway like a normal person? Tears rose in her eyes, blurring her vision.

Someone bumped into her, and she stepped to the side, forcing air into her lungs as spots danced before her eyes.

This was ridiculous. Gritting her teeth, she started down the steps, one foot after the other until she was in the station.

She fumbled in her purse for her MetroCard, wishing she'd thought to get it out ahead of time. She pulled it out and promptly dropped it on the floor. Her pulse echoed in her ears as she knelt to grab it. As she stood, her gaze caught on a man several feet away, cell phone up and aimed in her direction.

Fuck.

For a moment, she just stared at him, her mind gone totally blank. The rattle and chatter of the busy station faded away, leaving nothing but the thump of her pulse in her ears and the gasping breaths that sounded as if she'd just jogged a mile.

The next thing she knew, she was sprinting up the stairs toward the street. She speed-walked several blocks until her pulse had calmed and she was sure the man from the subway hadn't followed her. He would probably send those photos to one of the celebrity gossip blogs, but at least she hadn't had a full blown panic attack in front of him. His photos wouldn't show anything but a frazzled celebrity who didn't want to be photographed on her way home from the studio.

Too worked up to call an Uber, she walked all the way home instead. By the time she let herself into her apartment, she was tired and sweaty, and her feet hurt. Frustrated, she stripped out of her clothes and stepped into the shower, letting the warm water wash away as much of her discomfort as she could. Then she dressed in her comfiest pajamas and poured herself a glass of wine to go with the Thai leftovers in her fridge.

She wanted to call Chloe. Everything in her needed to hear Chloe's voice right now, but she'd just talked to her an hour ago, and Chloe was having a sleepover with her niece tonight. It would be rude of Piper to take her away from her time with Cait.

Instead, she turned on the TV and queued up *Grace and Frankie*. She desperately needed some comedic relief right now, and no matter how many times she watched this series, it never got any less funny. She laughed and ate spicy noodles while she polished off most of a bottle of wine.

About four episodes into her impromptu *Grace and Frankie* marathon, she made the flip turn from laughter to tears. It hit out of the blue, and before she knew it, she was curled on her side on the sofa, sobbing into the sleeve of her pajama top. Sometimes crying was its own form of stress relief, though, and by the time her tears dried, she felt somewhat calmer.

Drained from a long and emotionally exhausting day, she shut off the TV and went into the kitchen to chug a glass of water. Then she washed up and climbed into bed, asleep within minutes. The next morning, she indeed felt like a whole new woman. She worked another twelve-hour day, taking the car to and from the set to give herself a reset before she tried riding the subway again.

When she got home, it was almost nine. She ate a quick dinner and called Chloe, because apparently she'd become a person who needed to talk to her girlfriend every day.

"Hi," Chloe answered. "I was just thinking about you."

"Were you?" Piper settled on the couch, tucking her feet under herself.

"Yep," Chloe said.

"Well, obviously, you were on my mind too. How was your sleepover with Cait?"

Chloe let out a happy sigh. "It was so much fun. I can't

wait to have a million more sleepovers once I'm here full time."

"Just one more week, right?"

"Yes," Chloe confirmed. "I'll be in New York again on Thursday, but it's the last time."

"We'll have to do something fun while you're here, then," Piper said. "And we need to plan my trip to North Carolina."

"Yes to both," Chloe said. "After I finish flying next week, I'll be here pretty much anytime you want to come."

"*Defense* wraps for the season on the eighth, and I need to be back before the end of the month to get ready for *Tempted*, but I'm yours for as long as you want me in the meantime."

"Oh, I want you," Chloe said, her voice equal parts teasing and seductive. "Seriously, come for as long as you like. I miss you."

"Same," Piper said, surprised to feel the lump in her throat. "I could probably stay about two weeks if you're sure I wouldn't be overstaying my welcome."

"You could *never*," Chloe said. "I'll probably be waiting tables or something by then to pay the bills, but I'll try to be around as much as possible."

"I'm sure I can keep myself entertained with Mother Nature at my disposal," Piper told her. "Plus, you can put me to work around the house. You said it needs some fixing up, right?"

"Yeah, but you're going to be my guest. Bring your Kindle and your hiking boots."

"Do I need hiking boots?" Piper hadn't done much hiking before, but she definitely wanted to while she was in the Smoky Mountains.

"You can get by with sneakers, unless you want to do anything really adventurous."

"I doubt I'm that adventurous, but I might buy hiking boots just for fun, because they sound kind of badass," Piper said, picturing it. Suddenly, two weeks in the mountains with Chloe felt like the best vacation she'd ever planned.

"I think they'd look very sexy on you," Chloe said with a giggle.

"I don't know about sexy, but I definitely want you to take me hiking. I don't get much nature here in the city."

"Oh, I've got plenty of nature for you. We can hike. We could go zip-lining. There's the Biltmore Estate, which is as close to a castle as you'll find around here, and it even has its own vineyard. There's so much to do. We won't get bored."

And just like that, all the moodiness that had been lurking inside Piper this week evaporated. "Sign me up for everything you just mentioned."

She ended the call fifteen minutes later, already daydreaming about her visit to North Carolina. The next morning, Piper didn't have to be on set until nine, which was delightful. This morning, they had their table read for the season finale, where the cast would sit to read through the episode together for the first time. Piper picked up the script that had been left in her dressing room, eager to see how the season would wrap up.

"Oh my God, have you read through it yet?" Eliza asked, standing in Piper's doorway.

"Not yet. Is it good?"

"Good? It's *amazing*," Eliza said as she walked in and dropped onto the couch beside Piper. "See for yourself."

Piper skimmed through the pages. Sam would have a showstopping courtroom scene where she took on the head of a social media platform that had allowed her client—a rape victim—to be further victimized by her attacker, who happened to be a board member at the company.

After winning the case, Sam and her colleagues went out for celebratory drinks. Slightly drunk, Sam mistook a random guy in the bar for the man who'd shot her. She caused a rather unfortunate scene, which ended in her having a panic attack in the alley behind the bar.

"Shit," Piper mumbled, frowning. That struck a little too close to home, but of course, Benny didn't know about her panic attacks. This was logical character development for Sam after suffering a violent attack, and while it would be difficult, Piper could surely act the hell out of it.

"That's not the reaction I was expecting," Eliza commented. "You've been pushing for this all season. I thought you'd be thrilled."

"What?" Piper glanced at her, utterly confused because she'd never mentioned her panic attacks to her costars, let alone pushed for this storyline for Sam.

"Did you get to the last scene yet?" Eliza asked.

"Not quite."

"Oh, keep reading, then. You're going to love this." Eliza was grinning, and a funny feeling took hold in the pit of Piper's stomach, because there *was* a storyline Piper had pushed for. Surely, Eliza didn't mean...

Piper dropped her gaze to the script, skimming through the scene in the alley. Claire came outside to check on Sam, who lashed out at her in an attempt to hide her fragile emotional state. And then...

"Oh shit," Piper exclaimed.

"There it is," Eliza agreed happily.

"Benny really went for it. Sam and Claire are going to kiss!"

"And not just any kiss," Eliza said. "This one looks really hot."

It sure did. The final shot of the season involved Sam pressing Claire against a wall and kissing the shit out of her. Warmth spread over Piper's skin, but when she looked at Eliza, her embarrassment vanished. Her feelings for her costar were so far in the past now that it no longer bothered her to think of kissing Eliza.

"The Clairantha fans are going to lose their minds," Piper said as a grin slid onto her face.

"They sure are. I was kind of ambivalent about this idea when you first mentioned it, but now that I see it in the script, I'm excited. I think it'll be an interesting and important arc for both of our characters."

"So do I."

Piper went through her day with a newfound spring in her step. When she left the set that evening, she marched straight to the subway station, descended to the platform, and boarded a train almost as seamlessly as she'd done before the incident. Her knees wobbled as she exited the subway fifteen minutes later, jogging breathlessly toward the street.

Fuck fear. She still had a long way to go, but at this exact moment, Piper felt invincible.

17

Chloe couldn't remember the last time she had gone to the airport in street clothes, waiting for someone outside the security checkpoint instead of breezing through in her uniform. She was so ridiculously excited for Piper's visit, she was about to burst out of her own skin. Piper would be here in North Carolina for two whole weeks. That was more time than they'd ever spent together.

"Chloe? What are you doing here?"

She turned at the sound of her friend's voice, grinning when she spotted Nisha walking toward her. "I'm here to pick up Piper. Hey, stick around for a minute, and I'll introduce you."

"Oh my goodness." Nisha's eyes went wide. "I'd love to meet her, but I hope I don't get tongue tied and embarrass myself."

"You'll be fine," Chloe told her with a laugh. "She's just a regular person. Also, you and I need to catch up soon, because I miss you."

"Definitely. Let's plan something after Piper's visit."

"Oh, here she comes." Chloe had to restrain herself from bouncing on her toes as she caught sight of Piper walking toward them.

Her hair was tied in a side ponytail that draped over one shoulder. She wore black pants and a green top, and she broke into a huge smile as she spotted Chloe. "Hi."

"Hey." Chloe grabbed her hands, tugging her in for a quick kiss. "I am *so* glad to see you."

"Ditto," Piper said against her lips.

Chloe pulled back, keeping one of Piper's hands in hers as she turned toward Nisha. "This is Nisha. I just bumped into her and wanted to introduce you guys since we're all here. Remember when I told you about my friend who's a big fan of the show?"

"The friend you got Nate's autograph for," Piper said, grinning at Nisha. "It's great to meet you."

"Likewise," Nisha said, her golden skin growing a shade darker over her cheeks. "I've been watching *In Her Defense* since the first season, and you're amazing, but I'm also thrilled to meet the woman who's made Chloe so happy the last few months."

They chatted for a few minutes, and Chloe took a picture of Nisha and Piper with Nisha's phone before she headed for her car and Chloe and Piper walked to the baggage claim to retrieve Piper's suitcase.

"I can't wait to see your house," Piper said as Chloe led the way into the parking garage a few minutes later.

"Well, we've got a bit of a drive first, but I can't either."

"I don't mind the drive," Piper said, giving her hand a squeeze. "Something tells me we won't run out of conversation."

"I don't think we ever would." As Chloe met her gaze, she knew for sure this was love. There was just no other explanation for the warmth that filled her chest when she was with Piper or the soul deep contentment that filled her at the thought of spending the next two weeks with her, not to mention the heat that spread through other parts of her at the thought of having Piper in her bed tonight.

Based on the look on Piper's face, Chloe wondered if she was feeling the same thing. If not love, she was definitely feeling something happy. They climbed into the car together, and after a quick kiss, they were off.

An hour and a half later, Chloe turned onto Cicada Lane. The sun had just set, streaking the sky with pink and purple. Chloe had left a light on in the kitchen, giving the windows a warm glow as she turned into the driveway.

"Oh," Piper exclaimed. "It's even cuter in person."

"Thanks. It's got furniture now and everything."

"Fancy," Piper said with a grin.

They got out of the car, and Chloe helped Piper lift her suitcase out of the trunk before leading the way inside. She'd spent the last two weeks fixing the place up, and while it was far from finished, it was hardly recognizable from how it had looked when she bought it. It was amazing what a little paint and polish could do.

"Chloe, I love it," Piper said as she looked around the living room. "It's adorable, although I don't think that's quite the right word. It's got a funky vibe that feels very *you*, but at the same time, it's full of classic cottage charm. It's perfect."

"Thanks," Chloe said, beaming at Piper's compliment. "That's pretty much exactly what I was going for."

"I love the color of the walls," Piper said as she walked through the room.

"It's called dragonfly, and I was definitely swayed by the name, but it's the color I wanted too." The walls were a muted blue with just a hint of lavender, and she loved the way it offset the exposed wood beams in the ceiling. The fact that the paint shared its name with the bar where she and Piper met was just the icing on the cake.

Piper gave her a smile as she walked to the shelves along the wall, taking in Chloe's pictures and knickknacks. She held up the framed selfie she and Chloe had taken on the beach in the Caymans. "Aw."

"I couldn't resist."

"I need to print one for my apartment too, or maybe for my rental in LA."

"Where will you be staying while you're out there?" Chloe asked.

"A short-term apartment rental, nothing terribly exciting or fancy, but I hope you'll come for a visit." Piper crossed the room and pulled Chloe into her arms.

"I'd love to, if I can manage it," Chloe told her. "I've got a part-time waitressing job right now, which has let me have enough time to get the house fixed up and do lots of fun things while you're here, but I've got to either pick up more hours or find something more permanent after you leave."

"Well, if you can't make it to LA, I'll come back for a quick weekend visit, because I can't go three months without seeing you." The absolute sincerity in Piper's voice was like a balm on Chloe's heart because she felt the same way.

"I can't either," Chloe told her. "Are you hungry? Thirsty?"

"I'm fine for now."

"Bedroom's through here." Chloe walked over to grab

Piper's suitcase, rolling it down the hall. "That's the guest room, aka Cait's room." She gestured to the smaller room with light green walls and a white bedspread covered in pastel-woven flowers.

"Cute," Piper said, following her into the master. "Oh, nice."

Chloe had painted her room a pale coppery tone called new penny, and she'd paired it with gauzy cream-colored curtains and a matching bedspread. Her furniture was a rich mahogany which she'd re-stained to match the wood beams crisscrossing the ceiling. The effect was warm and soothing, or at least she thought so.

"This room is like an oasis," Piper said, tracing her fingers along the edge of the bed as she walked toward the windows overlooking the woods behind the house.

"That's what a bedroom should be, right?"

"Mm." Piper stood for a moment, staring out the window. "I love the city. I always have, but I think I'm going to love the mountains too. It's peaceful."

"The mountains have always been my happy place," Chloe said. "I can't wait to show them to you."

"I'm really glad to be here." Piper turned away from the window and, within moments, they were in each other's arms.

Chloe tugged the elastic from Piper's hair so she could bury her hands in it, anchoring herself there as their mouths met. "Missed you so much," she murmured, peppering kisses over Piper's gorgeous cheekbones.

"Same." Piper exhaled, resting her forehead against Chloe's as they held on to each other. "I've worked such long hours these last few weeks, and I'm not complaining, but God, I can't wait to just relax here with you for a few weeks."

"It's going to be perfect." She kissed a sensitive spot

beneath Piper's ear. "And you know what else? I've never had sex in this bed."

Piper gasped. "We'd better change that, then."

~

FLAMES DANCED before Piper's eyes, red and orange and yellow, sending an occasional burst of sparks into the night. The air hummed with the snap and crackle of the fire over-laid with a chorus of insects. She and Chloe sat by the fire pit behind her house, watching as the flames cast rippling shadows into the woods beyond.

"It's mesmerizing," she said quietly. After a grueling month and a long day, she could barely hold her eyes open. Exhaustion wrapped around her like a heavy blanket, but beneath it, she was happy. Content. And she wasn't going to let her fatigue ruin her first night in North Carolina.

"Isn't it?" Chloe said. "I don't sit out here much by myself, but I start a fire every time Cait's here. We roast marshmallows, and she tells me some surprisingly scary ghost stories."

Piper grinned. "I can't wait to meet her."

"I'm glad, because she definitely feels the same way."

"Marshmallows, huh?" Piper looked at Chloe, entranced with the way the flickering light from the fire danced over her face.

"Yeah. I've got a bag in the kitchen, and chocolate and graham crackers too, if you want to unleash your inner child and make s'mores," Chloe told her, eyes sparkling.

"Hell, yes," Piper said. "I haven't toasted a marshmallow since I was a kid."

"Spoiler alert, but it's just as fun as an adult, especially when you pair it with beer."

"Sold."

"Be right back." Chloe hopped out of her chair.

"Need a hand?"

"Nope." She waved over her shoulder as she disappeared into the house, pulling the screen door closed behind her.

Piper leaned back in her chair, wrapping her hoodie more snugly around herself. It got chilly after dark in the mountains, even in May. Before her, a log shifted in the fire pit, sending a plume of sparks into the air. Along the tree line, fireflies blinked. Piper sighed with contentment.

Behind her, the screen door slid open, and Chloe stepped out carrying a large Ziploc bag in one hand and two beer bottles in the other. There were two metal sticks tucked under her arm, with little forklike prongs at one end.

"Are those for the marshmallows?" she asked, incredulous.

Chloe nodded. "Part of my housewarming gift from my parents, probably because they knew Cait would be over here asking for s'mores all the time. Handy, huh?"

"That's...that's cheating!" Piper exclaimed as she stood to take one of the beers from Chloe.

She threw Piper an amused look as she set the rest of the supplies on the patio table. "I mean, you're welcome to forage in the yard for a real stick, but these are so much easier to use and more hygienic too."

"Fine, I'll use one of your fancy sticks," Piper said, accepting the one Chloe held toward her. "But for the record, I miss the innocence of youth when it never would have occurred to me to wonder if a stick I picked up off the ground was hygienic. I haven't made a s'more in ages."

"It's fun," Chloe said. "Cait brings out the kid in me."

"We should all stay in touch with our inner child, I

think," Piper said as she pushed a marshmallow onto the stick and walked toward the fire pit.

"It's true," Chloe agreed as she came to stand beside her.

Piper held her marshmallow over the flames, watching as it began to swell and turn a rich golden-brown. Chloe let out a yelp as hers caught fire, yanking it away from the flames to blow on it. Then, with a grin, she popped it in her mouth.

"Oops," she said, wiping a strand of melted sugar from her chin.

Laughing, Piper lifted her marshmallow and stuck it into her mouth too. They each ate several gooey marshmallows before they finally took the time to put together s'mores.

"Mm, this is so good," Piper mumbled around a mouthful. "I want to revisit my inner child every night I'm here."

"Sounds good to me," Chloe agreed.

"Probably shouldn't," Piper said as she brushed crumbs off her jeans. "I have to film a movie in a few weeks, and while I don't have to take all my clothes off for it, Jane hired a trainer for me this month to whip me into shape."

Chloe's lips pinched as she gazed at the fire. "How naked do you have to get?"

"I insist on a modesty clause in all my contracts. Usually, I wear something like a nude thong and pasties, depending how the scene is being shot."

"Ick," Chloe said, making a face.

"I know. I hate filming sex scenes. They're super awkward, but this movie only has one, and it doesn't sound too graphic. Plus, I got a good vibe from Landon during our chemistry reading. He seems like he'll be respectful and not creepy."

"Are actors sometimes creepy about that stuff?"

"Sometimes, although it's usually more of a problem

with the director and all the other people in the room, you know? You can tell who's there to work and who's there to watch."

"Ugh, Piper." Chloe sounded pained.

"This director has a good rep. It really should be fine. I'm not worried."

Chloe set her metal stick on the table and stepped into Piper's arms. "Am I a jealous asshole if I admit I hate thinking of you kissing other people and filming sex scenes for work?"

"No," Piper said as she brought her lips to Chloe's, tasting sugar and chocolate on her tongue. "As long as you don't get too hung up on it, because it's really just work, I promise."

"Even if you had to kiss Eliza?" Chloe asked.

Piper felt herself blush, although she wasn't even sure why. "Even Eliza."

"Oh my God." Chloe pulled back to stare at her. "You did, didn't you? You guys kissed?"

"Spoiler," Piper whispered. "But it was still just work, Chloe. I told you I don't have feelings for her anymore."

"Yeah, but I saw the sexual tension between you two in that scene in Sam's apartment. I was there. The air was crackling with it."

"Then we're both good at our jobs, because she's straight, and the only person I want to kiss these days is *you*." To prove her point, she nipped at Chloe's sugary lower lip.

"Sorry," Chloe murmured. "I trust you. It's just weird."

"I know it is, but you really *do* have to trust me."

Chloe nodded. "I can't believe Sam and Claire really kissed. The fans are going to be so excited."

Piper grinned. "I know. I can't wait to get their reaction.

For what it's worth, I don't think the showrunner's planning to take it any farther, at least at this point, but hey, we got a kiss between Sam and Claire before Sam kissed Tony, and that's something."

"It's amazing," Chloe agreed.

"It really is."

"Ready to head inside?" Chloe asked.

Piper nodded. "This was great, though, and the s'mores...yum."

"I'll be right in as soon as I put out the fire," Chloe said.

Piper gathered the s'mores supplies and their beers and carried them inside with her. She put the food away in the kitchen and brought their beers to the living room, where her attention was captured by the bottom shelf of the bookcase, which was filled with colorful, neatly stacked boxes. Piper walked over for a closer look and discovered that they were puzzles. Chloe had dozens of puzzles, cityscapes and mountains, an airport, the ocean, and even a field full of hot-air balloons.

Interesting. Piper wouldn't have pegged Chloe as the type to sit quietly and assemble a puzzle. That seemed more like something Piper herself might enjoy, although she hadn't worked on a puzzle since...well, she couldn't remember, so probably since she was a kid.

She sat on the couch with her beer and checked her phone, finding an email from her agent containing a more detailed shooting schedule for *Tempted*. After the initial production meetings, they would spend a week filming on location in Boston, which would allow Piper to drop in and see her family but also meant that potentially the first scene she filmed would be on a subway platform. After Boston, she'd be off to LA for the rest of the summer to film on the studio's soundstage.

The back door opened, and Chloe stepped inside.

"Puzzles?" Piper asked, waving her beer toward the shelf.

"One of my favorite hobbies," Chloe said as she came to sit beside her. "I find them very relaxing, and it's something Cait and I enjoy doing together."

"Are you working on one now?" Piper asked.

Chloe shook her head. "I haven't had time since I moved in. I was rushing to get the place livable before you got here and before my hours picked up, but I hope to do a lot of puzzles now that I'm settled."

"Have you put all of those together before, or are they new?"

"Some of them I've done before, but a lot of them are new. I've collected them over the years, birthday and Christmas presents, you know?"

"What do you do with them once they're complete?"

"Leave them on the table for a little while to look at. Then, if it's one I think I'd like to do again, I take it apart and put it back in the box. If not, I give it away."

"This is fascinating," Piper said, smiling at her.

Chloe's brow wrinkled adorably. "Why?"

"I don't know. I guess I've always wondered what people do with puzzles once they're done. Seems like a waste of time to work so hard on something and then take it apart and put it back in the box."

"Well, some people frame them," Chloe told her, "or take pictures for their Instagram or whatever."

"Hm." Piper shifted closer to her on the couch, resting her head on Chloe's shoulder.

"If I didn't know better, I'd think you want to put together a puzzle with me, Ms. Fancy Movie Star," Chloe said.

"I might, actually, but not tonight. I'm exhausted. Did you have something in mind for us to do tomorrow?"

"I have the next two days off, but after that I'll have to work at least a few hours most days that you're here," Chloe said with a slight frown. "It's a bummer, I know."

"No, that should actually work out fine, because I need to do some prep work for the movie, learning lines, researching my character, all that stuff. I can do that while you're at work."

"Okay," Chloe said.

That night, Piper didn't even need the sleeping pill she usually took when she was traveling. Snuggled in bed next to Chloe with a chorus of bugs singing outside and the mountain breeze whispering through the window, she closed her eyes and fell into a deep, dreamless sleep. A thump and a muffled swear from the direction of the kitchen woke her, and when she opened her eyes, she was greeted with soft morning sunlight.

She stretched with a sigh, feeling relaxed and rested, wishing she could start every morning exactly this way. Well, she would rather wake beside Chloe, but she wasn't going to complain about sleeping in, either. She'd needed it. In addition to all the other things she wanted to do here in the mountains with Chloe, she also hoped to sleep a *lot*.

She went into the bathroom to freshen up and then wandered into the kitchen to find Chloe at the table, coffee cup in one hand, phone in the other. She looked up at Piper with a smile. "Morning."

"Morning." Piper leaned in to give her a kiss before pouring herself a cup of coffee. "What do you want to do today?"

"Up for a hike?" Chloe asked.

"Definitely, although I never actually bought hiking boots."

Chloe grinned into her coffee. "It's fine. The hike I have in mind for us can definitely be done in sneakers. I know a little trail that leads to a waterfall where we could have a picnic lunch. How does that sound?"

Piper felt everything inside her relax just thinking about it. "It sounds perfect."

18

Piper's pulse pounded in her ears, and her heart thumped against her ribs, but unlike so many other times in her life, today she felt *great*. She panted beside Chloe as they climbed a steep portion of the trail beneath a brilliantly green canopy of trees. In the distance, she could just make out the roar of water.

"Okay?" Chloe asked, sounding breathless.

Piper nodded as she stepped over a tree root bisecting the trail. The air was warm and fresh, filled with the scent of fresh earth and vegetation, a world away from Brooklyn or even LA. This foray into nature was exactly what Piper had needed today.

"It's not far now," Chloe told her. She wore jean cutoffs and a blue-patterned tank top, her hair in a blonde ponytail piled high on her head. Their picnic was inside the backpack that she'd insisted on carrying, leaving Piper with nothing to do but follow along and enjoy the scenery.

And boy, was she enjoying it. She'd seen so many birds and even a lizard scurrying over a log. Chloe had warned her to be mindful of snakes, but luckily, they hadn't seen any of those. The sound of the waterfall grew louder through the trees, and Piper felt herself walking faster in anticipation of seeing it.

She'd never considered herself a nature girl, having grown up in the suburbs of Boston before oscillating between New York City and Los Angeles for her career, but right now, she couldn't be happier to be here in the woods with Chloe as her guide. The path dipped ahead, and they hiked downhill toward the sound of the water.

A few minutes later, they came out at a large overlook with a metal railing to keep people from stepping too close to the edge. A small crowd had gathered against the railing, and Piper could just see the waterfall beyond. It was about fifty or sixty feet high, with water careening over the sheer rock face to splash into a pool below.

"Wow," Piper said, awed by the sight even as she wished they could have it to themselves. She wasn't particularly worried about being recognized. No one they'd passed on the trail had given her a second glance, maybe thanks to the baseball cap on her head or maybe because spotting a celebrity was the last thing on their minds, but she'd envisioned a more private location for their picnic.

"Gorgeous, isn't it?" Chloe said as they made their way to an opening against the railing.

"So pretty," Piper agreed.

For a long minute, they stood with their elbows on the railing and watched the water cascade down the rock. It was hypnotizing. Piper could have stood here all day if it weren't for the crush of people around them. Laughter and conversation and the occasional shriek of a child filled her ears, muffling the waterfall. When she looked around and saw cameras and cell phones in the air, an all-too-familiar chill spread over her skin.

"Follow me," Chloe said, turning away from the overlook.

Wordlessly, Piper followed Chloe down a smaller path to their right, wishing she'd gotten to spend more time at the waterfall even as she was glad to be away from the crowd. As Chloe led them farther down the river, the pressure in Piper's chest eased. Chloe made an abrupt right, leading Piper into the trees on what might be a path, or it could just be a gap in the underbrush.

"Where are we going?" she asked, gazing uneasily over her shoulder toward the well-marked path they'd left behind. She absolutely did *not* want to get lost in the woods.

"It's sort of a well-kept secret, just for us locals." Chloe kept walking, leading them farther into the woods on their maybe-a-path. They started to climb a rocky hillside.

"You're sure you know where you're going?"

Chloe's head bobbed in affirmation. "I've been coming here my whole life. Trust me."

"I do," Piper said immediately. She'd trusted Chloe since that first night, when she'd been terrified and hiding beneath her wig, afraid even to share her name. Instead, she'd shared so much more and formed an immeasurable bond with this amazing woman.

Chloe led her over a rock formation that almost made Piper question that trust, but then Chloe grabbed her hand and pulled her onto the rock, and *whoa*. They were on top of the world, or at least that's how Piper felt when she stood and got her first good look around.

The forest surrounded them, trees blanketing them from prying eyes, and to the left, they had the most perfect view of the waterfall. They were just high enough to be separate from the chatter of hikers, but not so high that they couldn't hear the roar and splash of the water.

"This is perfect," Piper said. "I'm glad you're a local so we aren't stuck down there with the crowd."

"Me too," Chloe said. "Of course, it was a gamble that there wouldn't be another local up here, and lately, the word has sort of gotten out. I'm pretty sure it's listed on a website with 'best hidden spots' or something, but we lucked out, at least for the moment."

Piper reached for her, pulling her in for a quick kiss before Chloe bent to set her backpack on the rock. She unzipped it and pulled out a purple-and-black-patterned blanket, which she spread out for them.

They sat and pulled out their lunch, avocado sandwiches, chips, grapes, and bottles of water. Piper had worked up quite an appetite on their hike, and Chloe must have too. Between the two of them, they devoured all the food they'd brought, and then sat watching the water plunge over the rock. A rainbow shimmered in the mist hanging over the pool.

"It's so beautiful," Piper murmured, as calm now as she'd been frazzled in the crowd. She could sit here all afternoon, just watching the water and listening to the sounds of nature.

"Lie flat on the blanket," Chloe said, "and close your eyes."

Intrigued, Piper did as Chloe said. The rock poked uncomfortably against her skull even through the blanket, so she put one of her hands behind her head. Then she closed her eyes.

"Now just listen," Chloe murmured. "And feel. Memorize it all, and then you can visualize it when you're on your movie set and feeling anxious."

Piper felt something warm bloom in her heart when she realized what Chloe was asking her to do. Dr. Jorgensen had given her a similar assignment once, so she knew the power of sensory memory, although she hadn't remembered to utilize it lately.

She lay on this rock on top of the world, and she listened to the steady roar of the waterfall and the way the water splashed as it hit the pool below. She heard the wind whispering through the trees and a bird calling overhead. She felt the warmth of the sun on her face and the way the breeze tickled her arms. She smelled evergreen and leaves and the faint floral scent of Chloe's shampoo.

"Come here," she whispered without opening her eyes.

There was a rustle of fabric, and then she felt Chloe beside her, the warmth of her body against Piper's skin a moment before Chloe's arm brushed against hers. She sought Chloe's hand, finding and gripping it.

"Now it's perfect," Piper whispered.

"Mm," Chloe responded.

They lay like that for several minutes, and the rhythmic sound of Chloe's breath became part of Piper's aesthetic. The warm press of her hand in Piper's tethered her to the moment while her mind soared with peace and contentment.

～

CHLOE GIGGLED into her beer as Piper twirled the windcatcher she'd bought in a shop on Haywood Street. After their hike, they'd gone home to shower and change, and then Chloe had driven them into downtown Asheville to poke through the adorable shops here. Now they were seated on the outdoor patio of one of the local breweries for dinner.

Piper's hair glistened coppery red in the sunshine, but

no one had seemed to recognize her today. That might change after she filmed *Tempted*. She'd be a big enough name to draw attention even out here in the mountains of North Carolina.

"I see why you wanted to put down roots here," she said, sipping her beer. "I've only been here twenty-four hours, and I'm already in love."

Twenty-four hours, and Chloe was more in love than ever, but she knew that wasn't what Piper had meant. "It's hard not to love it here."

Their food arrived—Chloe's cheeseburger and Piper's portobello burger—and they chatted comfortably while they ate. Afterward, they strolled through downtown Asheville and bought ice cream cones before heading back to Chloe's house for the evening.

"Let's work on one of your puzzles," Piper suggested as she walked to the kitchen for a glass of water.

"Really?" Chloe followed, intercepting her for a kiss.

"Yeah. I want to get to know all the things you enjoy while I'm here, and who knows, maybe I'll find a new hobby."

"Not that you have time for one," Chloe teased, absurdly thrilled by Piper's words.

They changed into their pajamas and opened a bottle of wine, which they brought with them into the living room.

"Which one?" Piper asked.

"You pick," Chloe said, curious to see which one Piper would choose.

She crouched in front of the shelf and looked over the boxes. When she stood, she was holding one Chloe hadn't opened yet, a field full of hot air balloons. "Colorful," Piper said as she set the box on the table.

"It is, and that should help us put it together too," Chloe

said. "Puzzles that lean heavily on one color take a lot of patience."

Piper stuck her fingernail under the lid to break the seal so she could open it. "What's your strategy? Or do you just dump out all the pieces and dive in?"

"I like to start by sorting out all the edge pieces and assembling them first. Then it's easier to fill in the middle of the picture."

"Sounds good to me," Piper said.

They sat side by side, sorting out all the pieces with a flat edge. Piper wore pink-striped sleep shorts and a matching tank top, looking casual and comfortable, and Chloe found herself imagining a future where this was their everyday life, an impossible scenario. Piper was already a star, but she was on her way to superstardom, and her career was always going to require her to split her time between New York and LA, at least as long as she was still filming *In Her Defense.*

"You're awfully quiet over there," Piper teased, nudging her shoulder against Chloe's.

"Tired, I guess," Chloe said.

Piper paused, sliding a glance in her direction. "Is that all?"

Chloe placed a hand over Piper's. "Just wish we didn't live so far apart, that's all."

"Me too," Piper said, flipping her hand to give Chloe's a squeeze. "But people make it work all the time. So will we."

"I hope so."

Piper sat up straighter. "You don't think we will?"

"That's not what I said." Chloe shook her head. "It's just, I was daydreaming about us living here together, and that probably won't ever happen."

"Not full time," Piper said, "but I can come for weeks at the time like this."

"I'm struggling with the long-distance aspect right now," Chloe admitted. "Having you here makes me realize how much I'm going to miss you after you leave."

Piper looked down at her hands. "I'm sorry."

"Don't be sorry. Like you said, we're going to make it work," Chloe said, hoping it was true.

"I have faith in us," Piper said as she held up a corner piece.

Two hours later, they were tipsy on wine and had assembled about half of the perimeter of the puzzle on Chloe's coffee table. There was something satisfying about finding two pieces that connected, watching the puzzle begin to take form. It was orderly and predictable, something her life had never been.

"Oh my God." Piper giggled as she yet again tried to force two pieces together that were clearly not a match. "I'm so bad at this."

"Better not quit your day job," Chloe teased.

"I have no future as a puzzle master," Piper said, "but I'm having fun."

"And that's all that matters." Chloe took a piece from Piper's hand and connected it to one of her own, completing the right-hand border of the puzzle.

"Ooh," Piper exclaimed, looking proudly at the section that Chloe had mostly put together herself. "It's really coming together."

"If we keep working on it a little bit each day, we should be able to finish before you leave. And Cait will definitely want to help when she comes over this weekend."

"Perfect," Piper said.

"You're sure you don't mind her spending the night?" Chloe asked. As much as she couldn't wait to have two of her favorite people here together, she also knew not everyone found ten-year-olds as charming as she did, and Piper had so little time off as it was.

"Are you kidding?" Piper said, giving her an incredulous look. "I can't wait. With the age gap between me and my brother, hopefully it'll be a long time before I'm an aunt, so I'll live vicariously through you this week."

"Hey, I became an aunt at nineteen, so you never know," Chloe said.

Piper made a face. "Let's hope James doesn't knock up any girls any time soon."

"Do you want kids someday?" Chloe asked, not sure where the question had come from or why she'd blurted out something so personal, but Piper just shrugged.

"I don't know. I haven't given it much thought, and it's been years since I've been in a relationship anywhere near serious enough to start thinking about things like marriage or children."

"But you have been in that kind of relationship before?" Chloe asked.

"Once," Piper told her. "An actor I met in New York. We dated for over a year, and things got pretty serious."

"Oh my God, who?" Chloe blurted. "Do I know him?"

"Nick Rossi," Piper said. "We used to shoot on the same soundstage."

"Mm." Chloe twisted her lips to one side. "The name is vaguely familiar."

"He played Philip on *Next Generation* for five seasons," Piper prompted, seemingly amused by Chloe's cluelessness.

"Ooh, okay, I think I know who that is." Chloe had a vague mental image of a tall, handsome guy with wavy black hair. "So what happened?"

"He moved to LA," Piper said as she tried to shove

another mismatched piece into the puzzle. "And we decided long distance would be too much work."

"Oh," Chloe said quietly.

"I was heartbroken about it at first, but I guess deep down, I knew he wasn't the one," Piper said, "or we would have tried harder to make it work."

Which meant she *did* think Chloe was worth that effort. Tears welled in her eyes as she gripped Piper's hands and pulled her in for a kiss.

19

Piper frowned at the half-assembled puzzle in front of her. She alternated between fascination and frustration with the multicolored bits of cardboard that seemed determined to stymy her. She and Chloe had been working on the puzzle for the better part of a week now, and it was really starting to come together, no thanks to Piper. She picked up a blue-striped piece, sliding it into an open spot in the blue balloon.

"Oh," she said out loud to the empty room. It was satisfying to place one correctly. She could see why Chloe enjoyed it as a hobby.

Pleased with her progress, Piper went down the hall to the bedroom and changed into her jogging gear. She should have just enough time for a run and a shower before Chloe got home from work. They were having dinner with Chloe's parents tonight and then bringing Cait home with them for a sleepover.

Piper had been in North Carolina for five days now, and she'd settled in nicely. Chloe worked at a café in town most afternoons, but that gave Piper time to prep for her new role, not to mention some much-needed downtime to relax and read. Yesterday she'd spent several hours reading the Clairantha fan fiction that Chloe's friend had sent her.

It was called *Skin Deep*, and it opened with Sam and Claire getting tattoos together, which led to celebratory— and flirty—drinks at a bar afterward. Piper had thought it might be weird to essentially read about herself, but on paper, Sam was just Sam, and by chapter five, Piper was completely engrossed in the story. She couldn't wait to see what happened next and when Sam and Claire would finally get together.

Piper left the house and set off down the street at a brisk jog. The air here was so fresh. She sucked in deep breaths as she ran, grateful to have such a beautiful place to spend her downtime. Piper jogged her usual route, avoiding the steepest parts of Cicada Lane. Jogging in the mountains was no joke. The first day, she hadn't paid attention as she ran downhill, and then she'd had to walk all the way home, because the incline was way too steep for her to jog back up.

But she had her route now, and between daily jogs, yoga, and the occasional hike with Chloe, she was keeping up with the fitness goals her trainer had laid out to help her prepare for the movie. Piper wasn't overly concerned with her figure, but she was definitely aware that she was about to take on her first big Hollywood role, and she needed to look the part.

At the top of the hill, she paused to catch her breath. She'd discovered this spot a few days ago. The road twisted sharply to the right, but if she stepped off the pavement and stood in just the right place, she could peer through the trees and glimpse the valley below. The rolling ridge of the Smoky Mountains smudged the horizon beyond. It was beautiful, but more than that, it was *peaceful*.

Piper had always been a city girl, but the mountains spoke to her soul in a way she hadn't anticipated. It hadn't cured her anxiety or her panic attacks. There was no such thing as a cure. Anxiety had always been a part of her life, and it always would be, but she was working her way toward managing it, the way she had before the incident on the subway.

She was getting there, and the mountains were definitely helping. The mountains...and Chloe. Because every part of her life felt brighter and just *better* as long as Chloe was in it.

With a happy sigh, Piper tore her gaze from the valley and started jogging back down the hill toward Chloe's house. She gulped more of that fresh mountain air, letting it fuel her body and her soul as her feet pounded the pavement. She rounded a corner in the road, catching movement in her peripheral vision as something rushed out of the woods toward her.

Her body immediately jerked to a halt, adrenaline tingling in the pit of her stomach before a deer dashed into the road ahead of her and Piper's alarm turned to awe. The brown-eyed doe also froze, and for a long moment, they just stared at each other, both of them panting for breath. Piper's lips stretched in a wide smile as a second deer walked out to join the first, and then, as quickly as they'd appeared, they raced off into the trees on the far side of the road.

"Whoa," Piper whispered, pressing a hand against her chest.

Still smiling, she set off with an extra spring in her step. Ten minutes later, she walked into Chloe's driveway. She stood in the kitchen and sucked down a glass of water before going down the hall to take a shower. Since she was meeting Chloe's family tonight, she spent extra time drying her hair and applying makeup. She was pretty confident that everything was going to go well. From what Chloe had told her, her family was as easygoing as she was, but it was still nerve-racking to meet her girlfriend's family for the first time.

Just as she finished, she heard the front door open. She put away her makeup case and walked out to greet Chloe.

"Wow, you look nice," Chloe said, eyebrows rising. "Like, *really* nice."

"Are you saying I haven't worn makeup often enough since I've been here?" Piper teased.

"Not even a little bit, but it's cute that you got all dolled up to meet my family." Chloe leaned in for a quick kiss. "Meanwhile, they're going to adore you, whether you showed up in sweatpants or those probably very expensive jeans."

"They're a little bit expensive." Piper rubbed a hand down the front of her designer jeans. She wasn't much of a fashionista, so she tended to shop in the kind of boutique store where a stylist would pick things out for her, suggesting outfits that complemented her figure and coloring.

"You're adorable." Chloe kissed the tip of her nose. "I'm going to take a quick shower, and then I'll be ready to go."

"Okay." Piper went into the living room and sat to spend a few more minutes with the puzzle. Five days in the mountains, and she'd become the kind of woman who bumped into deer on her daily jog and worked on puzzles for fun. And she liked this version of herself a *lot*.

"You got a lot done on that today," Chloe commented as she walked into the living room fifteen minutes later, dressed in light blue jeans and a yellow top, as sunny as Chloe herself.

"I'm starting to get the hang of it," Piper told her. "Are

you sure we don't need to bring anything tonight? I feel weird going to someone's house without bringing something."

"I'm positive. They're my parents, and until a couple of weeks ago, I lived with them. Besides, our contribution to the evening is bringing Cait home with us so my parents can enjoy a night to themselves."

"Okay," Piper agreed, standing to grab her purse.

"They're going to love you," Chloe assured her as they walked outside to her car.

"Well, I hope they like me, at least," Piper said, trying to make light of her nerves. It had been a while since she met the parents of someone she was dating, and she had rarely socialized outside of work and her own family since her panic attacks started. Already, she felt the uncomfortable heaviness of anxiety beginning to compress her lungs.

Chloe chattered happily as she drove, telling Piper about a family she'd served today with a trio of rambunctious kids who'd sent Hot Wheels rolling across the restaurant and almost caused Chloe to fall while carrying a tray of drinks. Piper listened, attempting to focus on Chloe's story instead of the increasingly frantic beating of her heart.

After about fifteen minutes, Chloe pulled into a driveway that led to a two-story white paneled house with gray shutters. The house was older but well maintained, with carefully tended flower beds out front. Almost before Chloe had parked and shut off the car, the front door opened, and a blonde girl Piper recognized as Cait came bounding down the steps.

Beaming, Chloe got out of the car to hug her niece. Piper stepped out of the passenger side as Cait rounded the car to smile up at her. "Hi, Piper."

"Hi, Cait. It's so nice to meet you in person."

"You don't look as much like Darcy as I was expecting," Cait said, giving her a discerning look.

Piper grinned at the reference to her character in *Teen Spy*. "That's because I filmed that movie about ten years ago. I guess I've grown up a lot since then." She looked up to find an older couple watching them from the front door, which Cait had left open.

Chloe stepped closer and took Piper's hand, leading her toward them. "Mom, Dad, this is Piper. Piper, these are my parents, Cathy and Rick."

"We're so glad to meet you, Piper," Cathy said, gesturing for them to come in.

Piper followed Chloe and Cait into the house. The wallpaper in the front hall echoed the colors of the forest outside, and there was a table full of family photos just inside the door. After a full round of introductions, Chloe's mom poured glasses of iced tea and ushered them into the living room to relax until dinner.

"Chloe tells us you're about to film a movie in LA," Rick commented as he sat in the armchair near the fireplace.

"Yeah," Piper said, darting a glance at Chloe, who had sat beside her on the couch. "It's pretty exciting."

"Who else is in it?" Cait asked. "Anyone famous?"

"Piper's famous," Chloe told her teasingly.

"I said, who *else*." Cait pulled a cell phone in a hot-pink case out of the back pocket of her jeans.

"Landon Wilkes is my costar. Have you heard of him?" Piper asked her.

Cait's eyes rounded comically. "Oh my God—I mean, gosh. He's been in all those superhero movies! Everyone knows who he is."

"That must be true, because even *I* know who he is," Cathy said. "And watch your language, Cait."

"Sorry, Gram," Cait said, reminding Piper that the people raising her were her grandparents. "Piper, do you want to meet my hamster?"

"Sure," Piper agreed.

She went upstairs, where Cait showed her a brown-and-white hamster named Oreo. Cait handed the hamster to her while she freshened up his food and water, since she would be spending the night at Chloe's. A lavender backpack was on the girl's bed, and she told Piper she was ready to leave as soon as they'd eaten supper. Apparently, she was pretty excited about her sleepover. Her adoration of her aunt was obvious, and Piper knew the feeling was mutual.

She sat on the bed, laughing as the hamster crawled across her lap while Cait explained all the ins and outs of hamster food. Apparently, it was important for Oreo to have a mixture of premade pellets and seeds as well as fresh fruit and vegetables.

"Hang on," Cait said before dashing out of the room.

"I think your owner spoils you," Piper told the rodent, who stared at her with big black eyes before hopping off Piper's lap to crawl across Cait's bedspread.

Cait was back a minute later with a slice of carrot in her hand. "Here. You can give him this if you want. He loves carrots."

"Thanks." Piper took the carrot from Cait and offered it to the hamster, who promptly shoved it inside his cheek pouch, making it bulge comically. Laughing, she placed Oreo back into his cage, and Cait led the way downstairs.

Cathy was just starting to serve dinner, with Chloe's help, as Piper followed Cait into the kitchen.

"Anything I can help with?" she asked.

"Nope," Cathy told her. "We've got everything under control here." She set a large pan of lasagna on a serving tray on the counter while Chloe placed a bowl of salad beside it. Chloe went to the fridge and took out several bottles of salad dressing, which she set next to the salad, while her mom started slicing the garlic bread.

"Mm," Cait said with appreciation, eyeing the spread. "I love lasagna. Pop! Dinner's ready!"

Piper was glad for the salad and the bread since she probably couldn't eat the lasagna. She didn't mind, though. This was how it always was for her when she visited someone's home. She'd have plenty, and she could always snack at Chloe's house later if she was still hungry.

"The lasagna is vegetarian," Cathy told her with a warm smile. "You eat cheese, right?"

Oh. "I do, but I hope you didn't go to any trouble just for me."

"It was no trouble," Cathy said, touching her arm. "What kind of host would I be if I cooked a meal you couldn't eat? There are meatballs on the stove if anyone wants to add some meat to their meal."

"Like me," Cait said with a sly grin as she grabbed a plate. "Sorry, Piper, but you're missing out, because my Gram's meatballs are the *best*."

"I'll take your word for it," Piper told her before turning to Cathy. "Thank you. I really appreciate this. I never expect anyone to cook something special for me."

Cathy waved her off. "Half of Cait's friends have one kind of dietary restriction or another, not to mention the allergies. I aim to please. All right, everyone, come get a plate, and let's eat."

They did just that. Everyone crowded into the kitchen to fix plates and then they all found seats at the table. Cait carefully maneuvered herself to sit next to Piper, asking her endless questions about what it was like to film movies and which celebrities she'd met. Chloe sat across from them, smiling between bites of lasagna.

Her family—as promised—were great. By the time they'd finished eating, Piper felt completely comfortable with them and had already accepted an invitation to come over again the next time she was in town. As she walked out to the car with Chloe and Cait later that evening, she was surprised to realize her anxiety had entirely dissipated almost as soon as she'd walked through the front door.

"We should bake cookies," Cait suggested as she buckled herself into the backseat.

"We don't have to have dessert every time you come for a sleepover," Chloe protested.

"Come on, Aunt Chloe. It's like our tradition."

Piper grinned. The girl was spunky and adorable, and the bond she shared with her aunt was really special. No wonder Chloe had been so determined to settle down here so she could be a more constant presence in her niece's life.

They went home and baked chocolate chip cookies before Cait lobbied unsuccessfully to watch *Teen Spy*, but somehow Chloe's compromise meant they ended up watching *He's the One*, a made-for-TV movie Piper had done before she landed her role on *In Her Defense*. It was cheesy as hell, but Chloe and Cait seemed to love it, and Piper was happy just to be here with them.

After the movie, Cait went to bed, and Chloe and Piper retreated to the master bedroom, both of them exhausted by the long day and the rambunctious girl in the next room. They changed into their pajamas and crawled into bed. Piper rolled toward Chloe, nuzzling her face into Chloe's hair. "You were right. Your family is great."

"I'm glad," Chloe said, wrapping an arm around Piper to

draw her closer. "Because I'm pretty fond of them...and you."

Piper closed her eyes, breathing deeply, relaxed all the way to her soul. "Me too."

∽

ON THE FOLLOWING FRIDAY, Chloe woke feeling uncharacteristically sad. Today was Piper's last full day in North Carolina. Tomorrow, she'd fly home to New York to finish prepping for her new movie, and from there she would be off to Boston and then LA for the rest of the summer. Who knew when they would see each other again?

Beside her, Piper stirred, blinking at her through sleep-glazed eyes. "Morning."

"Good morning." Chloe drew her in, glad she didn't have to work today. They had the whole day to spend together, and she planned to treasure every moment.

Sleepy kisses soon became more hungry ones. As birds sang outside the bedroom window, Chloe stripped Piper out of her pajamas. Their bodies pressed together, warm and soft with sleep, hands seeking to give and receive pleasure, fueled by the knowledge that this was their last morning together, at least for a while. The bedroom filled with moans and gasps as they brought each other to climax...twice.

When they finally made it out of bed, they showered and dressed in light sundresses for their planned day of sightseeing at The Biltmore Estate. The estate was close to an hour from Chloe's house, but she didn't mind the drive. The scenery was gorgeous, and the company was even better.

"Any leads on a job in interior design yet?" Piper asked, gaze fixed on the rolling hills outside the window.

"Not even a nibble," Chloe said. "I knew it might be hard to get my foot in the door somewhere, but I guess I didn't expect it to be *this* hard."

"Well, it's only been a month," Piper said, resting a hand over Chloe's.

"I know." Chloe sighed. "I talked to my manager at the café, and he's going to talk to the owner about moving me to the tavern down the street, which he also owns. I'd be working evenings and weekends there, but I'd have more hours and earn better tips. If that pans out, it'll get me by for now."

"It's just not what you want to be doing," Piper said, her eyes sympathetic.

"No, it's not, but I'm good at waitressing, so it's not terrible. I'd just rather be helping people decorate their houses."

"You will," Piper told her. "I have faith in you."

"Thanks." Chloe was happy to be here in North Carolina full time, to have Cait over for sleepovers whenever she wanted, to have a home of her own for the first time. But she hadn't expected the restlessness that was already building inside her. She missed having a job that fulfilled her. She missed traveling. And she missed Piper, even though she hadn't left yet. She already knew she was going to be heartbroken when they parted at the airport tomorrow.

They parked at the welcome center for the Biltmore and bought tickets before winding their way through the grounds toward the public parking.

"Wow," Piper said, sounding awed as the estate came into view. She looked down at the pamphlet in her hands. "It says this is the largest private residence in America, built by the Vanderbilt family in 1889."

"Just wait until you see the interior," Chloe told her. "It's really something."

"I can't wait."

They parked in one of the large public lots and walked toward the front of the estate. Its sloped roof and turrets reminded Chloe of the castles she'd seen in Europe. A lush green lawn in front of the main building was highlighted by a fountain where people had lined up for the perfect scenic shot with the estate visible behind them.

Chloe and Piper entered through the massive front door, having elected to go on a self-guided tour so that they could set their own pace and keep away from the other guests as much as possible for Piper's sake. This being the most famous location they'd visited in the Asheville area, it was also the place where she was most likely to be recognized.

Hand in hand, they strolled through the rooms inside the estate, perfectly preserved bedrooms and libraries and studies, like they'd been transported back in time. On the second floor, they came out onto a wide balcony with grand columns where yet more people were posing for photos. She and Piper walked to the railing, staring out over the grounds, rolling green hills and flower gardens with the Smoky Mountains as a backdrop.

Piper stood beside her, auburn hair whipping in the breeze and a peaceful smile on her face as she stared into the distance. She wore a gray knit dress that Chloe had seen before, and she loved that she knew Piper well enough now to recognize her favorite outfits.

"I'm really going to miss you after you leave," she said quietly.

Piper turned to face her. "Me too. So much."

Out of nowhere, Chloe was blinking back tears. "I just...I want..." She shook her head when the words failed her.

Piper reached out and touched her cheek. "I know. I feel it too."

20

After touring the estate, Piper and Chloe walked through the gardens outside, overflowing with colorful flowers. The sweet fragrance of roses hung in the air along with the warm scent of vegetation. Everything around her was bathed in the golden glow of the afternoon sun. It was beautiful and romantic, the perfect spot to spend their last afternoon together.

Piper knew what she'd seen in Chloe's eyes earlier. It had frightened her at first, the idea of hearing Chloe speak the words out loud. Piper had only said them once before, and that relationship had fallen apart in the face of trying to maintain a long-distance relationship. Now she and Chloe were in the same position, but this time, geography didn't feel like such an insurmountable hurdle. Chloe was worth fighting for, and Piper needed to tell her that before they parted ways tomorrow, because she'd seen Chloe's insecurity and fear.

Chloe bent to sniff a pink rose, and as she straightened, Piper took her hands, turning her to face her.

"Hey," Piper said. "I wasn't kidding earlier. I do feel it too."

Chloe blinked at her, pinching her bottom lip between her teeth.

Piper squeezed her hands, staring into the honeyed depths of Chloe's eyes. "What I'm trying to say is...I love you."

"Oh my God." Those gorgeous eyes welled with tears. Chloe blinked, and they spilled over her lids. "Really? I mean, I love you too."

Piper grinned, releasing one of Chloe's hands so she could wipe away her tears. "I know it feels scary that I'm leaving tomorrow, and we don't know when we'll see each other again, but we're going to make it work, okay?"

Chloe squeezed her eyes shut, nodding as more tears fell.

Piper drew her in for a kiss, tasting salt on her lips. They kissed for several blissful minutes, oblivious to the world around them. Finally, she pulled back, reaching out to smooth down a lock of Chloe's hair. "Ready to look for someplace to have lunch?"

Chloe nodded, but she stayed where she was, bottom lip trembling, eyes glossy.

"You okay?"

"I've never told a girl I love her before." She gave Piper a shaky smile. "Kind of a big deal."

Piper wrapped her arms around her, holding her close. She closed her eyes, breathing in the scent of roses mixed with Chloe's shampoo. "It's a big deal for me too. I've never felt strongly enough about someone to try to make things work with my crazy lifestyle."

"It's going to be hard," Chloe murmured into her hair.

"I know."

"It's already hard," Chloe whispered. "I've never been clingy or needy like this with someone before. I don't like it."

"You aren't needy or clingy," Piper told her. "I think you're pretty perfect."

"Stop it." Chloe pulled back to wipe away fresh tears. "I never expected you to tell me you loved me today. You've kind of blown my mind here."

"Well, it's true, and now that we've said the words out loud, we can enjoy the rest of our day knowing that we're two women in love."

"I like that," Chloe said, eyes still glossy. "Actually, I *love* it. I had been wanting to tell you how I felt, but I was afraid it was too soon."

"Never." Piper gave her another kiss before leading the way out of the gardens. She pulled up a map of the grounds, looking for restaurants, and found an adorable place called the Library Lounge inside the inn that had stunning views of the grounds. It was a bit on the pricey side, but what the hell? She could afford it, and she was in a celebratory mood. She clicked on the app and reserved a table. "I just made lunch reservations."

"What? Where?"

Piper showed her a photo of the restaurant on her phone.

"Whoa, that looks fancy."

"Well, we look fancy, and we're celebrating being in love, so let's go eat."

They wandered across the grounds from the estate house to the inn, where they were seated at a romantic table for two in front of the window. Piper had paid extra for the view, but she decided to keep that to herself. They ordered several small plates to share. Chloe was quieter than usual, a dreamy look on her face that said she was still a bit dazed by the words they'd exchanged outside.

After lunch, they went on a tour of the vineyard and then attended a wine tasting. Piper bought two bottles for them to take home, a sweet blush wine and a cabernet sauvignon. By the time they got home, it was almost dinner-time. They'd gone shopping earlier in the week so they could eat a quiet dinner at home for Piper's last night.

They opened the bottle of cabernet and worked together in the kitchen, preparing their pizza. While it cooked, they sat in the living room to put the last few pieces into the puzzle. Chloe let Piper have the honors, pushing the final piece into its spot. She stared at the completed puzzle proudly. "I can't believe we finished it."

Chloe's coffee table was now a colorful panorama of hot air balloons drifting over a green field. Piper took a picture of it to commemorate her first puzzle, and then they took a bunch of silly selfies in front of it. They'd taken a lot of selfies the last two weeks. Those photos were going to get Piper through until the next time she got to see Chloe in person.

After they ate their pizza, they refilled their wineglasses and snuggled on the couch together. Piper lay with her head in Chloe's lap, smiling up at her while Chloe told her stories about all the shenanigans she and Cassie had gotten into together in high school. Then she got out a photo album and took Piper on a visual tour of her childhood.

"It's wild to see the two of you together," Piper said, touching a photo of Chloe and Cassie when they were about Cait's age. Not only were they a mirror image of each other, but they bore a striking resemblance to Cait.

"People always told us they thought it must be weird going through life with someone who looks like you, but to us, that wasn't weird. It was normal. The weird thing was when I didn't have anyone who looked like me anymore." Chloe's expression grew distant. "For me, it's weird being unique. I was meant to be half of a pair."

"Oh Chloe." Piper reached up to touch Chloe's cheek.

Chloe turned her face into Piper's hand, kissing her palm. "It's okay. Every day, I feel a little more comfortable on my own, and you've made me part of an entirely different pairing."

Piper smiled at her. "I'm awfully glad to be part of this pair."

"We make a pretty good one."

"We sure do." Piper sat up, spinning to face Chloe so she could lean in for a kiss. "I love you."

"Love you too."

∽

PIPER HAD MADE it two full weeks in North Carolina without a panic attack, but not even two hours into her journey home, she'd had to lock herself in the bathroom on the airplane to try to get control before she had a breakdown at thirty thousand feet. She closed her eyes, hands braced against the walls of the small space, attempting to block out the unpleasant smells and the way the floor vibrated beneath her feet.

She wiggled her toes, but she was wearing her black ballet flats, no fluffy socks to give her the sensory feedback she needed. The walls were closing in around her. Tears pooled in her eyes, and her chest was so heavy, she could hardly hold herself upright.

"Listen and feel."

She heard Chloe's voice in her head, her words on that mountaintop.

"Memorize it so you can visualize it when you're feeling anxious."

Piper remembered the hard press of the rock beneath her and the warmth of the sun on her face. The rumble of the jet engine became the roar of the waterfall. Her ragged breaths were replaced with Chloe's gentle, rhythmic inhales and exhales as she lay beside Piper. She sucked in a deep breath, remembering the way the water cascaded over the rock to splash into the pool below.

Her eyes popped open, and she blinked at herself in the mirror, halfway surprised to find herself in the tiny airplane bathroom. She was even more surprised to realize the panic had retreated. She still felt dizzy, and her legs shook beneath her. Her breathing was somewhat frantic, but the pressure in her lungs had eased.

She made her way back to her seat, grateful for in-flight Wi-Fi so she could text Chloe and let her know her suggestion had helped. Then Piper put on her noise-canceling headphones and closed her eyes to block out the rest of the flight. She couldn't sleep—she was still wound too tightly to approach anything resembling relaxation—so instead she reminisced on her time with Chloe.

Once she'd landed in New York, she found the car she'd hired and went home. It was a relief to step into her apartment. She'd had the most amazing trip, but it still felt good to be home, even if she'd only be here a week. She went next door to retrieve Master from the neighbor who'd been feeding him while she was gone, laughing as he lunged at her fingers through the glass while she carried him to his spot on the shelf in her bedroom.

The next week was a whirlwind of movie preparation.

Piper spent countless hours working with her trainer, relieved that her hikes and daily jogs in the mountains had done a good job of preparing her. She got her hair done— just a trim and some highlights due to her *Defense* contract —and spent a day at the spa being waxed and plucked and polished to perfection.

And then it was time to return Master to her neighbor. She flew to LA for a whirlwind forty-eight hours of production meetings before she crossed the country again, this time landing in Boston.

She'd be staying with her family this week, and she was really looking forward to the chance to spend time with them, but she'd failed to take her nerves into account. Because as she sat in the backseat of her parents' car on the way home from Logan Airport, she was about two breaths away from another panic attack. Tomorrow, she'd be filming on a subway platform, and not only that, she'd be doing it for her first big-budget Hollywood film. If she fucked this up, the consequences could be devastating for her career.

She should have spent the last month in Boston riding the subway every damn day until she'd worked out all her kinks, but even so, she couldn't bring herself to regret the time she'd spent in North Carolina with Chloe.

"Tell us more about Chloe," her mom said from the front seat, turning to look at Piper.

She closed her eyes for a moment, focusing on her mother's question. "She's wonderful. I can't wait to introduce you to her."

"It's a shame she couldn't come up with you this weekend."

"Yeah." Piper pressed her fingernails against her thighs, letting the sensation ground her. Right now, she would have given anything to have Chloe here beside her. "It's challenging, living in different states."

"I'm sure," her mom said. "How do you plan to make it work?"

Piper shrugged stiffly. "We're just taking it week by week for now. I think things will settle down after I shoot this movie."

"Three months is a long time not to see someone this soon into a relationship," her mom observed.

"Yeah." Piper held in another sigh. "Hopefully, we'll be able to squeeze in a few weekend visits."

Her father turned the car onto the road where she'd grown up, and Piper was hit with a wave of nostalgia. She really should have tried harder to find a way to bring Chloe with her this weekend. Her parents' house came into view, a two-story beige colonial. It hadn't changed a bit for as long as she could remember, one of the only constants in her life.

Inside, she took her suitcase upstairs to her old bedroom, and then she joined her parents in the living room. Her younger brother James wandered into the room wearing artfully ripped jeans with a Rolling Stones T-shirt, his hair gelled within an inch of its life and cell phone in hand. He was *such* a teenager. It made her want to roll her eyes at him and hug him at the same time, because he looked so much more grown up than he had the last time she saw him.

"Hey, weirdo," she said affectionately.

He shot her an amused glance. "Hey, movie star."

"Missed your face." She drew him in for a quick hug.

He patted her back awkwardly before pulling away. "Yeah, I guess I did too."

Teenagers, man. She smiled at him. "What have you been up to?"

He shrugged. "Dad wants me to get a job, but I really just want to enjoy summer break, you know?"

"Well, if you want any spending money for the summer, you should look into that job," she told him. "I bet Scoops is looking for summer help, and you get free ice cream. It's a win-win. Plus, I happen to know that a lot of hot girls stop in over the summer."

He laughed. "Yeah, maybe."

"Decide on a major yet?"

He shrugged again. Her parents were having a fit that he'd finished his freshman year of college without deciding what he was studying, but Piper hadn't even gone to college, so she could hardly judge him for having trouble making up his mind. She'd been rebellious as hell as a teenager, confused about her sexuality or what she wanted out of life. Acting had been her emotional outlet, and sometimes she still couldn't believe she'd managed to turn it into a successful career.

"You should come visit me at the end of the summer, once I'm back in New York," she told James. "Explore the city. Maybe it'll inspire you."

"Yeah, that sounds cool."

"Great."

She went into the kitchen to help her mom with dinner, annoyed to see the chicken roasting in the oven. Yes, she'd initially become a vegetarian as a way of rebelling against her parents, but it was an important part of her lifestyle now, so it was frustrating when her mom still acted like it was a teenage whim.

"I've got a tofu dish as a side," her mom said. "And bread."

"That's fine," Piper told her. Her trainer had her on a strict diet this week anyway, but she wished her mom didn't always relegate her to a side dish. Would it have been so hard to cook a meatless meal tonight, the way Chloe's mom had done?

Briefly, she remembered the horrified looks on her parents' faces when she'd dyed her hair jet black her sophomore year of high school. She'd gone through a bit of a goth phase, which had probably inspired the wig she used as her disguise these days.

Sparing one last glance at the chicken in the oven, Piper blew out a breath and pushed it aside. She was letting her anxiety color her mood. Her parents might be staunch meat-lovers, but they'd always supported her, both in her career and when she'd come out, so she would eat her side dish and shut up about it.

After dinner, she excused herself and went to bed early. Tomorrow was going to be a *long* day and a stressful one.

As it turned out, though, she lay awake most of the night, tossing and turning, despite the sleeping pill she'd taken. She arrived at the studio's production trailer at eight the next morning for a meeting with the director, producer, and her costars, already feeling brittle and depleted, but determined not to let this day get the best of her.

By lunchtime, Piper was in the hair and makeup trailer, watching in fascination as the stylist transformed her hair into a mass of wild curls. She'd never gone this curly before, and she kind of loved it. Her spirits had rebounded by the time she left the trailer, buoyed by her new look and the positive attitudes of the other cast and crew.

She and Landon took a car across town to the out-of-service subway station where they'd be filming that afternoon. She rubbed her palms back and forth over the textured skirt the wardrobe department had dressed her in, trying to keep herself calm.

"Been to Boston before?" Landon asked beside her.

"I grew up here, actually. My parents still live in Concord."

"No shit, really?" He turned the full force of that million-dollar smile on her.

"Really," she confirmed. "A lucky coincidence, since I was overdue for a visit."

"Guess I don't have to ask where you're staying this week," he commented.

"Nope. And where are you from?"

"Toronto," he told her.

Now that he mentioned it, she did remember that he was Canadian. "Even colder than Boston."

"Great skiing, though."

They chatted the rest of the way to the station in Cambridge, which helped distract her from what she was about to do. All too soon, though, she was descending the steps to the platform. She'd successfully ridden the subway in New York about a dozen times now, and today she didn't even have to board a train. She just had to stand down here and film a scene. The only other people on the platform would be extras, paid to stand on their marks. No one was going to jump. She could do this.

Except she couldn't. Once she arrived at the platform, she had to stand around for almost an hour while the crew made last-minute adjustments, and her composure unraveled a little bit more with each passing minute. She stood there with a half dozen industrial lights aimed at her, illuminating all her fears, burning all the way to her soul. As the director finally counted her down, her lungs quit working. Her heart beat desperately in her chest, and spots danced across her vision. Air. She needed air. It was so hot down here, and she couldn't breathe.

"And...rolling!"

Piper looked toward the tracks. Any moment now, the train would slide into the station, and Landon would disembark. Her lungs screamed for oxygen, but she couldn't inhale, couldn't move, couldn't breathe. Sweat dampened her skin. Her head swam.

And then everything went black.

21

Chloe shrieked as she slammed her toe into the corner of the coffee table. She dropped onto the couch and grabbed her cell phone, which was flashing Piper's name. In her haste to get to it in time, she'd nearly sacrificed her poor pinky toe, which was now throbbing like hell. "Hey," she answered breathlessly as she connected the call.

"Hi," Piper said in her ear.

"How was it?" Chloe asked. Today had been Piper's first day on set, and she'd had to film a scene on a subway platform. Chloe had been thinking about her all day, hoping and praying everything had gone well. There was a faint sound on the other end of the line that sounded alarmingly like a muffled sob. Chloe's stomach plummeted. "Piper..."

"It's okay," Piper said, but her voice wobbled, and she was definitely crying. "I got through it."

"Oh good," Chloe said, pressing a hand against her chest. "Tell me everything, I mean, unless you'd rather not talk about it."

Piper was silent for several long seconds, probably

trying to get herself together, and it was killing Chloe that she couldn't reach out and hug her, couldn't wipe away her tears and help her through what had obviously been a difficult day. "Will you tell me about your day first?" Piper asked finally.

"Yeah, of course." Chloe rubbed at her sore toe. "I had an interview today, my first one for an interior design job, and I don't think it went very well."

"Why do you think that?" Piper asked, sniffling quietly.

"They were looking for someone with five to ten years of experience, which I obviously don't have. The woman who interviewed me goes to church with my mom, so I think Mom may have called in a favor for me."

"Sometimes all you need is to get your foot in the door for someone to realize you're the right person, regardless of your work experience," Piper said.

"Well, maybe, but I got a definite snooty vibe while I was there, like they were humoring me for my mom's sake, so we'll see what happens." She paused, and when Piper didn't say anything, she kept talking. "After my interview, I picked up Cait from school and took her for ice cream. And I may have broken my toe on my way to answer the phone just now."

"What?" Piper asked. "How?"

"Ran into the coffee table. I'm a klutz, what can I say?"

"I miss you," Piper whispered, and she sounded so sad, Chloe felt tears welling in her own eyes.

"I miss you too. First days are hard, Piper. Tomorrow will be better."

"I hope so." Piper sighed into the phone. "Literally the first scene we shot today was in the subway, and it just fucked me up more than I'd anticipated."

"I'm sorry," Chloe said, hugging her knees, wishing fiercely she was hugging Piper instead.

"I had a full-blown panic attack in front of the whole cast and crew." Piper's voice broke, and she sucked in a shuddering breath. "The director was trying to be understanding, but he was definitely frustrated with me. I was so embarrassed, and then they had to redo my hair and makeup because I'd gotten so sweaty, and I just…"

The sound of her tears was too much for Chloe to bear. Her own tears broke free, sliding over her cheeks. "Oh honey, I'm so sorry."

"Anyway, I delayed production and made a terrible impression on my first day, so yay me," Piper said bitterly. "But we did get through the scene eventually."

"I'm so proud of you for sticking it out."

"I just…I don't want to be labeled difficult."

"Surely the director didn't think you were being a diva," Chloe said, hoping it was true.

"I don't think he did, but I *was* difficult today. It's hard enough in this industry as a woman, especially a queer woman, and…I'm just disappointed in myself. It's not how I wanted my first day on set to go."

"I know it isn't," Chloe said. "But the important thing is that you got through the scene, and tomorrow can only get better, right?"

"Right," Piper repeated, her voice hushed, but she didn't sound like she was crying anymore. "We're filming on the street tomorrow, so that should be easier."

"Yes," Chloe said. "Maybe it was for the best that you got the hardest scene out of the way first, rather than having it hanging over your head."

"Well, we do have to film on the subway platform again later this week, but I have a few days to prepare. If it's not too late when we finish filming tomorrow, I should probably spend some time in the subway on my own."

"If you think it would help, but sleep is important too," Chloe reminded her.

"So is talking to you," Piper said, and *poof*, Chloe's heart turned to gooey mush inside her chest.

"I'm so glad you called." They'd barely talked since Piper left North Carolina over a week ago, and Chloe was already pretty sad about it. Hopefully, once Piper settled into hew new routine on set, they'd be able to talk more often.

"Just needed to hear your voice before I went to bed," Piper said.

"You must be exhausted."

"I didn't sleep much last night," Piper admitted.

"I won't keep you, then," Chloe said. "Call me again tomorrow if you can, okay?"

"Mm," Piper agreed.

"I'm working from four to eleven, so if I miss you, leave me a message so I can at least hear your voice."

"Yeah," Piper said. "Night, Chloe. I love you."

"Love you too." Chloe ended the call and sat for a minute in her living room, just staring at the phone in her hands. She missed Piper so much. She wanted to be there with her on these hard days. Hell, she wanted to be with her *every* day, even if that was impossible given Piper's career. Even if Chloe moved to New York, Piper would still be away for months at the time on location shoots. And Chloe couldn't leave North Carolina. It was her home and the heart of her family.

Before she knew it, she was crying again. The only time she could remember feeling something similar to this was when Cassie dropped out of college. When it came down to it, Chloe wasn't very good at being away from the people she loved. And she feared loving Piper from afar was slowly going to break her heart. Would it ever be enough?

With a sigh, she dried her tears and went down the hall to her bedroom, limping on her sore toe. That was going to be a bitch tomorrow when she had to wait tables all evening. She wasn't quite ready for bed, so she changed into her pajamas and curled up with a book, hoping Piper was already soundly asleep and that she had a better day tomorrow.

But as it turned out, Chloe didn't hear from her the next day, at least not before she had to be at work, and she had to leave her phone in her purse in back while she was waiting tables. She was working at the tavern downtown now, which meant longer shifts and better tips. It was enough to pay her bills, and that would do for now. She worked her whole shift with Piper at the back of her mind, wondering how she was and how her second day on set had gone.

When she finally got off that night, she forced herself to walk out to her car before she pulled her phone out of her purse. There were no missed calls, but she did have a text message, sent an hour ago.

Sorry I missed you. I'm going straight to bed again. Talk soon. xx.

Chloe swallowed her disappointment over not getting to hear Piper's voice. She hadn't said that today was better, but hopefully it had been. Chloe started her car and drove home, using that time to convince herself not to call Piper. She'd said she was going straight to bed, and it would be selfish of Chloe to wake her, no matter how badly she wanted to hear her voice.

At home, she sent Piper a quick text instead.

Hope today was better. Call me tomorrow, no matter what time. Love you!

And then, she queued up an episode of *In Her Defense* on her TV, hoping it would help her to feel closer to Piper.

∼

PIPER ARRIVED in Los Angeles feeling like a hollowed-out shell of a person. Last week in Boston had been brutal. Her confidence had been shaken that first day on set, and she'd let it throw her off her game for the rest of the week. Hopefully, her anxiety wouldn't show during those scenes in the finished movie. The hours had been long, and the work had been hard—especially the scenes on the subway platform—but she'd done it.

She'd developed a rapport with the director and with Landon, and her time in LA was going to be a fresh start. Working on a soundstage on the studio lot wouldn't be that different from her work at *In Her Defense*.

"At least I hope so," she muttered to herself as she walked to the window of her new apartment in West Hollywood. Too bad she hadn't decided to spend the extra money on a rental within walking distance of the beach. If she went out now, she'd be on a busy street full of people who would recognize her. This was Hollywood, for crying out loud. Celebrity spotting was like a professional sport out here, not to mention the paparazzi.

Up until now, she'd flown mostly under their radar. There weren't many professional paparazzi in New York, and they didn't tend to bother with television stars. There had been a bit of a flap when she came out, but that was old news now. This movie was going to change things for her, though.

In fact, she'd already noticed an uptick in the celebrity gossip stories about her. Jane sent her the more interesting ones, things she should be aware of. She'd seen several photos of her and her "mystery blonde," both in New York and in the Caymans. And there were already photos circulating of Piper filming scenes from *Tempted* in Boston.

Rather than pace her apartment until she gave herself another panic attack, she dialed Chloe. It was just past noon on Tuesday, and hopefully, she hadn't left for work yet.

"Oh my God," Chloe said in lieu of hello. "I can't believe you finally caught me."

"Took the red-eye from Boston to LA last night, but I don't have to be on set until later this afternoon," Piper told her. "And hi."

"Hi," Chloe said, and Piper could hear the smile in her voice. "You took the red-eye last night, and you still have to work today?"

"Just for a few hours...hopefully." She was tired, so fucking tired, but she'd known it would be like this. Hollywood moved at a frenzied pace. It always had, and it always would.

"It's so good to hear your voice," Chloe said. "How are you?"

"I'm okay," Piper said, remembering with a pang what a mess she'd been the last time she and Chloe spoke on the phone. "Last week was really hard, but the rest of the shoot should be easier, at least anxiety-wise. The hours will be long, but it's just work."

"I'm glad," Chloe said. "How's Landon?"

"He's great, actually. Really professional and hardworking, which is a nice surprise. You never know about these Hollywood types," she said with a laugh.

"Hey, *you're* a Hollywood type now too," Chloe teased. "Hopefully, your head won't have grown by the time I see you next."

"I'll be exactly the same."

"Just don't forget about your small-town girlfriend." Chloe said it jokingly, but Piper heard something vulnerable in her tone.

"Not a chance," she said. "On the contrary, I'm going to hassle you until you agree to let me fly you out here for a weekend, because now that I've seen my schedule, I don't think there's going to be time for me to fly to you."

"We'll see," Chloe said, but it sounded like a no. "I'm working weekends now, and I can't afford to lose those hours."

"It's only three months, Chloe," Piper said, even as she felt a pang in her heart at the thought of spending so long apart. "I'll still be yours at the end of it, as long as you're willing to wait for me."

"You know I am," Chloe said.

They talked for a few more minutes before Piper ended the call to get ready for work. Exhaustion was starting to set in, because of course she hadn't slept on her red-eye flight, so she brewed a pot of coffee and hopped in the shower in an attempt to revive herself.

Two hours later, she arrived on set. Her first stop was her own trailer, where she dropped off her things. It was fancier than her dressing room in New York, but she was in Hollywood now. She stretched out on the overstuffed couch and snapped a silly selfie, which she sent to Chloe. There was a small bedroom in back, which didn't bode well for her upcoming schedule. It meant she'd be crashing here between shoots when there wasn't time to go back to her apartment to sleep.

The fridge and pantry in the kitchenette were well stocked, and she grabbed a bottle of water before consulting the map of the soundstage on her phone so she could find her way to the hair and makeup trailer. She introduced herself to the team and settled in for them to sculpt her hair into Tara's signature curls using continuity photos sent by the team in Boston.

An hour later, she walked onto the set, exhausted but firmly in control of her emotions. It was time to repair the crew's initial impression of her and prove she had what it took to make it in Hollywood.

22

Chloe sat with her phone in one hand, beer in the other, trying hard not to cry as she stared at the photo on the screen. Piper and her costar Landon Wilkes had been photographed dining together at a fancy restaurant in Hollywood with the caption, *More than costars?* The accompanying article documented their romantic evening and included a few other grainy photos of Piper and Landon around town, purporting to show a budding romance.

It wasn't true. Chloe knew Piper wasn't sleeping with her costar, but the photos hurt. Piper had been in LA for a month now, and while she and Chloe still texted every day, they were usually only able to chat or FaceTime on the weekends.

During those conversations, Piper talked about her long hours and apologized for not being around more, but there was a sun kissed glow to her skin that brought to mind the way she'd looked during their weekend in the Caymans. Why did Piper have time to sunbathe but not to call her girl-friend? And those photos...

It wasn't just the photos of Piper with Landon either. There seemed to be an endless supply of paparazzi pictures of Piper lately, all dressed up at fancy events or hanging out with her famous friends. And for whatever reason, they made Chloe feel very small. They made her feel left out, and she hated that feeling.

She didn't know *that* Piper, the Piper who walked red carpets and hung out with celebrities. Piper had promised she'd still be the same person after she finished filming this movie, but what if she'd been wrong? While Chloe sat in her little house in the mountains pining over her, Piper was in Hollywood doing God knew what with God knew who.

And yes, Chloe knew she was being petty and irrational. She hated herself for it. But she couldn't help how she felt, not when she was sitting home alone on a Friday night, looking at photos of her girlfriend with another man. Blinking away her tears, Chloe swiped the photo off her screen and dialed Piper, hoping against hope that she might actually catch her this time.

But, as usual, the line rang unanswered until it went through to Piper's voicemail.

~

PIPER WAS SO TIRED, her bones hurt. She often worked sixteen-hour days during the week, sometimes crashing on the bed in her trailer, too tired to make it home before her call time the next morning. But despite her rather disastrous start in Boston, she'd settled into her role now and became more comfortable as Tara each day.

Landon had been a big help. He was funny and easy to work with, and they'd even gone out for a couple of meals together at the request of their publicists, looking to generate buzz for the film and its stars.

Saturdays were Piper's only real day off, and she often spent them walking the quieter stretches of the coastline or hiking in the Hollywood Hills. On Saturday nights, she caught up with some of her friends in the area, going out to eat at flashy places to give the paparazzi a chance to photograph them. This was all part of the Hollywood game, and she only had to play it for a few months before she could go back to New York…and to Chloe.

Piper's publicist had put together a comprehensive plan to elevate her status and visibility as she looked ahead to the premiere of *Defense*'s fifth season and her big screen debut. It meant she'd have to get used to a lot more publicity over the next year or so, events and interviews and appearances on primetime talk shows, but she was ready for the challenge.

Her Sundays were spent preparing for the upcoming week of filming. She had a *lot* of new lines to learn each week, but it was nothing she couldn't handle. Everything was going well, except her relationship with Chloe. They were still struggling to sync their schedules, and Piper could tell that Chloe was upset about it, although she didn't know how to make it better. Chloe worked all weekend, and Piper was working every waking minute during the week.

As June became July, Piper was missing her more than ever. She was about a third of the way through filming, which meant it felt like she'd been in LA forever, but it also still felt like forever until she got to go home.

That Sunday morning, she lay in bed with her script and her phone, hoping to catch Chloe before she left for work. Between the time difference and Piper's desperate need to catch up on her sleep during the weekends, she sometimes didn't wake before Chloe started her shift at the tavern.

"Morning," Piper said when the line connected, already smiling in anticipation of talking to her.

"Speak for yourself," Chloe said in a teasing tone. "I've already had lunch."

"Yeah, yeah, you're three hours ahead of me. How are you?"

"Lonely," Chloe said, suddenly serious.

"Me too," Piper said with a sigh, snuggling deeper into the covers.

"You don't *look* very lonely," Chloe said carefully.

Piper frowned. "What's that supposed to mean?"

"Nothing. Sorry, I'm just in a pissy mood today."

"Chloe..."

"It just seems like you're always out with Landon and all these other famous people, and yet you never seem to have time for *me*." Chloe's voice grew muffled at the end, as if she'd buried her face against her sleeve, or maybe a pillow.

Piper sat up in bed, staring blankly at the script in her lap for a moment of shocked silence. Of all the things she'd expected Chloe to say...

"I know that's unfair of me, so just forget I said it, okay?" Chloe said quietly.

"Well, I can hardly forget it now that you've said it." It came out harsher than she'd meant for it to, but seriously, what the hell, Chloe? "I'm working my ass off out here, and you're upset that I went out to dinner with friends a couple of times?"

"I'm sorry," Chloe mumbled.

Piper climbed out of bed, pacing the room while she tried to figure out how to respond. Without warning, tears sprang to her eyes. "Chloe, talk to me. What the hell is going on?"

23

Choe pressed a hand over her eyes, blinking back tears. Piper sounded angry, and worse...hurt, and Chloe hadn't meant to cause either. Why hadn't she kept her stupid mouth shut? Or better yet, why hadn't she learned to control herself and stop googling Piper's name to see what she was up to out in Hollywood?

But she'd started this conversation, and now she was going to have to finish it. She blew out a breath. "It sounds petty now that I've said it out loud, but it just feels like every time I look online, there are more photos of you, and that one article said maybe you and Landon were starting an off-screen romance, and—"

"Chloe!" Piper's voice hit a note Chloe had never heard before, and she wished immediately that she never had. "What the fuck are you accusing me of?"

"Nothing, I'm not...I know you aren't sleeping with him," Chloe said, waving a hand in front of her face as if Piper were there in the room with her. "It just feels like you're out there partying in Hollywood with all your famous friends, and I'm here watching from the sidelines and wishing you would call me."

"Well," Piper said, and her voice sounded harsh, but not in a mean way, more like she was trying not to cry. "I guess we have a problem."

"We do?" Chloe hugged herself miserably.

"Chloe, I'm working about eighty hours a week on set, and I am so tired, I can hardly see straight, but I haven't complained about it, because this movie is my *dream*. I've been working up to this moment my whole life, and I have to do the publicity that comes along with it, even if it means going out and being photographed when I'd rather be sleeping. I'm sorry if you read something that said I'm dating Landon. I don't have time to read the headlines, and I...I thought you trusted me." Her voice cracked at the end, and Chloe wanted to die.

"I do trust you." She swiped furiously at her tears. "I'm sorry, Piper. I didn't mean to fight with you."

"I don't want to fight with you either." Piper sighed into the phone. "But I'm also not going to apologize for catching up with a few of my friends while I'm in LA. I hate that you and I haven't been able to talk more often, but I'm only home on the weekends, and that's when you're at work. It sucks, but it's only for a few months. I don't know what else to say."

"I hate this whole conversation," Chloe admitted. "I'm so sorry I got weird and jealous. I just miss you."

"I miss you too," Piper said quietly. "Can you take a weekend off and come visit me? Then the paparazzi photos can be of you and me."

Chloe pressed a hand over her eyes, shaking her head in her empty living room. "I can't afford to take a weekend off yet. That's where I earn most of my tips."

"And I can't manage a trip to North Carolina right now, Chloe, I—"

"Stop," Chloe said. "I know you can't. We'll see each other after you wrap filming, okay? I'm really sorry for ruining this phone call. Let's start over. Tell me about your week."

"Well, it was exhausting, but we got a lot done. The sex scene wasn't bad at all, not that you probably want to hear about it." There was still some bite in Piper's tone. Chloe had hurt her feelings, and she felt awful about it. "I was covered by a sheet the whole time, and Landon was super respectful."

"I'm glad," Chloe said.

"I had dinner with a couple of friends yesterday, but I feel like you already know about that. I won't tell you not to cyberstalk me, because I have nothing to hide, but you need to make sure you're doing it for the right reasons."

"You're right. It's obviously making me weird and petty. I should stop."

"That's up to you," Piper said. "But you can't use it to guilt me like this. It's not fair."

"I know it's not." She'd been out with her own friends plenty of times over the last month, probably more often than Piper had, but no one had written about it in the gossip pages. She was being an asshole. "I'm really sorry."

They talked for a few more minutes, and when they hung up, everything was ostensibly fine between them, but Chloe had a nagging feeling it wasn't. She needed to get a grip before she ruined their relationship. Piper was doing the best she could, working a million hours while dealing with anxiety and panic attacks, and Chloe had just bitten her head off for no reason.

And as the week progressed, it became obvious the

damage she'd caused. Piper texted less often, and while they usually exchanged at least a few missed calls during the week in an attempt to catch each other, that week Piper didn't call.

Chloe reined in her cyberstalking, but by the following weekend, her curiosity had gotten the better of her. She searched Piper's name and found...nothing. She hadn't been photographed in public a single time all week.

Dammit.

This was Chloe's fault. She picked up her phone and dialed, hoping to catch Piper at home since it was Sunday.

"Hi," Piper answered just when Chloe had decided the call was going to go to voicemail.

"Hi. How are you?"

"Tired," Piper said with a sigh. "We did a location shoot yesterday that didn't wrap until after midnight."

"On a Saturday?" Maybe Chloe had been reading things into Piper's silence that weren't there.

"Yeah. We needed to shoot a scene in an office building, and it's occupied during the week. Anyway, it went well, just long. How are you?"

"Still waiting tables and missing you."

"No leads on an interior design job yet?" Piper asked. There was a rustling sound as if she'd just snuggled into bed with her phone.

"Nothing," Chloe answered. "It's been harder than I expected. I guess not as many people hire interior decorators out here in my little town as I thought, or at least, no one wants to take a chance on the new girl."

"Well, that sucks," Piper said quietly. "I'm sorry. I hope something comes along for you soon."

"So do I."

But as she ended the call a few minutes later, she realized her job situation was part of the problem. She'd given up an exciting job she loved to wait tables, and right now, it was keeping her from seeing Piper. If she had an interior design job—or any job with regular hours—she would probably have been able to fly out and visit her for the weekend. At the very least, she'd be less frustrated with her life so that she didn't take out her unhappiness on Piper.

With a sigh, she got off the couch and got ready for work. She served food for the next eight hours, keeping a cheerful smile firmly in place, determined not to let her frustration with her current situation affect her tips.

The next morning, she spent several hours potting colorful flowers in the hanging boxes on her house. Mondays were her day off, and she cherished the chance to be outside. After lunch, she changed and went for a hike, hoping it would help her burn some restless energy. Without deciding on her destination ahead of time, she wasn't surprised to find herself hiking toward the waterfall where she'd taken Piper.

She took the hidden path to the rocky hilltop where they'd shared their picnic. As she sat there, staring out at the mountains and the waterfall below, she felt a sudden clarity. Maybe interior design should wait. If she expanded her search, surely there was a nine-to-five job out there that she was qualified for, because working nights and weekends at the tavern was never going to allow her to see Piper.

She could keep hunting for an interior design position, even if she took another office job in the meantime. It was just a steppingstone on her path. In fact, maybe her recent struggles with Piper were part of the same journey. Chloe had never been in love before. Everything about a serious relationship was new to her, including the hard parts, like jealousy and geography.

She was learning. She was growing. And she was going to find a way forward with Piper. Feeling much better, she stood and shimmied down the rock. She hiked back to her car and drove home for a shower before she headed to her parents' for dinner.

Cait was waiting at the front door to whisk her upstairs to play with Oreo until dinner was ready, and Chloe had to admit, she was getting pretty fond of the furry critter. And she was so glad to be here with her niece. Her waitressing job at the tavern was also keeping her from seeing Cait as much as she wanted to, which was all the more reason to look harder for something new.

After dinner, she sat in the living room with her mom while her dad and Cait went outside to look at fireflies.

"How are you, Chloe?" her mom asked. "You seem sad lately, and I'm just wondering if things haven't worked out quite the way you wanted them to."

"They haven't," Chloe admitted. "But I think I figured out a way to make it a little better. I need to expand my job search beyond interior design. I could be a receptionist or something, anything with regular weekday hours so I'll be around for Cait more and able to take a weekend to fly out and see Piper. This waitressing job is killing my social life."

"That's one option," her mom observed.

"You have a better idea?" Chloe asked. "Because I'm all ears."

"Tell me this," her mom said. "If you took me and your dad and Cait out of the equation, what would you want, and where would you be living right now?"

"Well, that's an impossible question," Chloe said. "Because you *are* in the equation, and I want to be near you."

"I don't know what it's like to lose a twin, Chloe. I do

know what it's like to lose a daughter, and I know that for a long time after Cassie died, I held on to you and Cait a little tighter than I probably should have to compensate for missing her."

"Mom..." Chloe's voice wobbled. Where was this coming from?

Her mom's eyes were glossy, but her voice was steady. "I worried so much about how you would manage without her, because you and Cassie were two halves of a whole, but you seemed to get by as well as any of us did. I know you started working as a flight attendant because it was what you and Cassie had planned to do together. She was so adamant that you carry on with the plan after she had Cait, and you went along with it. But I'm not sure any of us ever asked you what *you* wanted, Chloe."

"I wanted to be a flight attendant," Chloe said, fingers twisting in her lap.

"Did you really? Or were you just living Cassie's dream?"

"I...I don't know, but I did love that job, Mom."

"And then you gave it up because you decided you needed to be here for Cait."

"That's not the only reason," Chloe said, tears blurring her vision, and where was her mom even going with this conversation? She was confused and emotional, and she just wanted to go home and cry.

"I think you've always tried so hard to be what Cassie wanted you to be, and after she died, you transferred that devotion to Cait. But you can't live your life for someone else, Chloe. You need to go after what *you* want for once."

"I want to be here with you guys," Chloe said, swiping at her eyes. "I want to live in my little house and help decorate other people's houses and have Cait for sleepovers on the weekends."

"And what about Piper?"

"I want to be with her too. I'm miserable without her, as you've probably noticed, but I don't know how to make it all work. I've tried, and I've tried, and I just can't figure it out."

"Oh sweetie, come here." Her mom moved to sit next to her on the couch, wrapping an arm around her.

Chloe snuggled against her like she'd done when she was a little girl, tears streaming over her cheeks. "I'm afraid we'll only ever have a long-distance relationship, and I'm afraid that'll never be enough for me and eventually it'll ruin everything."

"And that's why I think you should quit your waitressing job and go to her. Live for yourself for once. There are so many more interior design jobs in the city than there are out here in the middle of nowhere. Go."

"But I live *here*," Chloe protested. "I bought a house. I promised Cait..."

"Sweetie, Cait will be fine, and your girlfriend is rich. Keep your house, and you two can stay in it when you visit. In fact, we'll expect you to visit a lot, but you should live in New York with Piper. Dream big. Go get your girl."

24

P iper accepted the flower arrangement the awkward teenager on her doorstep held toward her. She thanked him before stepping backward into her apartment so she could close and lock the door behind her. The flowers were lovely, an arrangement of what looked like wildflowers in a variety of bright colors. She didn't have to look at the card to know who'd sent them. She should be *thrilled* to get flowers from her girlfriend, but...

A tender place in her heart was still hurt by the way Chloe had acted last week. These flowers felt like an apology, and she hated that she needed one. She hated that Chloe was jealous of her life in Hollywood, but she was doing her best to move past it. Hopefully, they'd find their rhythm with this new chapter in their relationship. And the flowers were nice. They were lovely, actually.

Piper carried them to the kitchen table and plucked the card attached to the vase.

Miss you. Love you. See you soon. ~ Chloe

Soon was a relative term. Piper had six long weeks left in California, and then she would fly straight to New York for scheduled meetings with her agent and publicist. Maybe Chloe could at least meet her there, and then Piper could fly back to North Carolina with her for a little while before she returned to the *Defense* set at the end of October.

She sighed, dipping her head to inhale the sweet scent of the flowers. They brought to mind afternoon hikes in the mountains, peace and happiness so complete she'd never wanted it to end. Would they be able to recapture it?

Piper sent a quick text to thank her for the flowers, and then she got dressed to drive to the set. This film had taken a lot out of her. It had been weeks since she had a panic attack, but she was living in a constant state of lowkey stress that, combined with her long hours, had left her more tired than she'd ever been in her life.

Once she arrived at the lot, she headed to the hair and makeup trailer to have Tara's curls done, and then she slipped into the little red sundress she'd be wearing today. This morning, they'd be filming several scenes on an outdoor section of the lot that had been designed to look like a park, complete with flower beds and decorative benches.

It was hot today, and by the time the director called "Rolling!" on their first take, she was already sweating. She and Landon strolled through the park, exchanging flirtatious banter before an extra released a little white dog that charged toward her. Tara had an irrational fear of dogs, so Piper dodged to the side, almost falling into the fountain. At the last moment, Landon steadied her with an arm around her waist, pulling her in for what would be their characters' first onscreen kiss.

"And...cut."

She took a step back, bending to adjust the strap on her right heel, which was digging into her skin. Immediately, she and Landon were surrounded by stylists, adjusting their clothes, blotting away sweat, and reapplying makeup. Piper also needed frequent spritzes of sunblock to keep her from turning as red as her dress.

They filmed the scene twice more, but the dog had a mind of his own and kept running up to Landon instead of Piper, making her near-fall seem improbable. Consequently, for the fourth take, she held a dog biscuit discreetly tucked against her left palm. The trainer let the dog sniff her hand to discover this fun fact before the extra walked him to the far side of the park.

The crew called out their marks. "...and we're rolling."

Piper strolled beside Landon, and on cue, the little dog came charging right at her. She squealed in fear as she jumped sideways, left heel squarely on her mark. The dog planted his front paws on her dress and yipped, and she tumbled backward.

"Tara!" Landon lunged for her, but the dog dashed between his feet. Landon tripped, dropping to his knees.

For a moment, Piper was too stunned to react. By the time she'd realized he wasn't going to catch her, it was too late to catch herself. She plunged into the fountain, smacking hard against the concrete bottom of the pool. The cold shock of the water combined with the impact of her fall jarred her back to her senses, and she scrambled to sit up, surfacing with a gasp.

"Dammit." Landon was halfway into the fountain, one hand extended toward her. "Piper, I'm so sorry. Are you okay?"

She was sitting in chest-deep water, her vision obscured by soggy curls of her hair. Her back was on fire, and her lungs weren't working right. It almost felt like a panic attack, but this was different. She swiped hair out of her face. "Got the wind knocked out of me," she managed, pressing a hand against her chest as she waited for the sensation to pass.

Within moments, she was surrounded by a crowd of concerned cast and crew, hovering over her where she sat. Landon helped her to her feet, and she climbed out of the fountain.

"I'm fine," she said, attempting to ward off the crowd as she caught her breath.

Landon rested a hand against her back, and she winced at the contact. His eyes narrowed in concern. "You fell pretty hard. You should get checked out."

"Just bruised," she said. "Really."

"He's right, Piper," Sydney, the director, said. "You should go to the medical trailer. We'll resume filming after they've cleared you. Damn dog," he muttered. "This is exactly why I hate working with animals."

"I'll walk you," Landon offered, one hand resting lightly on her shoulder. "God, I'm so sorry. I can't believe I dropped you like that."

"Not your fault," she told him with a small smile as they walked across the lot toward the medical trailer. "Blame it on the dog."

Her feet slipped inside her sandals as she walked. She was dripping wet from head to foot. She'd have to change and have her hair and makeup redone before they could resume filming. It could take hours. *Ugh.* Her back throbbed, and now that the shock had worn off, she realized she'd hit the back of her head too. It was going to be a long day.

~

CHLOE HAD BOOKED this flight on purpose, because it allowed her to fly with Nisha. Her friend winked at her as she pushed the drink cart past Chloe's seat. It was weird flying as a passenger, wearing jeans and a tee, for reasons that were solely her own. This would take some getting used to. When the plane touched down at Dallas/Fort Worth International Airport, she and Nisha hugged in the terminal before heading to their respective gates.

"Good luck," Nisha told her. "For the record, I think you're doing the right thing, and I am so insanely happy for you right now."

"Thanks," Chloe said. "I'll text you later, okay? And we still need to meet up for dinner the next time I'm home."

"Definitely to both." With a wave, Nisha was on her way, heels clicking over the polished floors.

Chloe turned in the opposite direction, sneakers squeaking as she made her way toward the gate where she'd board her flight to LA. Her stomach swooped as she spotted her destination illuminated on the screen.

I'm really doing this.

She'd spent days thinking over her mother's words, torn between the desire to throw caution to the wind as her mom had suggested and the need to stay the course. She'd just started this new chapter of her life in North Carolina. How could she even think of leaving?

And how could she forgive herself if she didn't?

So here she was, on her way to Hollywood, without a job and knowing exactly one person in the entire city. This was either one of the bravest or stupidest things she'd ever done, maybe both. Hopefully at the end of the day, brave would win out.

She waited, toe tapping nervously, for her flight to board. After enduring a delay that was only thirty minutes but felt more like thirty hours, she was finally on the plane and on her way. She'd been bored out of her mind on her first flight, having realized belatedly that she had no idea what to do on an airplane when she wasn't working, so this time she made sure to download an eBook onto her phone before she had to put it in airplane mode.

Then she attempted to pass the next three hours without going crazy with anticipation. Finally, the plane touched down in warm and sunny Los Angeles. Chloe had been here dozens of times, although she'd rarely left the airport. She certainly didn't know her way around Piper's probably fancy neighborhood, but that wasn't going to stop her.

Somehow, she'd decided that showing up unannounced was the way to do this, and it was too late to change her mind now. She went into the restroom to touch up her hair and makeup, and then she made her way outside, where she called an Uber to take her to Piper's address.

Here goes nothing...

Her stomach was a massive swarm of butterflies as she climbed into the Volkswagen sedan the app had summoned for her. The ride was longer than she'd anticipated, especially with LA traffic to contend with, and it was over an hour later when she finally arrived at a nondescript apartment building in West Hollywood.

She located the stairs leading to Piper's unit, grateful that it was accessible from the outside so she wouldn't have to call Piper to let her in. That would have been an anticlimactic way to announce her arrival. Piper's apartment was on the third floor, and as Chloe approached her door, adrenaline flooded her system. Her fingers shook as she lifted her hand to knock.

She tapped her knuckles against the door and then stood back to wait, but when she peeked through the window, Piper's apartment was swathed in darkness. It was past eight, which felt like eleven to Chloe. Was Piper still at work, or had she gone out?

Hoping her suitcase made her look like a visitor and not an intruder, Chloe sat on the top step to wait. If Piper hadn't come home by nine, Chloe might have to give up the element of surprise and call her. In the meantime, she sat and waited. And waited. At some point, she scooted backward to lean against Piper's front door, resting her head against the cool wood. She closed her eyes, lulled by the sounds of the city around her.

"Chloe?"

She jerked awake at the sound of Piper's voice, lurching to her feet almost before she'd opened her eyes, and then she blinked furiously at the woman in front of her. Piper's hair framed her face in a wild array of red curls. She wore a blue jumpsuit that showed off all her curves, and like... whoa, did she have all those curves before?

"Um, hi," Chloe stammered, grinning at her.

Piper smiled back, but there was something hesitant there, like she wasn't entirely sure why Chloe was here, and that was probably fair. Things had been a bit rocky between them since she started filming the movie, thanks to Chloe. Piper's makeup was different too. It was more exaggerated than Chloe was used to seeing, even when she was dressed as Sam. Beneath it, she looked tired. Really tired.

Chloe stepped forward, reaching out to touch her curls. "Crunchy," she said with a goofy laugh. Oh God, what was she doing right now?

Piper reached up and covered her hand, bringing it to her lips. "This is a surprise."

"I missed you," Chloe whispered, stepping closer.

Piper smelled the same, the feminine scent of her

perfume wrapping around Chloe like a welcome hug, enveloping her in a whirlwind of memories from Brooklyn to the Caymans to North Carolina and back again.

"Missed you too," Piper said quietly, pressing her lips against Chloe's. "Can't quite believe you're really here." She reached behind her and unlocked the door, motioning for Chloe to go inside. "Want to tell me *why* you're here?"

She stepped into the foyer of Piper's rental, sweeping a quick glance around the place before returning her attention to the woman she'd just crossed the country to see. "I quit my job at the tavern."

"What?" Piper's brow bunched adorably. "Did you find an interior design job?"

Chloe shook her head, fidgeting with her hands as Piper lingered a few feet away, waiting for Chloe to explain herself. "No. I think...I think I was focusing on the wrong things."

Piper crossed her arms over her chest. "How so?"

"Like trying to find a job in North Carolina when maybe that's not where I want to live," Chloe said, having lost the ability to think. All her carefully prepared words evaporated into the LA smog as she faced Piper, looking so glamorous and gorgeous and...vulnerable. Chloe wanted to sink her fingers deep in those auburn curls and kiss her for the rest of her life.

"But you just rearranged your whole life to live in North Carolina."

"I know, and it was a mistake," Chloe told her. "I've been miserable ever since, except for the two weeks you were with me. I miss traveling, but more than that, I miss *you*."

"I don't understand," Piper said, eyes glistening, bottom lip trembling. "You bought a house, and what about Cait?"

"Once my mom helped me sort out my priorities, Cait

was fully on board with me coming here. I'll still see her lots, and I'll be so much happier when I do."

"What exactly are you proposing?" Piper asked.

"Well, I'm not *proposing*," Chloe said, and then shook her head helplessly, because what the hell was she doing right now? A nervous laugh escaped her lips, and Piper was just staring at her like she'd lost her mind. "Remember when I visited you on set in Brooklyn?"

"Of course."

"I hung out with Monica from the props department, and she basically offered me a job as a set dresser if I ever moved to New York, which felt ludicrous at the time, but Piper, what if it isn't ludicrous at all? I don't know if she can actually get me a job, but I know I can find work in the city. There are a million more jobs there than in small-town North Carolina."

"Holy shit." Piper shoved a hand into her curls, pushing them back from her face.

"We'll live in Brooklyn and stay at my house in North Carolina when you're not working, and I don't know... I mean, is that what you want too? Because I definitely had a more organized speech planned, but I think you get the gist, so..."

Piper stepped forward then, eyes locked on Chloe's. She closed the gap between them, yanking Chloe against her for an all-consuming kiss. "Yeah, it's what I want. Fuck, Chloe, it's all I've wanted since the moment I met you."

"Oh," Chloe gasped, finally giving in to her need to bury her hands in Piper's hair.

Piper winced, moving Chloe's hands to her shoulders, but not before she'd felt the knot on the back of her skull.

"Jesus, Piper! Are you okay?"

"I took a pretty nasty fall on set earlier. Just bruises. I'm okay."

"Oh my God. What happened?"

"I fell in a fountain." Piper shook her head. "Long story. I'll tell you later, but...you're really here to stay?" Tears spilled over her eyelids.

"Yeah." Chloe pressed their lips together, sparks sizzling in her veins, her whole body coming alive now that she had Piper in her arms, and her mom was the smartest woman on the planet, because of course this was right. Of course this was where she was meant to be. "I'll waitress for a few weeks here in Hollywood and try to line up something more permanent by the time we get to New York."

"And your family?" Piper asked, her tear-streaked cheeks stained almost as pink as her lips.

"You have a few months before you're back at *In Her Defense*, right? Depending what I have going on jobwise, maybe we can stay at my house for a while this fall. We'll just bounce back and forth between New York and North Carolina, whatever makes sense."

"Yeah," Piper said, grinning through her tears. "I love that. I love *you*." She pressed closer, exhaling, and Chloe could swear she felt something leave Piper, like that metaphorical weight had been lifted from her shoulders. "It's so perfect, Chloe. We're going to be so happy."

"I think so too," Chloe said as her gaze caught on something on Piper's kitchen table. "Is that...a puzzle?"

Piper glanced over her shoulder. "Yeah. I'm absolute shit at it, and I was never going to finish on my own. It's a really good thing you're here to help."

Chloe looked at the pile of puzzle pieces on the table, realizing it was a mountain scene, and her heart grew almost too big to contain in her chest. "Oh my God, I love you so much."

Piper rested her forehead against Chloe's. "My head and back are killing me. We should really go out to celebrate, but...how do you feel about delivery?"

Chloe grinned, holding Piper gently, careful not to hurt her. "We'll go out another night. Right now, it sounds like what you really need is a back rub, and I want to hear everything about your day...starting with how you managed to fall into a fountain."

"Mm, back rub," Piper murmured. "Yes to all of that, but first, I want to make sure you know how hard I fell for *you*."

"**M**s. Carson, could I see you in my office please?"

Chloe stared at her phone for a moment in confusion because Piper didn't have an office on set, and why did she sound like...*oh*. "I'll be right there, Ms. Whitaker."

A tingle of anticipation spread through her belly as she hurried toward Piper's dressing room. They'd talked about making up for the time they'd been interrupted in their attempt at Sam Whitaker role play, the day Piper had been cast in *Tempted*, but they'd never gotten around to finishing the game.

And if that was what Piper had in mind tonight, then... fuck yeah, Chloe was on board. She was *so* on board. She rushed into the props office to close up for the night. For the last six months, she'd worked as a set dresser both here on the set of *In Her Defense* and next door where the studio filmed a teen drama, and honestly she loved her job so much that sometimes she still couldn't believe she was lucky enough to do this for a living.

She had a few interior design clients on the side, but as

it turned out, dressing sets was her true passion. She loved using her eye for design to help bring these characters to life, or at least, bringing to life the rooms they would inhabit on the show. Next month, *In Her Defense*—and the teen drama—would wrap for the season, and Piper and Chloe would spend their summer in North Carolina. Cait was going to stay with them for a whole month, and Chloe was so excited, she could hardly stand it.

It had been just over a year since their anonymous encounter at Dragonfly, the most crazy awesome whirlwind of a year. Piper had recently signed on for another movie, which she'd film at the end of the summer, and *Tempted* had been such a box office smash that she'd been able to triple her already impressive paycheck. If she'd been a star when Chloe first met her, she was a superstar now, and Chloe was so ridiculously proud of her.

After locking up the props department, she hurried toward Piper's dressing room. The door was closed, and while Chloe would usually go right in, given Piper's phone call, she stopped at the door and knocked. "Ms. Whitaker?" she called.

"Come in." It was Sam's voice, and the sound of it sent a delicious shiver down Chloe's spine. She'd met Piper first, but now she was a certified Sam Whitaker fan, and she was about to live out one of her hottest fantasies.

She pushed the door open to find Piper in a rose-colored skirt suit, leaned against the table with her arms crossed over her chest, her expression dialed to Sam at her most deadly. Chloe felt herself grow wet at the sight.

"You're late," Piper said.

"Sorry, Ms. Whitaker. I got here as quickly as I could." Chloe took a hesitant step forward, hiding her smile as Piper pushed off from the table to stand in front of her. Her white blouse had navy pin stripes, and it was distractingly pretty beneath that pink jacket, drawing Chloe's attention to the swell of Piper's breasts.

"Your performance today was unacceptable," Piper said icily, and Chloe really couldn't get enough of hearing Sam's voice come from her mouth. "I'm afraid I'll have to let you go."

"Isn't there anything I can do?" she asked, batting her lashes at Piper. "Can I beg for another chance?"

"Well..." Piper dragged her gaze from Chloe's mouth to her toes, lingering everywhere in between. "I suppose it never hurt to beg."

"Please, Ms. Whitaker," Chloe said, taking another step toward her. "I'll do anything you say."

"Anything?" Piper lifted one delicately plucked eyebrow.

"Anything," Chloe confirmed.

Piper reached down and began unfastening her jacket, releasing each button with a distinctive pop that made Chloe quiver with anticipation. The jacket gaped open, revealing more of that pin-striped blouse, and the black bra Piper wore beneath it.

"Just show me what to do," Chloe said breathlessly.

Piper reached out and took one of Chloe's hands, bringing it to her breast. Chloe felt Piper's nipple harden beneath the shell of her bra.

"If you want another chance, you're going to have to work for it," Piper said throatily. "Show me everything you've got."

Chloe traced her hand down the center of Piper's blouse all the way to the waistband of her skirt, and then she kept going, fingers trailing lightly over the silky fabric, watching as Piper pinched her bottom lip between her teeth, her cheeks getting pinker by the moment. "By the time I'm finished with you, you'll give me anything I ask for."

Piper gasped, hips arching into Chloe's touch. "That's probably true."

"Probably?" Chloe teased, momentarily losing the game.

And when she looked up, she saw Piper staring at her, not Sam. "I've been yours for the taking since the moment we met."

ACKNOWLEDGMENTS

First of all, a huge thank you to my family for putting up with me when I'm buried under deadlines. This year has been a challenging one, and I appreciate your support more than ever.

I am endlessly grateful to every reader, blogger, reviewer, and friend who has supported me along the way, whether it's by reading one of my books, leaving a review, following me on social media, or sending me a Tweet or an email. Your support means more to me than you could possibly know!

Thank you to my editor, Linda Ingmanson, for making this book shine. And as always, a huge thank you to my critique partner, Annie Rains. I honestly don't know how I would write a book without you!

xoxo
Rachel

KEEP READING

If you enjoyed *Come Away with Me* but haven't read the rest of the series yet, turn the page to read the first chapter of *Don't Cry for Me*, the first book in the Midnight in Manhattan series.

DON'T CRY FOR ME
CHAPTER 1

Eve Marlow's heels clicked confidently against the polished floor as she strode down the hall toward her producer's office. She paused outside the door, running her fingers over the front of her dress to smooth any wrinkles before lifting her hand to knock.

"Come in," Greta called from inside.

Eve grasped the handle and pulled the door open. Greta sat behind her desk, glasses perched on her nose as she looked up from her computer screen. But she wasn't alone. Bruce Koslowski, *Life & Leisure*'s director of advertising, stood beside her. "Greta," Eve said with a polite smile. "Bruce, this is a surprise."

"Hello, Eve," Bruce said with an equally polite nod.

"Have a seat." Greta gestured vaguely to the guest chairs in front of her desk.

Eve sat, placing her laptop on the edge of the desk.

"I'm afraid I have some bad news," Bruce said.

Eve nodded. "Greta told me this morning that the ratings for our season two premiere weren't as high as we'd hoped, but I've put together several proposed adjustments to *Do Over*'s advertising plan that I think should—"

"Actually, that's not why I'm here," Bruce interrupted. "You can discuss advertising with Greta later."

More bad news? Eve straightened in her seat, clasping her hands loosely in front of herself. "All right."

"We have to pull episode eight," Bruce said.

"The ice cream shop?" Eve said, incensed. "That's one of our strongest episodes. Why on earth would we scrap it?"

His lips drew into a frown. "The owner has been charged in a sexual assault."

Fuck. Eve felt a heavy sensation in her stomach, as if the remnants of her lunch had hardened into concrete. "That's...not good."

"I know," Greta agreed. "It's a publicity nightmare. There's no way we can air it."

"Is there time to shoot a replacement?" As the CEO of Marlow Marketing, Eve had built an empire helping under-performing small businesses reach their potential. Two years ago, the *Life & Leisure* channel had offered her a television show—*Do Over*—that followed her as she worked. Each episode featured a different business, offering viewers the chance to become invested in their success as she helped them rebuild. Season one had been a runaway success. So far, season two was off to a lackluster start, and without this episode, she might be in real trouble.

"It's possible," Greta said. "But the timing would be extremely tight."

Bruce's frown deepened. "I'm afraid there's no room in the production budget to reshoot, even if you were able to fit it into the schedule."

"I'll make room in the budget," Eve said automatically. This

was what she did for a living, after all. She saved failing businesses, and now she would save her television show, because if
she didn't get her ratings up, *Do Over* would never get renewed
for a third season. "I'll draw up a revised advertising plan."

"If you're able to make room in the budget, I'll think
about it, but I'm not making any promises," Bruce told her.
"Have it on my desk by the end of the day."

She nodded. "Consider it done."

Bruce left, and Eve slumped in her chair. "How much
time do I have to find a new client and shoot a replacement
episode?"

"Not much," Greta told her apologetically. "You'd need
to bring me the client's name by Friday, with filming to
begin next week."

Eve pressed her knuckles against the edge of the desk in
front of her, letting the cold wood bite into her skin,
providing an outlet for her frustration. "Friday, as in the day
after tomorrow?"

"Yes. And first, you've got to make room in the budget
and have Bruce sign off on it," Greta reminded her.

"I'll do that right now." Eve stood, picking up her laptop.

Greta nodded, waving a hand in Eve's direction. "Go
work your magic. You'll pull this off. I have full confidence
in you."

"I will," Eve confirmed. She left Greta's office and strode
down the hall toward her own. They had hundreds of leftover applications from their season two casting call. The
trick would be finding someone who could bring her the
ratings she needed, when she'd already chosen what she'd
believed to be the ten strongest applicants from the bunch.
Hopefully, she'd overlooked a potential breakout star.

First things first. She closed the door to her office and
spent the next two hours reallocating funds from *Do Over*'s

already stretched advertising budget to allow her to shoot the replacement episode. As much as she needed those advertising dollars, she needed a full season more. She emailed the revised budget to Bruce and settled in to sift through previously rejected season two applications.

But as the sun slid behind the Manhattan skyline outside her window, she was no closer to finding a replacement client and her stomach had begun to growl obnoxiously. Stifling a growl of her own, she packed up to head home. She'd find something to eat, change into her pajamas, and keep working.

Preferably with a glass of wine.

Since it was going to be a late night, she stopped in the break room to fix herself a coffee for the ride home. She spent her thirty-minute subway ride making notes on her phone, outlining ways to maximize what remained of her advertising budget. While Marlow Marketing wasn't in any trouble, *Do Over* was dangerously close to cancellation. She enjoyed filming the show. It had become an important part of her brand, and perhaps most importantly, it had tripled her income. She wasn't going to lose it, not when she knew it could be saved.

Her cell phone rang as she exited the subway, and Greta's name showed on the screen. Eve connected the call. "Please tell me you're calling with good news."

"I am, actually," Greta told her. "They've signed off on your revised production budget. All you have to do now is bring us a new client in time to get the replacement episode filmed."

"Excellent." Eve exhaled in relief as she dodged a bike messenger, stepping aside to let him pass. "I'll let you know as soon as I have a name."

"Friday," Greta reminded her.

"Got it." Eve tossed her empty coffee cup into a nearby trash can. A tiny, muffled cry echoed from somewhere, and she paused. "Did you hear that?"

"Hear what?" Greta asked.

"Nothing. Listen, I'll check in with an update tomorrow morning, okay?" She strode down the street toward her building, intent on getting upstairs, out of these heels, and warming up something for dinner. Where had that cry come from? Had it been something on Greta's end of the line? It hadn't sounded human, more like an animal. Probably someone nearby on the street was watching a video on their phone or carrying some kind of exotic pet. This was New York City, after all. She'd once seen a man carrying a tiny pig in a backpack.

But an uneasy feeling deep in her gut worried that the sound had come from inside the trash can, and it only grew stronger with each step she took. Holding in a sigh, she turned and walked back to the bin. It was filled almost to the top with garbage. Eve couldn't believe she was even contemplating poking around in a public trash can. God knew what was inside, but it was sure to be disgusting.

She grimaced as she stood there, listening. Other than the steady hum and honk of traffic, laughter from a couple passing by, and the distant roar of a jet overhead, she couldn't hear a thing. She was being ridiculous. Hours of work awaited her in her apartment, so she had no idea why she was standing here, staring at a trash can. To satisfy her conscience, she turned on the flashlight on her cell phone and shined it inside.

There was her coffee cup, laying on a plastic grocery bag at the top of the garbage pile. No animals. Nothing but gross, smelly trash. She wrinkled her nose, shining the light quickly over the rest of the bin, but...did that bag just twitch?

Oh, hell.

It twitched again. A sick feeling washed over her, all thoughts of ratings and clients wiped from her mind. With her free hand, she reached cautiously into the bin, nudging aside her coffee cup to uncover the bag beneath it. She hesitated before touching it. What if the movement was caused by a rat, rooting through the rubbish? Or something even less friendly?

But that stubbornly uneasy feeling in her gut made her grasp the knot where the bag had been tied shut and lift it out of the bin. Something inside squealed, and Eve's heart slammed into her ribs. Her skin prickled. Oh God, there was really a live animal trapped inside this bag. What kind of sick joke...

She knelt and placed the bag on the ground. Cautiously, she tore a hole in the plastic, keeping her fingers well away from the opening in case whatever was inside tried to bite her. She'd just free the rat and be on her way. But the tiny creatures inside weren't rats. The bag was full of some kind of baby animals that looked like...were those kittens? Tiny newborn kittens, eyes closed and barely moving.

Eve exhaled harshly, as if the wind had been knocked out of her. She ripped the bag all the way open and reached inside. Her fingers brushed soft black fur, and the kitten mewled softly, rooting its head toward her hand. It was cool to the touch.

"Jesus," she murmured, scanning the rest of the animals. She counted six total, a mixture of black, gray, and one solid white kitten. Not all of them were moving. Oh *fuck*. Were they even alive?

She stripped out of her blazer and laid it on the ground. Carefully, she lifted the kittens out of the bag one by one and placed them inside her jacket, trying not to notice how cold and stiff they felt beneath her fingers. The temperature hadn't quite reached seventy today, average for mid-April in Manhattan. She needed to get them inside and warm, and then...what?

She'd call the animal shelter. Yes, that was the logical next step. She eyed the bag they'd been inside of. Should she take it with her? Was it evidence? Was it a crime to throw a litter of kittens in the trash? She sure as hell hoped so. And so she balled up the empty grocery bag and tucked it inside her blazer, which would be going straight into the wash—if not the trash—once she got home. She scooped the edges of the fabric together, forming a makeshift sack for the kittens, and hurried toward her apartment building.

A cool breeze whipped through the thin material of her blouse, and she shivered. Several people gave her strange looks as she cradled her blazer in front of herself. She resisted the urge to tell them off, reasoning that in their position, she'd give herself an odd look too.

Eve Marlow, up-and-coming reality television star, behaving bizarrely among rumors that Do Over's *second season is off to a disappointing start.*

This day could really just stop now. She'd had enough. Walking briskly, she rounded the corner and approached her building. She'd take the kittens inside, call the shelter, and get them on their way to help and veterinary care. Then she could get back to work.

Morris, the doorman, held the door open for her. "Good evening, Ms. Marlow."

"Evening, Morris. Thank you." She offered him a brief but grateful smile on her way to the elevator. There hadn't been a peep out of the kittens since she'd put them in her blazer. No wriggling. God help her if she was carrying a jacket full of dead kittens up to her apartment right now. What if they were covered in fleas? Or had rabies? Was she endangering herself by bringing them inside?

She punched the button with her elbow and waited, toe tapping impatiently, until the elevator arrived. It carried her swiftly to the eighth floor, and she let herself into her apartment. There, she stood for a moment, unsure what to do next and halfway terrified to look inside her blazer.

But her discomfort was no excuse for further endangering their lives. She lay her blazer on the kitchen table, spreading it flat. A few of the kittens stirred, mewling as they scrambled toward each other for warmth.

Several of them didn't move at all.

She shuddered. They were so cold. Thinking fast, she went into the bedroom, rummaging through her closet until she found the heating pad she used when her back started acting up. She carried it to the kitchen table and plugged it in before laying the jacket full of kittens on top of it. "Now to find someone to take you."

She washed her hands—just in case—then sat at the table and pulled out her phone. She looked up the nearest animal shelter, only to receive an automated recording that it was closed for the night. Same story at the next shelter. And the next. It was only seven o'clock. Wasn't there any place to take abandoned animals after hours? These kittens wouldn't make it until morning. Not to mention, she didn't have time to deal with this, not in general and especially not tonight.

Eve stared at the furry pile of kittens. What the hell was she going to do with them? She'd never had a pet, never cared for an animal in her life. She had no idea how to care for these, but they were obviously too small for solid food.

They probably needed milk. Maybe she could warm up some of the half-and-half she kept in the fridge for her morning coffee, but what would they drink it out of?

They were so small, so helpless.

Irritation warred with concern inside her as she typed "what to do if you find abandoned kittens" into the search bar on her phone. The top result was a YouTube video with the thumbnail of a woman with lavender hair holding a kitten about the size of the ones Eve had found. For lack of a better option, she pressed Play.

"Hi, everyone. It's your favorite kitten rescuer, Josie Swanson, here to tell you what to do if you find an abandoned kitten or litter of kittens," the woman in the video said.

Eve leaned back in her seat as the knot in her stomach loosened. This video might be exactly what she needed. Josie was pretty, with warm eyes and an endless smile. Eve had never been a fan of unnatural hair colors, but the lavender seemed to work for Josie, accentuating her bubbly personality.

Unfortunately for Eve, the video mostly covered how to care for newborn kittens rather than where to take them. But, worst-case scenario, it might help her keep them alive through the night until she could drop them at the shelter in the morning.

"The important thing to remember is to never bring a litter of orphaned kittens to an animal shelter," Josie said, staring earnestly into the camera. "Most shelters aren't staffed to care for bottle-fed babies and will have to euthanize them. The best thing to do is to reach out to local animal rescues and ask for their help. I've included a list of resources in the description below."

Well, this wasn't good news, but that seemed to be the

theme of Eve's day. Then again, maybe she could find an animal rescue that would take the kittens tonight. She scrolled through the links below the video until she found a kitten rescue in New York City. According to the contact information, Josie herself ran it. Maybe Eve's luck had turned. She'd give the kittens to Josie and be done. Josie would know exactly how to care for them. She had over a million subscribers and countless videos detailing all the kittens she'd saved.

Eve clicked on the contact button and composed a quick message detailing her situation, adding URGENT to the subject line, because she wasn't sure these kittens would survive another hour without intervention, let alone overnight. And as much as she needed to get to work and find a client for her replacement episode, she did *not* want a pile of dead kittens in her kitchen...or on her conscience.

Not knowing what else to do, she rewatched Josie's video while she waited. They'd need kitten formula, which she could apparently get at most pet stores. So much for the half-and-half in her fridge. She had just pulled up a list of local pet stores when her phone rang with an unknown Manhattan exchange.

Eve connected the call. "Hello."

"Hi," came the vivacious voice from the video. "This is Josie Swanson. You've found a litter of abandoned kittens?"

"Yes," Eve told her gratefully. "Someone dumped them in a trash can."

"It happens all the time, unfortunately," Josie said. "About how old are they, if you had to guess?"

"Newborn, maybe," Eve said. "Their eyes are still shut, and I think their umbilical cords are still attached. Can I bring them to you tonight? I'm honestly not sure how long they're going to survive otherwise."

"I'm so sorry, but I can't take them. I'd be happy to meet you, show you how to care for them, and give you some supplies, though."

Eve's stomach clenched in a combination of disappointment and frustration. She'd been so sure Josie was going to help her. She was tired and hungry, her feet ached, and she needed these kittens out of her apartment so she could get back to the mountain of work awaiting her. "I don't understand. You run a kitten rescue. Why can't you take them?"

"I really wish I could, but I own a bar in Brooklyn, and we're short-staffed at the moment. I'm tending bar twelve hours a day, and these guys will need round-the-clock care."

Eve bristled at the implication. "I work full-time too. I can't keep them."

"Look, you're in Manhattan, right?" Josie asked.

"Yes."

"Tell you what. Bring them here. I'll make some calls while you're on your way and see if I can find someone to take them for you. If not, I can give you some formula and show you how to care for them, at least temporarily."

"Bring them to your bar?"

"Yes," Josie confirmed. "Sorry, but I'm working all night."

Eve's entire body tensed, and her pulse quickened. She couldn't handle walking into a bar, especially not tonight. Her gaze fell on the kittens. What choice did she have? But if she brought them to Josie's bar, she was going to convince her to keep them, because there was no way Eve was bringing them back home with her. "I'll be there in half an hour."

ALSO BY RACHEL LACEY

Love in the City

Read Between the Lines

Vino and Veritas

Hideaway

Midnight in Manhattan Series

Don't Cry for Me

It's in Her Kiss

Come Away with Me

Almost Royal Series

If the Shoe Fits

Once Upon a Cowboy

Let Your Hair Down

Rock Star Duet

Unwritten

Encore

The Stranded Series

Crash and Burn

Lost in Paradise

The Risking It All Series

Rock with You

Run to You

Crazy for You

Can't Forget You

My Gift is You

The Love to the Rescue Series

Unleashed

For Keeps

Ever After

Only You

ABOUT THE AUTHOR

 Rachel Lacey is a contemporary romance author and semi-reformed travel junkie. She's been climbed by a monkey on a mountain in Japan, gone scuba diving on the Great Barrier Reef, and camped out overnight in New York City for a chance to be an extra in a movie. These days, the majority of her adventures take place on the pages of the books she writes. She lives in warm and sunny North Carolina with her family and a variety of rescue pets.

facebook.com/RachelLaceyAuthor

twitter.com/rachelslacey

instagram.com/rachelslacey

amazon.com/author/rachellacey

bookbub.com/authors/rachel-lacey

CPSIA information can be obtained
at www.ICGtesting.com
Printed in the USA
BVHW050157071022
648916BV00010B/47